Shadowbane

Age of Aelfborn

Paul Francois

DEDICATION

For my son, Nicholas, who always continues to amaze me with his intelligence, confidence, and leadership abilities.

Table of Contents

ACKNOWLEDGMENTS

I would like to thank the following individuals for their part in the creation of this novel:

Casey Renee Miller for copyediting.

Jeffrey Kimbler for his impressive cover illustration. You have a remarkable talent. Not only with creating amazing works of art, but also with teaching those who wish to learn.

Kelly Francois for content editing and the impressive recommendations of future rewrites. You really shaped this novel.

Last, but certainly not least, I would like to thank God for allowing me to write this novel and still maintain the illusion of wisdom.

Prologue: Heritage, Honor, and Sorrow

More than one hundred years have passed since the Age of Strife began. More than a hundred years since the betrayal of the High King Cambruin, which left him for dead against the great Stone Tree of Life. The world entered an era of chaos and conflict on that dreadful day in Kierhaven. Over time, some have sought the remains of the High King to claim the mighty but cursed sword, Shadowbane. All whom attempted to claim the weapon from the Tree of Life had failed. The tales from the last quest to Kierhaven were disastrous as the fallen Elven fortress was no more. Kierhaven once stood atop the enchanted Mount Telorinadreth. Now, only a vast sea dwells in its place. The great sword had risen and fallen several times over the ages. Many had taken on pilgrimages seeking the heir of Cambruin, but once again, they only discovered sorrow. Even in these times of chaos, life had endured.

On the outskirts of Aerynth, lay the small village of Fort Viatrus. A humble place where chaos and wars are whispered rumors when children are in their beds. Families here are farmers, not Warriors. One stone structure three stories tall stands in the middle of the settlement. This building is the gathering place for its people. Life here is content and peaceful in comparison to most of the known world. It is the perfect place to raise a family, at least Aedan and Vanya thought so.

Vanya is an Elven woman from the sea wayfaring Elven tribe known as the Gwaridorn. Due to her heritage, she had a pale green tint to her skin, as all Gwaridorn Elves did. Megildur and Aranel were her only offspring. Her husband Aedan was Human. As such, the children were both of the Aelfborn race, half Human and half Elf. The children did not have the same pale green skin as their mother. What they did have was mystical tattoos covering their bodies. Mixing Human and Elven blood did not always blend well. Typically, Aelfborn offspring have a pale golden skin tone and their facial features are those of their Elven half. Aelfborn have sharp eyes and keen pointy ears but from their beginning, this breed has had a curse upon them.

The Elven Queen Silesteree Allvolanar placed a curse of madness on her own Aelfborn offspring, whose father was none other than the All-Father himself. In her anger toward the All-Father, for his act of treachery, she doomed all Aelfborn during the Age of Twilight, and henceforth. The tattoos placed on the Aelfborn offspring at birth calm the curse of madness. As for their Human contribution, they inherit greater physical strength than most Elves but Aelfborn are not as tall as Elven folk. The final abomination to the curse, besides the madness, was that Aelfborn were sterile and unable to produce any offspring.

Since their world Aerynth was in constant turmoil; some days Megildur would follow his father, Aedan, on his voyages to the nearby safehold, New Mellissar. It was a safe haven for Humans, Aelfborn, and even Half Giants. While his father gathered food, clothing, and other supplies, Megildur overheard tales of great nations attacking each other to gain land and resources. Some battles were because of the hatred between warring factions. And for some wars, there was no reason at all.

Aedan was a strong capable man who the other villagers looked up to. He was the leader in their small but noble settlement of Fort Viatrus. He brought Megildur along as part of teaching the boy responsibility. Aedan always hoped that his son would assume his responsibilities and take on a leadership role within the village. Megildur felt safe and secure when his father was around, due to his keen intellect and Warrior prowess. Though he did not project his combative skills, Aedan did possess excellent ability with an axe.

Vanya, Aedan, their son Megildur, and their young daughter Aranel lived life hoping that the outer world would not consume their blissful family existence.

CHAPTER 1: Siblings

Megildur was young, still yearning to be a man. He stood proud in the fact that he was the man of the family, in his father's absence. Megildur was not as big in status or in physical prowess, but that did not deter him from wielding his father's axe, when possible. What he lacked in stature he made up for with valor and kindness, especially when it came to his little sister, Aranel.

On days Megildur does not accompany his father to New Mellissar, he tended to the daily chores his father ordered before leaving. Megildur cared for the livestock, meaning he fed and watered them. His father instructed him to clean up after the animals as well, this chore he despised the most. The stench of the animals was so foul, he not only tied a cloth around his face, but he also shoved more material up each nostril. He finished the job, but definitely not to his father's standards. His next chore was to chop firewood for winter, but his sister had other plans.

Aranel spouted off, "Megildur, you promised we would go down to the water today." She was several years younger than Megildur, and her sole responsibility was to be a handmaiden to Mother.

"I said no such thing you silly girl! Now stop annoying me during my chores or I will have to answer to Father for not completing my tasks!" Megildur loved his sister but she made it impossible to complete his chores when she was around. Vanya emerged from their home, "Mother, can you find a task for Aranel?"

"Take care of your sister, Megildur. She is young and full of spirit," Vanya replied to her son. "You were once the little one demanding my time, not so long ago."

Aranel retorted, "See Megildur, there is nothing wrong with me."

Megildur grumbled, "Nothing a visit from an Orc would not fix."

Aranel screamed and ran for her mother, "Mother, did you hear him?" Megildur dropped his axe and ran for Aranel. Due to her size, he restrained her with ease.

Megildur pleaded, "Wait. Do not tell Mother what I said. Please, my dear sweet sister." His mother had warned him before about teasing his younger sister.

"As you wish," Aranel replied with a sinister sneer. "But it will cost you big brother. I want to go down to the water, right now." Aranel was now demanding, since she knew her brother could not deny any request of hers.

Megildur grunted, "No! I am too busy!"

Aranel screeched, "Oh, Mother!"

"Alright," Megildur conceded. "Just keep quiet!" Aranel gave a satisfied smile and bound off to collect her clothes for playing in the water. Megildur knew he would have to answer to his father for not completing his chores. However, having to answer to Mother for being mean to his sister was a greater challenge he would prefer to avoid.

Megildur picked up a small dagger and lashed it to his belt. He carried this weapon everywhere since Father gave it to him in celebration for being fourteen years old. That was over two years ago. That was also the first time his father told him he was a man now and that his primary responsibility was to protect his family, especially his little sister.

"Alright you little menace, let's go!" Megildur commanded Aranel to get moving. He wanted to get back before dark.

Megildur and Aranel proceeded through the dense forest where their village lay hidden away from the main road. They cleared the last of the trees and both saw the water off to the west. It would still take some time to get closer to the water, but Aranel kept getting more and more excited during the long trek. Once they were close enough to smell the kelp, Aranel ran for the waves. "Be careful you little imp, you are going to hurt yourself and Mother will blame me!" It would not be the first time she injured herself being mischievous and Megildur was to blame.

Aranel was about to jump into the water in her dress when she remembered how her mother scolded her in the past for getting her good clothes muddy. She scanned the area looking for a safe place to change. Megildur chuckled. "Behind that rock, you'll be safe there." He pointed to a large mound of rocks.

"You won't leave me, will you?" Aranel asked. Her older brother teased her before. One time he even threw rocks into a puddle of water near where she was standing just to annoy her.

Megildur scowled, "Just go and make haste, or I will leave now!" She scurried behind the largest boulder and changed her clothing. Megildur scouted the area. Granted they found a secluded area, but he wanted to be certain. Aranel darted out from behind the boulder and ran for the water squealing like one of their animals back in the village. Once content with the safety of the surrounding areas, Megildur climbed upon a nearby rock, perched like a large bird, and began to watch over his little sister playing in the water.

Megildur stood proud on top of his rock, drew his dagger, and fantasized it was a mighty sword in which to slay his enemies. Slashing and slicing to and fro, the formidable Aelfborn vanquished all who opposed him. He prepared to strike his lethal blow upon the easily defeated Chaos Demon, and then he heard a faint giggle in the distance. Awakened from his fantasy of glorious battles, he saw his sister reposed below the boulder. She failed at containing her laughter.

Megildur grumbled, "Be gone you banshee!" He stormed off to escape embarrassment. He turned to face his sister; she was still jeering him. "If you do not cease at once, I will take you home now!" With that said Aranel turned and ran back into the water. Megildur smirked and then continued, camping out atop of another rock, further away from his bothersome sister. He continued with his daydream of being a colossal Warrior but kept it to himself, to avoid persecution. Aranel continued playing in the mild waves and diving for shells. She enjoyed lining them along her bed and everywhere else, even in Megildur's room.

After what seemed like an eternity, he decided they needed to leave before the sun set. Megildur knew he needed to get home and face his father about his incomplete chores. Also, his father would be even angrier if Megildur brought his sister home after dark. Aerynth was bad enough during the daytime, but at night screams and explosions heard off in the distance were a constant reminder of the turmoil and conflict around them. He shouted, "Let's go Aranel, and be swift about it. We need to get home!" He picked up his dagger and secured it to his belt again. He waited for Aranel to exchange her wet clothing for her clean dress. She finished, and they began the journey home.

However, soon after they began their trek, Aranel shuffled her feet and slowed her pace until she stopped walking and sat upon a large boulder. With her head held low, and shoulders slumped, she released a long sigh. A day full of swimming wore the young Aelfborn out, which Megildur did not anticipate. He did his best to get her back up on her feet and continue. The sun was setting and time was of the essence.

"Get up, we need to arrive in the village before dark," Megildur pleaded with his sister.

Aranel whined, "But I'm tired!" She used her sad eyes to beg Megildur. "Give me a piggy-back ride?"

Megildur lashed back, "I'm not carrying you! Get up or I'll leave you!" The boy was bluffing, but he hoped his sister would not notice. Megildur just stood there. Aranel held her arms up for her brother to pick her up. After a few moments, he turned and continued walking toward home. It did not take long before Aranel started crying.

Aranel screamed out as her brother vanished from sight, "Megildur!"

"Be quiet, you whelp!" Megildur yelled back, reappearing before his sister. "If someone hears you, we both will be in trouble! The woods are full of robbers and Thieves after the sun goes down." Megildur noticed the sun was fading. "I'll give you a piggy-back ride if it will keep you quiet." He rolled his eyes and picked her up upon his back. He had no other choice.

Between their bickering and slow pace because of Megildur carrying his sister, night set in before they made it home. A large moon filled the night sky, peering up over the trees. The moon was so bright that it even cast large animated shadows behind them. However, another light puzzled Megildur, an intense aurora emanating over the trees, coming from their village. Megildur heard loud noises that were indistinguishable at first. His heart began to race, beating stronger with every step. Something was amiss. Megildur was afraid, but he dared not show that emotion to his little sister. One distinct noise pierced the night air. It was their mother crying out their father's name…"A E D A N!"

CHAPTER 2: All is Lost

Megildur knew that cry meant one thing, trouble. Megildur cautioned his sister, "Aranel, you stay here behind this shrub and don't move!" He hid her away and moved in to investigate the commotion. Aranel had a look of terror in her eyes, but Megildur had to leave her. If his mother was in peril, he needed to defend her. Once he felt his sister was safe, he crept in. Megildur approached the village and could see that many of the small huts were burning. He positioned himself behind one of the larger trees on the edge of the village. He could still hear screaming and something that sounded like wild beasts. Megildur was unsure what this sound was. He knew if he stayed next to the tree, he would not be able to scout the area. He crawled in closer next to one of the burning huts and saw a familiar body lying down. "Father!" He screamed. Megildur slid next to his father on the ground and noticed a pool of blood around his body. There was a gaping wound on his father's side. His father leaned in to whisper in Megildur's ear.

Aedan gasped, "Protect your mother and sister, you are the man of the family now. Do you swear to uphold this vow?"

Megildur replied, "I swear I will protect them Father!" With that, Megildur could tell his promise brought his father relief.

"I am proud of the man you have become, Megild..." Aedan whispered to his son with his dying breath. Megildur pulled back to see his father was no longer among the living. Megildur was about to cry but he knew mourning his father would have to wait; he had a vow to keep. He scanned the area looking for his mother. In the dark, it was hard to see his mother or the ones plundering his village. He could still hear the sound of wild beasts but could not tell where it was coming from. He knew their livestock would not make that sound. He tried to remain undetected, but came to the realization...he failed. Someone grabbed him from behind. The assailant turned Megildur around. The figure stood two feet above Megildur, until the attacker lifted him off the ground. Now they were eye to eye. Megildur could tell he was an Elf due to his sharp eyes and ears that gathered to a point. Megildur shared similar facial features with this Elf, though this Elf had pale alabaster skin. He threw Megildur to the ground several feet away and pounced atop of him. The Elf drew his dagger from his sheath and sneered at the boy.

The Elf bellowed, "I shall end your miserable existence half-breed! May the All-Father be damned for siring a spawn of Chaos like you!" He began to bring his weapon in for a fatal blow. Megildur cringed, believing his life had come to end, but he only partially closed his eyes. He wanted to meet death as his father did, with his eyes open. Megildur felt the close sweep of a blade and watched something severe the Elf's hand from his arm. The shocked Elf looked up from his severed hand, now lying next to Megildur. The same sword then impaled his chest. He slumped over to the side. Now, Megildur could escape. A familiar hand reached down to help Megildur to his feet; it was his mother.

Megildur shouted, "Mother, I am happy you are still alive!" He hugged her and then withdrew. Megildur said with sorrow in his voice, "Father has passed on." His mother had a look of terror in her eyes; they were now alone in this fight.

"He was courageous, defending our village. I am pleased that you are still alive. What of your sister?"

"She is safe, waiting just outside the village," Megildur replied. "I must get..." Warm blood spattered across Megildur. He focused on his mother and could see the tip of a bloody sword protruding from her chest. Vanya stared at her son in shock, collapsed to her knees, then toppled to the ground. Megildur looked up from his mother's lifeless body and first saw hooves. Panning up from the hooves, he discovered a savage fur covered beast standing on two legs. From the stories his father told him growing up, his mother's killer was a Minotaur. They were the beasts making the wild sounds that Megildur could not place.

Enraged from his mother's brutal slaying, Megildur drew his dagger and plunged it into an opening he found in the Minotaur's armor. The beast let out a resounding roar and backhanded the Aelfborn with his armor-covered fist. The boy dropped to the ground. The beast knocked him senseless for a moment. Megildur gazed up at the brute standing over him. With the dagger still protruding from its armor, the Minotaur raised its hoof over the boy. Using all his might, he trampled Megildur. The pain was so intense Megildur screamed out with what breath he had left. Megildur heard the scream of a small child, the Elven invaders found Aranel. He watched, helpless as an Elf dragged his little sister, handing her off to a Minotaur thrall.

"Put this half-breed with the other slaves," the Elf commanded the Minotaur. "And the next time you annihilate someone who is good stock for the slave pits it will cost you your life, Thrall!" The Elf glanced over at Megildur while making his threat. The Minotaur turned and carried off Aranel. Megildur was powerless to come to her rescue. He had sworn an oath to protect his mother and sister, but failed in both instances.

Megildur lay there, dying and wishing the pain would end, and then fate granted his wish. The pain subsided to a tingling feeling, much like when a limb falls asleep. After a few moments of this new feeling, it faded and Megildur welcomed death.

A calming voice resounded, "Have no fear, my child." Megildur felt a warming sensation on his shoulder. This calmed and soothed the confused boy. "You will soon return to Aerynth and start on the path to your destiny."

A puzzled Megildur thought to himself, "Return? Am I not dead?"

Much to Megildur's surprise, he was within his body again. He opened his eyes to see he was beside a giant stone obelisk. It had carvings laid into the stone but he could not distinguish its markings. He stood on his feet, which amazed him to see he still possessed and backed up to gaze upon the massive object that stood twice as tall.

"Watch your step, you half-breed twit!" Megildur spun around to see he had just stumbled into an Elf. He reached for his waist but found he was without any weapon. The Elf just glared at him and pushed past. Megildur turned in his direction, since he did not want to show an Elf his back. Megildur noticed he was in a much larger area. He watched the rude Elf walk around a colossal broken decaying sea vessel. Megildur did not want to trust an Elf, but he needed to know where he was. Reluctantly, he decided to follow the same path the Elf did. He moved around the broken down ship to find an entire town on the other side. His first thought was...where was his family?

In the town's center resided an ancient tree. It had few limbs and looked near death but still stood tall. To the right stood a tall tower made of stone but looked decayed over time. Past the tree, he noticed a circular stone platform with steps leading up to the center of it. Around the platform, on three points, were more stairs leading up to a circular walkway above the lower platform. Megildur, never having seen anything such as this, stared at the strange object for quite some time. Some people would walk up to the lower platform, make a motion with their hands, chant, and an unusual symbol would glow on the surface in front of the person. They stepped on the new symbol and vanished from the platform. Megildur walked closer to the platform until someone shouting to the left of him diverted his attention. The noise was emanating from a large structure on the edge of this murky town. Megildur decided to enter the building, hoping he could find an answer to his question. Why was he in this strange place?

"Ye call this ale, Wench?" A local patron yelled, Megildur stood in the doorway. He had to sidestep a flying mug that landed on the wall near the entrance. Megildur was unsure of what to think of the place he had just walked into. The air was thick and smoky. The stench in the room reminded him of animal stalls back in his village, just before they needed a cleaning. The center of the room accommodated some damaged tables with some small isolated rooms around the outside of the main chamber. In addition, he saw a counter with taller stools on the far end of the room with a ratty looking man behind the counter. Maybe he would find some answers there.

Megildur walked around the tables and felt like he was the center of attention. This was attention he did not need right now. He was especially trying to avoid one of the creepier looking characters on the far end of the room. It was a man with a dark cloak and red bloodshot eyes. He sat in one of the isolated areas on the edge of the room but he looked like trouble. Megildur kept his distance from the cloaked figure and made his way to the counter. Now he needed the man's attention behind the counter.

"Excuse me Sir," Megildur hailed and raised his hand, motioning for awareness from the man behind the counter. The man just ignored him, so Megildur continued waving his hand until frustration overwhelmed him. After getting nowhere with this tactic, he lowered his hand abruptly and into the mug of a large fellow next to him, knocking the mug to the floor. The owner of that tankard turned to face Megildur. He stood from his stool and Megildur could see he was taller and his skin was red, like blood. His skin was actually steaming, as was his temper. He grabbed Megildur by the shirt but the boy squirmed out of his grip and managed to tear off most of his shirt in doing so. With his skin now exposed, so were his mystical tattoos branded on him by his mother at birth.

The red-skinned man bellowed, "You half-breed fir'khanim! I will gut you for your insolence!" He grabbed Megildur by the hair and revealed some type of weapon mounted on his fist. He gripped the armament and spikes protruded from the lead edge of the device, which now pointed at the Aelfborn. He pulled his arm back to build force for bludgeoning the boy. Just at that moment, Megildur witnessed a bolt of energy coming from across the room and striking the red-skinned assailant, throwing him into the adjacent wall. The boy turned his attention toward the other side of the room and spotted the source. There stood a person covered in a tattered robe. It was the mysterious man with the bloodshot eyes. His hands were sparking with some type of energy field and he was glowing. Some yellow energy, drawn from the red-skinned man, was fueling the aura of energy. Megildur began to thank his newfound defender, but the robed protector dashed to his side of the room and grabbed him.

The man behind the counter bellowed, "Hey, you can't just ruin my establishment and run out!" The one in the robe, who still had not revealed his identity, turned to face the man behind the counter.

The robed fellow resounded, "Restrain your tongue Zaphire or I will silence you myself!" He turned to the entrance and hauled Megildur away. They moved through the doorway together and over near an isolated shack. "Speeak yur name booy and wheere diid yoou git thaat marrking?"

He muttered, "My name is Megildur and my mother marked me upon birth."

The robed man slurred, under venomous breath tainted with ale, "Don't beee coy wiith me chillld, only a foool doesn't knoow that Aelfborrrn must have thee mysstical tattoooos, and I ammm no fooool!" His breath could have toppled an Orc. He thundered, pulling Megildur's shirt back and exposing his shoulder, "I reeferrr to thees marrrk!" Megildur scrutinized his own shoulder and noticed a new mark branded into his skin, three interlocking circles. They emitted a shimmering light and appeared more mystical than even the tattoos his mother placed upon him at birth.

Megildur proclaimed, "I have never seen that mark before!" The robed man sneered at the boy in disbelief.

The drunken man uttered in suspicion, "Naive! Ye knooww nottt of thee All-Father? Weell I ammm undeeeciided if I shoould feed yee to a spaawwn of Chaaaos or hearrr morre of yurrr tale, but I gueesss I cannn usse somme enterrrtaainmennt." The elderly sloshed fellow turned to the round platform Megildur eyed before and walked off. "Come onn boyyy, wee havve morre converrrsing to doo. Follooow meee." He led Megildur over to the platform and stopped him on the edge. He began to chant and move his hands the same way Megildur observed others doing. After the process, a new symbol was glowing on the platform. The man looked at the boy, as if he was waiting for him to proceed, but Megildur was cautious after the events that had unfolded earlier today. Perturbed with his procrastination the old man shoved Megildur onto the radiant symbol and his reality faded into darkness.

CHAPTER 3: The Old Man

During Megildur's journey, the darkness lifted and he could clearly see a circular shape with unusual markings along the outer ring. It had smaller circles on the inside that shone different colors. In the center was a handheld weapon of some sorts. It looked like a small dual sided axe to him. The symbol faded and Megildur could see he was somewhere else entirely. It appeared to be an island with water surrounding him. Moving forward he looked down and noticed he was on an identical platform to the last location. Megildur continued to survey his surroundings and the old man appeared.

The old man grumbled, "Alll rriight boyyy. If yoou arre done restinng wee shoulld giit movinng." He grabbed Megildur and headed out toward the Northern shore. They walked past some trees and into a clearing. In front of them was an old castle in ruins. It looked like one strong wind could knock over the entire structure. In the front of the castle, Megildur saw three dragons guarding the ruins. They paced back and forth before the disheveled castle. Each of the scaly beasts looked hungry and malicious.

Megildur began to pullback from the old man. The elderly man muttered, "Keeep movinng. Theey will noot harrm you." The boy did not trust the old man, but if he wanted him dead, the drunk could have accomplished this back at the last place when that red-skinned man had threatened his life. He definitely possessed the ability. They moved closer. Megildur could see the dragons ignored them, but the old man was leading them straight through one of the beasts. Megildur threw his hands up to soften the impact of running into the dragon but instead he passed right through it. The old man could see his astonishment and began to chuckle. "Theey arre juusst an illuussion I crreaated to safffeguarrd myy castllle, whillle I ammm awayy."

The old man took him into a larger room in the center of the castle. There he walked near a hearth on the far side of the room. The man waved his right hand and a flame kindled inside the fireplace. The fire swelled which the battered Megildur found comforting. The Aelfborn tried to warm himself by the fire until he noticed some movement to the side of him. He turned with haste to see a creature in the corner of the room. It was almost the height of a man and had red skin and horns protruding from its body.

Megildur exclaimed, "What is that thing?"

"Thaat is myy minnion, hee iss a wizarrd's familliarr. Hee woon't harrm yee, unleesss I commannd it." The man removed his dark cloak and began to pour warm broth for both of them. "So booyy, let's heearr yurr taalle."

"Well, I come from a small village named Fort Viatrus, near New Mellissar," Megildur began to explain. The old man seemed disinterested so far. "My sister and I were returning from an afternoon along the shore. The sun had just began to fall away behind the trees, so dark was upon us. We reached the outskirts of our village, I could see burning huts, and many were screaming, including our mother. I left my little sister hidden on the outskirts, and I proceeded alone. I arrived and found my father wounded, slumped out on the ground." Megildur swallowed and took a deep breath to contain his emotions. Then he continued with his tale. "I went to my father's side. With his dying breath he made me swear to protect my family, which I failed to do." By this time, Megildur could no longer hold back his feelings. After a momentary release of emotions, he continued. "A Minotaur slaughtered my mother from behind. I tried to avenge her death but my small dagger was no match for the might of the beast. He knocked me to the ground and plowed my body into the dirt with his hoof. I laid there too weak to move. I watched as an Elf carried off my sister." This part of the story finally caught the old man's interest. He lowered his broth and listened with more intrigue. "I faded into a hazy mist. I found myself floating in an empty space, filled with voices and chanting until I asked who was there. A voice replied..."

The old man demanded, "Yes, yes! What did the voice say?" He was on the edge of his chair by this point, awaiting the conclusion. Also, Megildur noticed the broth seemed to improve the old drunk's speech as well. Or perhaps that was due to the lack of ale.

"The voice told me to have no fear and that I would return to Aerynth and start on the path to my destiny. I felt a warm sensation on my shoulder, as if someone had touched me," Megildur continued. "The next place I awoke was at the strange place where I found you and that irate red fellow, whatever that was."

The old man exclaimed, "By the All-Father! Well allow me to fill in some of the gaps in your tale," the old man stood and began to pace as he educated Megildur. "The place where you found me is Sea Dog's Rest. Many races gather in this port. It is a haven for all, where no one will battle for land or power. However, that tavern you walked into is not a favorable place for a boy. As for that 'irate red fellow', as you referred to him, he is an Irekei. They are a desert dwelling race long divided from their Elven kin. Aside from their hostile nature, their other noticeable difference from the Elves is their skin tone. They vary from a crimson red to pitch black. Oh, and they detest any markings on the body, so you can see why he would despise an Aelfborn such as yourself."

Megildur inquired, "Well, I am accustomed to the half-breed reference, but what was that name he used for me? What is a..."

"Fir'khanim translates to rain bleeder," the old man interrupted. "The Irekei emanate so much heat from within they do not sweat, their skin steams instead. They refer to all others as rain bleeders. The Irekei are fierce and ruthless, they hate all non-Irekei."

"What was the device you used to bring me here?" Megildur asked, figuring he could gather many answers so long as the elderly man was willing.

"That was a runegate," the old man replied and began waving his hands in front of Megildur. He displayed one of them in a layer of mist. "Since the Turning, and Aerynth's division, we use runegates to travel between landmasses."

Megildur queried, "What of the marauders that attacked my village? Who are they and why did the Minotaur kill me?" He was no longer interested in the Irekei and the runegates. His interests now were with retrieving his sister.

"The ones who attacked must have come from Aelarnost. It's their safehold to the north of your village, comprised of Minotaurs and the Dar Khelegur Elves," the old man told Megildur what he wanted to know. "These Elves are the High Ice Lords who dwell in the frozen mountains of the north. They founded the Deathless Empire. They use the Minotaurs as thralls to carry out their bidding."

Megildur roared, "Then that is where they took Aranel and where I must go!" He stood and advanced to the door before a strange force dragged him back to a seated position. He looked down and could see some sort of energy surrounding his body. Upon following the energy beam back to its source, he could see the old man was the culprit. He gave a bewildered look toward the man. "What's the meaning of this? Am I to be your prisoner?"

"Relax my eager one. One young and impish Aelfborn cannot take on the entire Deathless Empire alone," the old man spouted. "Besides, you don't have enough facts yet. You still have no clue on why you have returned, who brought you back, or what your destiny is." Megildur, not seeing he had much choice, decided to sit back and let the old man continue. "Let me explain why that Minotaur's hoof didn't permanently plant you in the ground. Since the Turning, the gates to Heaven and Hell are no longer open." The old man observed Megildur's confusion. "Did your parents not tell you of the Turning or the Age of Kings? That is what is wrong with children in this day and age, they're all ignorant!" Megildur looked scared at the old man's ranting. He could see Megildur withdrew after his last statement, so he sighed and sat down to educate the boy, calmly. "At the end of the Age of Kings one of Cambruin's own Knights betrayed the High King of Men, using his own weapon...Shadowbane. To this day, nobody knows who the vile Traitor was, but his act of treachery brought upon the Turning. It caused the world to tremble, separating into several continents, divided by vast seas. It also closed the doors to Heaven and Hell, since the All-Father turned his back on Aerynth. For better or worse, we are immortal. The Tree of Life that our parents bind us to in life is where we arrive once we experience death. Think of the experience as a type of rebirth."

"I do not recall my parents binding me to any Tree of Life and we have no special tree in our village," Megildur replied. "Who's this All-Father and what is this Shadowbane you speak of?"

"All-Father? You ask who the All-Father is? That would be like asking about the sky and the dirt below your feet. The All-Father is in all living entities around us. He created Aerynth and all we touch and feel. He is the creator of life, in all forms. The All-Father even created the World Tree, in which He found his beloved Braialla. The Traitor pinned Cambruin to this same tree using Shadowbane. I believe the voice you heard during your rebirth was that of the All-Father. I can only assume from the marking He gave you upon your shoulder, that you are the heir to the High King Cambruin. He has sent you to me so that I may guide you to your destiny."

"You are mad!" Megildur professed. "I am no royal heir, I am a simple peasant! No more! Unless you count the fact that I'm also a half-breed, which everyone I meet seems pleased to remind me! Now you claim that the gates to Heaven and Hell closed after the Turning. Then my parents might have experienced rebirth as well?" The old man nodded in agreement with Megildur's inquiry. "Then I must make haste in returning to my village." Megildur stood and looked at the elderly man, who seemed to offer no resistance. The boy walked for the door and proceeded outside.

Megildur knew by looking at the sun that he was further north from the mainland. He needed to head southeast but was unsure of how to cross the vast sea once he made it to the water's edge. On his way to shore, he saw the runegate again. The Aelfborn stepped onto the platform and tried waving his hands in an attempt to open a portal. Frustrated because it did not work, he walked off and sat at the shore for a moment. He felt a force of energy nearby and raised his head to see the old man appear before him again.

"If you seek the way to your village I can guide you," the old man proclaimed. "Follow me." The old man led him to the platform that they arrived on for this island. "Once I open this gate you will be back in Sea Dog's Rest. Proceed to the old tree in the center of the port and look for the runemaster. He will be standing next to the tree. Tell him you seek passage to New Mellissar and he will oblige. Once back in New Mellissar you may travel north to your village." The old man waved his hands and chanted. The symbol once again illuminated on the platform. "Place both hands around this runestone, and I will know you need my assistance." The old one placed a stone in Megildur's hand; the symbol upon it looked like a flame.

"Thank you for your guidance and tutelage," Megildur said to the old man. Then he stepped onto the symbol and once again faded into darkness.

CHAPTER 4: Along for the Ride

The display during transport mesmerized Megildur, but he once again arrived in Sea Dog's Rest as the old man had promised. He stepped off the runegate, and the first place he noticed was the tavern where he first met the old man, and the furious Irekei. Steering away from that disheveled place, he spotted the old tree he was seeking and the runemaster below. He approached the runemaster to interact with him. "Ahoy, stRanger! You have found our refuge. What can I do for you?"

Megildur resounded, "I seek passage to New Mellissar, Sir."

"Granted," the runemaster replied. With that, he waved his hands and Megildur transported to New Mellissar.

Upon arrival, Megildur recognized the area from when his father would bring him there. With no delay, the boy began his journey to Fort Viatrus...or what remained of it. The sun was directly above him when he started heading north. Megildur did not dare follow the main road, since he had heard tales of Thieves and Assassins laying waste to travelers. He stopped once or twice to gather some water from any source he could find; he had not prepared for such a journey. Normally his father would have packed accordingly for such a trek.

Night began to fall when Megildur reached the outskirts of his village. He made one full circle around the perimeter, being apprehensive of more invaders left behind. The entire village looked abandoned and charred. All that remained of the huts were faint outlines of their existence, so Megildur made his way to the stone building. Since his father was the village leader, his family used this building for their residence. It was three levels tall but had a small footprint, especially in comparison to the castles and fortresses Megildur had seen in drawings. The invaders did not leave anything unturned while rummaging through the stone building either. Megildur made his way to his room. It was also in disarray with his bed overturned and the few belongings he owned damaged. The boy picked up a drawing of his sister and him that their mother, Vanya, had drawn. He dropped to his knees and wept for the sister he could not save and for the parents he had lost. He felt a hand on his shoulder, which caused him to back into what remained of his bed.

An elderly woman from his village whispered, "I am sorry, Megildur, I did not mean to startle you. Your father and mother were here this morning looking for you and your sister."

Megildur burst out. "They live? Where did they go? Did they find Aranel?"

"Slow down," replied the woman. "After rebirth they returned to find both you and Aranel were gone. They did not know if the Deathless Empire seized you both, but I was able to tell them that they took Aranel. They grabbed what provisions they could and began the journey for Aelarnost."

Megildur declared, "That is where I must travel to." He stood and proceeded to the armory on the first floor. His father never permitted him in the armory before, but everything had changed now. Determined to keep his vow to his father, he equipped himself with some leather armor. He also armed himself with a sword, dagger, food, and as much water as he could carry. He trudged through the halls to the front door where the old woman met him at the exit.

The woman pleaded with him, "Do be careful. These roads are not safe anymore since the Deathless Empire trampled through. Scavengers have swarmed the roads since they know the Dar Khelegur demolished most of the villages in these parts."

Megildur replied trying to restrain his dread, "Do not fret. I shall be triumphant in my journey." He placed his hand on the old woman's arm and pushed the door open. He pulled the hood over his head to insulate him from the cold night air and started heading north to Aelarnost.

Megildur walked far away from the view of the road, keeping the sea in sight. The moon was his torch, since he dared not light a fire. After walking for a great distance, Megildur began to see the sun peer up over the horizon. He had not slept in quite some time, but he could not waste time now with sleep. He did need to stop briefly to adjust his armor. Otherwise, he would surely die of the wound his sword would make digging into his side. He found a fallen tree to rest his weapons on and adjusted his armor. While he was doing so, he caught the reflection of a metallic object out of the corner of his eye. He knew this could not be good. Megildur reached for his sword only to have an arrow obstruct his path to his weapons. He followed the path of the arrow back and caught a glimpse of a Scout fade from his view.

He knew he must move with haste, so he once again reached for his weapons but this time he spotted an adversary even closer. There was a Half Giant standing just on the other side of the fallen tree. The brute unsheathed a sword. He emitted a light from his body as bright as the sun. The Half Giant grew wings of fire that stretched longer than Megildur could see, being that close. The boy stumbled back to gain some distance from this new aggressor and in doing so he felt pain to the back of his head. The light of the morning sun faded, Megildur plunged to the ground. This time he was in total darkness…this time, there was no calming voice telling him to have no fear nor did he see a spectacle of lights.

Megildur felt a force against his belly. This was not a feeling of hunger, but a familiar feeling. It reminded him of a simpler time when he and Aranel went down to the sea and they ate too many berries. After that they got…oh no. Megildur abruptly opened his eyes and before he could see his surroundings, the contents of his last brief meal came bursting out of his mouth. The taste was less satisfactory coming out as opposed to the time it went in. He wiped his mouth with his sleeve. When he did this, he detected he was over the shoulder of the Half Giant that confronted him earlier. The giant man threw Megildur to the ground and attempted to glance over his shoulder, to see what mess the boy had made.

Megildur could hear laughter, but knew it could not be the brute he just expelled his meal on. Megildur observed a man appear out of thin air, when once there was nobody except him and the Half Giant. He observed this Scout before losing consciousness. He heard that they could blend into their environment and vanish from sight.

Looking at the brute, the Scout jeered, "It's a good look fer ya!" He noticed the boy staring at him in disbelief. "Cease yer gawking boy or I'll carve out yer eyes!" He turned back to the Half Giant. "Now, let's git this pagan back to the safehold before I disembowel him!" The Scout walked away laughing, fading away once more.

The Half Giant snatched Megildur. Fortunately, this time, he threw him over the other shoulder. Unfortunately, this action dislodged the runestone the old man had given him. The object fell to the ground and Megildur doubted the brute would let him stop and pick it up. Bouncing up and down, off the giant's other shoulder, Megildur noticed that they traveled on sand but could not tell where they were. Hopefully they would reach their destination soon. This desert heat was unbearable, nearly as unbearable as the view from the back of this brute. Megildur thought it might almost be worth having this savage kill him, just to reduce the time they carried him like a side of meat. Whenever possible, he would bend in such a fashion so he could see something new in the direction they traveled. He did not do this often since it upset the Half Giant and he would bounce Megildur on his shoulder even harder, causing great discomfort to his belly. The last thing he needed was to heave all over the brute's back once more. That would surely lead to a slow and painful torture session.

Megildur began to hear voices and realized they must be approaching their destination. For better or worse, the journey was over. It was starting to get dark but he could see the gates, once they had cleared them. The Scout had once again reappeared, Megildur assumed since he could hear his raspy voice again. The brute once again dropped him to the ground, made a grunting noise, and walked away. Someone forced him back down when he attempted to stand.

The Scout grumbled, "Git down, ye pagan! We'll purify ye soon nuff!" To Megildur, purification sounded pleasant enough. Maybe it would remove the stench he now had from that brute carrying him over his back. The Scout dragged the boy along the dirt to a nearby tent. The Scout bellowed to a young girl already inside the tent, "Slave, clean this pagan so I can offer him to the High Confessor!" She just bowed to the Scout and gathered her container to collect water he assumed.

Once the tent was vacant, he peeked outside to see if he could find an escape route. However, the guard, who he did not see in time, had other plans and smacked him in the head with the pommel of his sword. After rubbing his head for a bit, the girl returned to the tent. She was around Megildur's age with blonde hair and tanned skin. Megildur assumed this was because of her desert lifestyle. When she walked past the Aelfborn, her scent filled the room and aroused Megildur. She smelled like flowers in a meadow near his village, and this reminded him of a more peaceful time in his life. She now had her container filled with water and a cloth to cleanup Megildur, seemingly impossible in this waterless desert. She avoided eye contact with him.

She requested, "Please remove your leather armor and shirt." Megildur did not want to in front of a girl, but he figured if he denied her request she would call for the guard. He preferred to avoid him if possible. It was not difficult to remove his armor now, since they already stripped him of his weapons. He dropped the leather chest piece to the ground and removed his shirt. Megildur glanced back at the girl and caught her peeking at him. She made an unexpected sound and turned away, due to embarrassment. Standing there half-naked with only his tattoos covering him, she turned back around and began to scrub his body. Now Megildur was the one trying to avoid eye contact due to embarrassment.

Looking away was not possible when she stopped upon reaching his right shoulder and gasped, "By Saint Malorn!" Her eyes grew wide and she stared at Megildur. She dropped the cloth she was using to clean the boy and ran for the tent opening. Megildur knew it would not be in his favor when she returned. He put his shirt back on and grabbed his leather chest piece when the girl returned with an older woman. The older woman pulled back his shirt, exposing his right shoulder and she too gasped. Megildur was beginning to feel like an exhibition.

"Where did you get that marking upon your shoulder boy?" The older woman queried.

Megildur was fearful of her reaction, since he thought the girl was going to pass out after she viewed the mark. He did not want to mention his meeting with the All-Father. "A Minotaur's stomp crushed me into the ground and upon my rebirth I heard a voice tell me to have no fear. The same person who told me this also laid his hand upon my shoulder." The woman gasped, as the girl did, and they both receded near the back of the tent to converse amongst themselves. Megildur used this opportunity to finish getting dressed. Once Megildur nearly finished getting dressed, the older woman confronted him once more.

The old woman pleaded with the boy, "You must leave this place! It will mean certain death if you do not."

"All they mentioned was purification, which does not sound bad," Megildur speculated.

"The High Confessor achieves purification with fire," the old woman explained and Megildur's eyes widened. "If you survive, they will then either test you further or just slaughter you for being Aelfborn.

31

The Temple of the Cleansing Flame insists outsiders undergo purification for the sanctity of the religion."

"On second thought, fleeing sounds like the more survivable choice at this time," Megildur replied. He finished getting the last of his armor on. The woman explained to him that she would have her daughter guide him out through an opening in the fence. The woman said she would distract the guard outside the tent so he could escape. "Thank you for your assistance, but why are you doing this?" Megildur asked.

"Anyone with the mark of the All-Father deserves our help, not cleansing. Your heart is pure. Fulfill your destiny and bring peace to this fragmented world," the woman replied with a warm smile and went outside to distract the guard. Apparently, she knew the mark of the All-Father without Megildur telling her.

Megildur turned to the young girl and said with a slight grin, "Shall we?" The girl smiled back, lifted the back of the tent material, and they both crept out of the tent.

They followed along the perimeter until a large brute in armor halted them in their tracks. Megildur panned up the massive length of the guard's body just in time to see him raise his sword. The boy froze with panic, unsure of what to do. The sword came down but before it could reach him, an arrow struck the guard in the chest. He dropped his sword and looked past Megildur, just as another arrow struck him and he dropped to the ground. Megildur looked behind him to see the young girl holding the bow that killed the guard. This impressed Megildur, and aroused him at the same time. He loved seeing strong women who could handle their own battles. Before the boy could give a compliment on her aim, energy bolts started flying across the encampment. They seemed to appear out of nowhere. Megildur scanned the area and found the source was a hooded figure in the middle of the camp, atop of some structure. His newfound distraction was attacking guards within the camp. Megildur and the girl took that opportunity to proceed to an opening in the perimeter. Once there, the girl moved aside and allowed Megildur access to the escape route. He inquired, "You are not going any further?"

She looked at Megildur with sorrow in her eyes. "This safehold is my home. No matter how bad it is, I must stay with my mother," she replied, glancing at the ground.

The Aelfborn lifted her chin gently. "I understand, I am fond of my home as well," Megildur responded. Her skin was soft, like a flower petal. "May I know your name?"

She responded, "I am Zabrina. My mother named me from the desert flower."

"Well Zabrina, I will not forget you. Nor will I forget what you have done for me," Megildur replied. The Aelfborn could resist her scent, and beauty, no longer. He leaned in and kissed her on the lips, pressing firm against her. He would always remember her, and his first kiss.

He then turned away and forced his way through the small opening in the fence. Because of the hooded figure's attack, it was easy to sneak off amid the chaos. He did not know which direction to travel, but he surmised anywhere was better than here amongst the heretics. How could a place be so treacherous, and yet contain such a gentle soul as Zabrina? He just started running, assuming that would take him away from certain death by purification.

CHAPTER 5: The Lost Child

The sun was now peering up over the sand dunes. He wondered the desert all night. The sand in his boots ground against his flesh, causing intense pain and discomfort...and not to mention driving him crazy. He stopped momentarily to rub his feet and to remove as much sand as possible from his boots. Megildur could now survey the land better and detect predators. This also let him know the direction he traveled was east. As a child, his father helped him track and observe his surroundings, as well as how to read maps. He knew directions well, but he had never been to this uncharted desert before. The temperature surged as Megildur trudged through the desert. He was able to bypass most of the encampments with beasts, which helped him live a little bit longer, but that would be meaningless unless he found water soon. The heat was now getting unbearable, and Megildur knew he must find shelter from the sun if he was going to survive.

He found a large rock formation that provided some shade. The day turned to night as Megildur lay sleeping against his newfound shelter. Because of the distance, he covered in one day, Megildur slipped deep into sleep that night. So deep, in fact, that he began to dream. Before him, he saw a girl standing with her back toward him. She had golden blonde hair, and he assumed it was Zabrina. He moved closer behind her and placed his hand on her shoulder. She spun around and thrust a sword into the Aelfborn. Terrified, Megildur looked down at the sword protruding from his chest and stared back up at

Zabrina, a Minotaur now stood before him. The beast opened his mouth to speak and asked one question, "Why didn't you save me, Megildur?" The words emanated from the creature in front of him, but the voice was that of his sister.

Megildur screamed out, "Aranel!" He sat up from the ground. The thought of his sister suffering at the hands of the Elves hurt Megildur. However, the Aelfborn realized it was not the dream that hurt but the hundreds of ants crawling all over him and biting. He leapt to his feet and whisked off the ants. Dancing around like a drunken fool, the Aelfborn realized the ants were not just on the surface of his clothing. With a panicked scream, he dropped his trousers and began carefully brushing off the more delicate areas. After removing the last of the pests, Megildur inspected his clothes and put them back on.

Night again was now upon the Aelfborn and the temperature plummeted. He knew he must continue on, and the frigid nighttime temperature was preferable to the scorching daytime swelter. He thought for a moment and then remembered the direction he was traveling under the sun. He found the path was clearly visible under the bright moonlight, but it was difficult to see far ahead. Desolation surrounded Megildur, as did isolation. His thoughts kept wandering off to the girl who freed him, Zabrina. How could she want to stay in such a dreadful place? He realized it was because of her mother and that reminded him of his family. That was why he continued, no matter how bad the conditions were. After walking for hours, the sun began to peer up over the sand dunes in front of him. Another day was upon him, and he wondered if he would find food or drink today.

This vicious cycle of night and day continued another seven times for Megildur. He was able to find a desert plant a few days into his journey, but it only provided a minor amount of bitter liquid. Megildur's pace was dragging and he started to see deceptive visions that he was back home. One moment he was walking through the arid course sand, and the next he was playing in the water with his sister. When he briefly phased back into reality, he discovered that it was not water but sweat pouring off his body. After his isolation in this forsaken desert for over a week now, the Aelfborn was sunburnt, weak, suffering from massive headaches, and chaffing due to the sand in his pants. The sand was in his clothes and in his teeth as well. Megildur would attempt to spit the sand out, but he was so dehydrated and thirsty he needed every bit of moisture left just to keep moving. The only thing that kept him going was the thought of rescuing his sister and of course, the sweet smell of the girl who saved him, Zabrina.

The Aelfborn removed the leather armor covering his chest to use for shade, but it was not enough. He was about to begin looking for a safe haven from the sun, when he realized the temperature dropped. He glanced down to see shade from the sun below him, but the shape of the shadow was unusual. He turned around and discovered a desert beast had crept up behind him. The creature was three times his height with a furry mane and a stinger for a tail. Megildur recognized the creature from stories he heard in New Mellissar and screamed out, "Manticore!"

Without thinking, Megildur used the only weapon he possessed, the leather chest piece. He smacked the creature across the face, but this just aggravated the manticore. The beast batted the armor to the ground and let loose an intimidating roar, proving his dominance over Megildur. Tired and defenseless the boy did what anyone in his predicament would; he turned and ran! He ran until the furry aggressor was no longer visible and then he dropped to his knees, exhausted.

He observed some birds flying over him and knew they must be scavengers, just waiting to pick the flesh from his bones once he died. Megildur focused on one of the birds and surmised they were not scavengers but the same ones he used to see near his home. This type of bird lived around...water! He leaped to his feet and ran toward the birds. Crawling over the sand dune ahead of him, which felt more like a steep mountain, he gazed into a vast body of water. Stumbling down the sand dunes, he landed face first into an oasis. He had never been so happy to be so clumsy. The water felt so cool and refreshing to this weary traveler. Forgetting how fatigued he was, Megildur first started to gulp the water and then began to splash around like a small child. His stamina dwindled and he sat down on the shore wondering what to do now. Scanning the area, he noticed an island in the middle of this body of water. There was shade from trees and vegetation. He drifted out to the island and slumped before the first plant. He gorged himself on as many berries as his mouth could hold, and then he exceeded that amount. Juice from the berries ran down his drenched shirt, appearing like bloodstains on his clothing. This mattered not to the boy; he was just happy to find cover from the intense heat and food to fill the enormous void in his belly.

Megildur got his fill of berries and planted himself under the large tree on the island to relax for a bit. Since the sun was still high in the sky, Megildur used the intense light to examine his surroundings, from a seated position of course. He noticed to the east, the direction he was originally traveling, another coastline, as well as one to the south. He gathered that this body of water must be an inlet from the main sea. The water was slightly brackish, but still potable. He was still unsure if he was traveling toward some sort of settlement or deeper into oblivion. Megildur lay against the tree for so long that the sun disappeared and night settled in. Between the night air and breeze off the water, the boy began to tremble and shake. His wet clothes aggravated the freezing situation. He found some light dried up wood to start a fire. He piled most of the wood, minus two pieces for starting the fire, away from the tree and berry plants. He did not want to destroy his only source of food or shade. He began to rub for some time until smoke appeared, followed by a spark. His father's training was successful...he had created fire.

Once Megildur dried his clothes from the heat of the fire, he sat back against the lone tree and contemplated his journey. So far, he died trying to save his mother, he let the Deathless Empire abduct his sister, almost beaten severely by an Irekei, and finally religious extremists captured him. In addition, they wanted to roast him alive. He narrowly escaped because of the kindness of a girl and the desert was not any better. His journey so far did not appear to be going in his favor. He grew frustrated thinking of his journey and fell into a deep slumber. That night, he did not have any visions.

It was the belief of his people that Saedron the Fate Weaver planted the visions you see during sleep. She was a Goddess who resided in a great palace on the Silver Moon, so the legend goes. The tales also revealed that Saedron first taught Sorcery and

Wizardry to the Elves back in the Age of Twilight. However, her sanity and compassion faded as of late because of the death of her twin sister, Volliandra. The Dragon, who destroyed the Golden Moon, also killed Volliandra whose palace resided there. Megildur's mother, Vanya, used to tell these tales to him and his sister at bedtime.

The dark skies gave way to the bright desert sun in the morning. This did not wake the boy for some time. In fact, he did not wake until the sun was at the highest point in the sky. He opened his eyes and realized he had slept through the entire morning. He stretched and reached for some berries for his midday meal. Leaning back on the tree, he decided not to leave today since it was unwise to travel under a midday sun in the desert. He spent the rest of the afternoon weighing his options and dreading the thought of returning to the blistering heat and course sand of the desert. The only time Megildur was around sand back home was when he and his sister would play down by the water. He tried to focus more on the happy times of his childhood, but his thoughts kept returning to his sister in peril. Megildur thought of his sister in danger. He enjoyed his cozy little oasis, but this thought gnawed at him. He could also not stop thinking of what the old man said to him about being the heir to the High King Cambruin.

Since his thoughts would not allow him to sit there peacefully, Megildur decided he must continue his journey that night. He tore a small patch of cloth from his shirt and laid it on the ground. He grabbed several handfuls of berries and piled them on the cloth. He pulled up the corners and tied them to each other forming a small satchel of berries. He attached the satchel to his waist and then proceeded east to the water's edge. Megildur knew the water would be cold. He figured it was better to begin the day wet and cold in the desert then hot and sweaty. He swam through the water and climbed ashore. He ascended the sand dune to resume his trek. He was unsure why he journeyed east but he felt compelled, no pulled, to continue through the desert. The boy walked until the sun began to rise. He glanced ahead and observed some large creatures in his path. Since the encounter with the manticore before, he decided it would be unwise to walk through the creatures. Instead, Megildur chose a path around the camp. Several creatures wandered around some ruins in the sand. Megildur watched them closely since he did not want to interact with any of them. After he made some distance past the ruins he returned to his original course.

He walked for a bit when he noticed some sort of haze to the sand before him. It grew in size and intensity until it was finally upon him, a sandstorm. He pulled his shirt up as far as he could and tried to walk in the same direction, but that was impossible. The wind pounded the harsh sand against the boy as if he was a stain in the desert and someone decided to rub him out. Unable to withstand the force of the winds, Megildur was catapulted head-over-heels into a sand dune. Disoriented and battered, the Aelfborn braced himself for more punishment. In the corner of his eye, Megildur thought he saw something, or someone, in the storm. He quickly raised his head but the sand enveloped his eyes. Megildur could have sworn by the All-Father that he saw a figure moving about. Megildur tried to clear the foreign matter from his eyes. When he finally did, the strange figure was now gone, vanished in the storm. Was he imagining the figure in the sand? Was this an elaborate mirage? He searched the area in front of him without success.

Megildur felt a sharp pain to the back of his head forcing him to the ground. He spiraled to the hot desert surface staring up at his newfound assailant. He had on a black hood and his skin was just as dark. The boy tried to reach for a nearby rock to use as a weapon, but the injury to his head rendered him unconscious. Megildur, once again, slipped into a veil of darkness. What else could go wrong?

CHAPTER 6: Buring Blood

During Megildur's time in darkness, he had no visions. He experienced a feeling of warmth, which was not hard to find in a hot desert. At least this let him know he was not dead...yet. He opened his eyes and tried to move his arms, only to discover they were bound by rope. He tried several times to break the bindings but was only able to create a commotion. This raised the attention of a guard, who peered inside the tent. The guard muttered something Megildur did not understand and closed the opening. However, he did recognize the race of his captors, Irekei. The guard had the same bright red skin the Irekei in the tavern did, when the old man first saved him. Since his first encounter with the Irekei race almost ended with a beating, the boy was not optimistic. The tent flap flew open once again and a woman stood in the opening. Her skin was black like coal and her eyes raged with fire. She grumbled some words that the boy did not understand but knew they did not convey good times were ahead for him. The woman pulled out a dagger, grabbed him by the back of his head, and pressed the sharp blade to his throat. Megildur did not close his eyes but instead spoke harshly. "Kill me if you want, but after I finish off the Elven scum who destroyed my village, I will be back for you!" With that said, he spit on the sandy floor and prepared to die once more.

A voice bellowed from outside the tent but once again, Megildur did not understand the language. The Irekei woman glared toward the new voice and sheathed her dagger. He could tell this other person's order did not please her. She dragged the Aelfborn outside the tent into the blazing bright sun. Megildur would have shaded his eyes from this sun, if his hands were free. His eyes eventually adjusted to the new brightness levels and he could see a large man with coal black skin, much like the woman still restraining him. He motioned to the woman and she dropped Megildur, pulled out her dagger again, and cut the bindings on his hands. She snorted at Megildur and turned away.

The man jeered, "So boy, you want to destroy the entire Deathless Empire?" All the others around him found this question humorous and responded with laughter. This one appeared to be the leader, since everyone circled around him and laughed when he did. "One impish Aelfborn outcast against the mighty Elven armies?"

Megildur snarled, "I would not call any army mighty when they attack at night, I call them cowards. Nor do I hold any Elf in high regard who steals little girls and slaughters women!" He knew this might get him killed, but right now rebirth anywhere would be preferable to confinement in this forsaken desert. He tired of the games others played, with him as the pawn. "So if you are going to kill me, be quick about it! You are starting to bore me!"

The Irekei leader halted and glared into Megildur's eyes. The boy knew he must not waver from this contestation or he would remain a prisoner indefinitely. After what felt like an eternity, the Irekei broke eye contact and chortled. Then his followers joined in the jovial response. "I like this half-breed! So tell me boy, why do you hold such hostility toward the Elven nation? Other than the already cursed blood running through your veins, why do you hate them so?"

"The Elves from the Northlands came down and devastated my village. They also took my sister with them," Megildur replied. "I began the journey to find her some time ago, but marauders intercepted me and dragged me to this horrid desert. I am even unsure where in Aerynth I am!" The boy threw up his arms. The long trek exhausted and disheveled Megildur. Moreover, they abducted him twice, which did not help his situation.

The Irekei leader observed Megildur's frustration and decided to take pity on the young Aelfborn. The Irekei thundered, "Follow me boy, I think I can give you more bearing on your journey." He led Megildur to a large building in the middle of the camp. They proceeded up a short set of stairs and into a large chamber. At the entrance were two rather disgruntled guards who both departed from view after the Irekei leader waved his hand and spouted some order. He guided the boy to the far side of the room where, spread out across most of the wall, was an enormous map of their world, Aerynth. The maps size and detail amazed Megildur. The Irekei showed the boy where in the desert he was. He was down in the far southeast of Aerynth. "The fir'khanim that brought you down here were from the Gray Sands safehold here." The Irekei pointed west of their current location. "They call their guild the Temple of the Cleansing Flame. You must have journeyed for over a week across this desert before we brought you to our safehold, Kaal Tharkhan."

"Yes, the cleansing flame part sounds familiar." Megildur remembered the trial by fire they wanted to perform upon him. Then he looked a bit puzzled by the name of the Irekei safehold since it sounded more Elven. He was almost too afraid to ask. He knew the hatred the Irekei had toward the Elven nation, so the name baffled him. "Please do not take offense to this question; the name of this safehold almost has an Elven dialect to it. Is it named after them?"

The Irekei leader sneered at Megildur for a brief moment and replied, "The Irekei and the Elven people share an ancient heritage." The leader eased his hostility knowing the boy did not know any better. "During the Age of Twilight both races were one, but many felt their blood burn. Some of us had a yearning for action and conquest, not to just sit around and debate the needs of the people casually. The weak elvish nobles, who banished us stronger ones to the burning deserts, looked down upon this burning blood. They feared us because of their own ignorance and hatred for anyone different, and they consider themselves highly intellectual!" The Irekei collided with a nearby table and was having issues controlling his rage. Megildur could see his skin was steaming as he paced back and forth in the room, agitated and ranting about the Elven people.

Megildur knew he must diffuse this tense situation somehow. He provoked, "So are you going to kill me now or just torture me? I must get on with my journey and this desert heat is rather tiresome."

The Irekei leader ceased his pacing and scowled at the boy. However, it did break the tension in the room. The Irekei leader broke out in laughter at Megildur's remark. "I like you boy, you have a flare to you!" He walked over to the boy and vibrantly patted him on the back. He pulled Megildur in close and began to walk with him out of the building. "I will not kill you today, but I can get you back on your journey." This news intrigued the boy. "I will grant you temporary access to our runemaster. Now he will not be able to transport you to your safehold but he can get you to Sea Dog's Rest. You can get passage to your safehold from the runemaster there. Sound good or do you prefer death?" The Irekei glared at the boy, looking to get a rise out him.

Megildur countered, "Oh no, I prefer the first option." The Irekei once again burst out a hearty laugh, guiding the boy over to their tree in the middle of the safehold. On their way to the runemaster, they walked past two Irekei Warriors wearing only trousers and engaged in battle with each other. Megildur stopped to watch in amazement. The two Warriors fought with no weapons, just fists against fists. He turned to the Irekei leader, "Why do they fight each other? Did they have some disagreement?"

He boasted, "It is the Irekei way boy! Our blood burns for conflict, we thrive on war. They do not need a dispute with one another. The conflict is already in them." The Irekei leader allowed Megildur to stand and watch for some time since he could tell their fighting prowess amazed the boy. One of the Warriors dealt a devastating blow to the other, knocking him to the ground. Once the one on the ground was slow in lifting himself up, the victor went to him and gave a hand, helping him to his feet. "You see Aelfborn, we are not without honor. We battle because we must. It is who we are, who we must be. Everyone has their roles in life. Ours is conquering enemies in battle." He gave a slight sneer to Megildur and turned him back toward the tree.

The Irekei stopped him a short distance from the runemaster and continued alone. He spoke with the runemaster and pointed to Megildur during the conversation. Megildur noticed at that time, that all the runemasters looked alike. They appear Human and wear the same modest white hooded robe. Then the runemaster nodded to the Irekei leader, accepted the orders, and the Irekei motioned for the boy to approach. Megildur walked to the runemaster, the Irekei leader shook his hand.

The Irekei leader bellowed out, "Good hunting on your journey Aelfborn! May Kryquo'khalin, the Holy Source of the Sun, shine his blessing upon you." The Irekei leader sneered and walked off, leaving the boy with the runemaster.

"So my master has ordered me to transport you to Sea Dog's Rest," the runemaster said to Megildur. "Are you ready?" The boy nodded and the runemaster waved his hands to begin transporting Megildur. Upon arriving in Sea Dog's Rest, the Aelfborn wasted no time with loitering around that place. He approached the runemaster near the tree and requested passage to New Mellissar, but he was unsure of what he must do next.

CHAPTER 7: *Zeristan the Wise*

Once he arrived in his own safehold, Megildur dropped to his knees, overwhelmed to his very core. He had never even left his village for more than an afternoon before this whole disaster began. Only sixteen years old, expected to save his sister, and to fulfill some destiny was too much for the young Aelfborn. The boy sat there uncertain of what to do next, when a cloaked figure approached and spoke to him.

"So how did you enjoy your first visit to the deserts of Aerynth, boy?" The cloaked figure inquired. The voice sounded all too familiar, but Megildur was unable to see the face of the stRanger. It was impossible to see with the sun in his eyes and the cloak shading the stRangers face. The stRanger drew back his cloak and Megildur could see the elderly man who saved him from the Irekei in Sea Dog's Rest.

Megildur queried the old man, "Who are you old man, and how did you know I was in the desert?"

The old man chuckled, "You mean besides the sand pouring from your boots? We can discuss that after you clean up and get some sustenance, let's go Aelfborn." The old man guided the boy into a building. He tossed a gold coin to the woman behind the counter and pushed Megildur into a backroom. "Alright boy, clean that wretched desert off of you and then we can talk." The boy found a washtub in the room filled with water and some cloth to dry with afterwards. Before he could remove his clothes the elderly man entered with some clothing and fresh boots. "Here, put this on once you clean yourself." He walked back out and Megildur removed his clothes and jumped in the water. It was the first time he has been clean in weeks.

His mother would have never let him get that bad. Mother...it was the first time he thought of his parents in some time as well. Did they find his sister? Did they have better fortune than he. The boy wasted no time in cleaning the entire desert off him. He wanted to get out of the washtub and find out why this old man kept showing up. What does he want? He removed as much dirt, sand as possible, and stood from the washtub to dry his aching body. He put on the oversized clothing and boots and walked into the next room. The elderly man bellowed, "Now you look more presentable, boy! Here, come sit down before you collapse from starvation."

Megildur sat down at the old man's table but wondered how much he already had to drink. "I thank you for your assistance but I must know, who are you and why do you keep appearing out of nowhere?" Megildur now demanded to know the identity of the old man.

The old man let out a deep sigh and set down his drink, seemingly reluctant to talk about himself. "Alright, it seems only fitting I tell you my tale, especially to the heir of Cambruin." He winked at Megildur but he thought the old man was crazy about him being royalty. "My name is Zeristan..."

Megildur lashed out, "Hold your tongue, old man! You expect me to believe you are Zeristan the Wise, Wizard and Counselor to the late High King Cambruin? A drunk like you is the mightiest Wizard in all of Aerynth?" The boy began to laugh.

The old man sneered at the boy and waved his hands. Megildur opened his eyes after laughing. He was in hovering in midair outside of the establishment. The boy plummeted a short distance to the ground. He landed in some soft hay meant for livestock. Fortunately, the hay was clean but it stuck out of his hair and clothing, giving him the appearance of a scarecrow. He looked upward to see the old man descending from the sky, more graciously than him. The Wizard, of course, proved his powers of teleportation and levitation. "What I expect from you, boy, is the respect I have earned! I am older than anyone in Aerynth and more powerful, do not forget that!" Megildur nodded in amazement at him. Zeristan transported them back to their table after reaching the ground. "Now, if we can continue without any more disrespectful outbursts!" Zeristan glared at Megildur but the boy looked away, hoping to avoid any more demonstrations of his powers. "So you have heard of me from your parents then?"

The boy replied, "My father used to tell me the tales of Cambruin during the Age of Kings."

"Ah yes, I remember those days well," Zeristan responded. "Those were glorious days, once High King Cambruin possessed Shadowbane." He stared off remembering days long past when mighty kingdoms sought his counsel and powers. Megildur could see he was reminiscing, but he needed his assistance here and now.

Megildur interjected, trying to bring Zeristan back to this reality. "You spoke of Shadowbane before being the sword that the Traitor used to pin Cambruin to the Tree of Life? What's so special about a sword?"

"Shadowbane is no mere sword!" Zeristan retorted. "Thurin, the God of Forge and Craft, constructed Shadowbane during the Age of Twilight. He created it to battle an ancient evil so powerful and so feared that the eldest of Elven brethren referred to it as the Terror of Terrors and the Irekei called it Kryquo'khalin."

"Terror of Terrors?" The boy asked even though the name alone struck fear in his heart. "What is this ancient evil?"

"A dragon who laid in slumber beneath the ground, deep inside Aerynth," Zeristan described the early encounter with the dragon. "Nobody recalls what woke the creature but his might and fury shook the world. It toppled many of the great Elven cities and its fiery breath alone created the Sun in the sky. Before this tragedy, Aerynth bathed in constant moonlight from two moons, one was Gold and the other Silver. Thusly, they named that period of time the Age of Twilight." Zeristan continued, Megildur sat there listening in awe. "It took the combined power of The All-Father, Thurin, and another mighty God, Kenaryn the Hunter, in order to subdue the dragon back into Aerynth. Kenaryn even broke the tip of his mighty spear into the eye of the beast. Once they wounded the beast, it withdrew into a deep slumber near the core of the world. The Elves thanked the Gods for their help. However, the Elves feared they would be defenseless if the Terror ever woke again. Fearing for the Children of Braialla, Thurin promised to construct a weapon so powerful that it would have no equal. The light emanating from Shadowbane would subdue all shadows."

"Shadowbane!" Megildur interposed. "Besides the fact that a God made Shadowbane, what makes it so special?"

Zeristan stared at the boy in disbelief. "Well, apparently your father did not tell you the most important details. I guess that is why the All-Father sent you to me." The old Wizard shook his head and waved his hands. A vision of the sword appeared before Megildur. He just sat, staring at it in wonder. "The blade is as black as the deepest depths in Aerynth. No other weapon is stronger nor does it possess the same metal. Thurin forged Shadowbane using a mixture of adamant, truesteel, and truesilver, which the Dwarves ground from the Bones of the World. Thurin took the blade and quenched it in the acidic blood of the dragon. He tempered the weapon, in case the beast ever emerged again. Look closely at the hilt and you will see the mark of the Terror on the guard. On the opposite end...the mark of The All-Father on the pommel. Around the grip, tightly spiraled, is golden wire fashioned from a lock of hair that Malog gave to Thurin. That was all that remained of his beloved wife, Volliandra. She died in her palace on the Golden Moon when the Terror unleashed his fiery breath, before the Gods drove the beast back into the pit from which he came."

Megildur inquired, "So Shadowbane never fulfilled its intended design? Since they never used Shadowbane against the dragon, what became of the sword?" The tale of the mighty sword intrigued the boy.

Zeristan jested, "Well, I see I have your full attention now." Megildur gave him a perturbed look but he could not deny his fascination for the saga of the weapon crafted by the Gods. The Wizard continued, after seeing the annoyance on the boy's face. "To put the Elves at ease with the thought of the dragon returning, Thurin presented the sword to the Elven King Sillestor. Sillestor named the sword Shadowbane, the mighty sword with a light to vanquish the Shadow of Oblivion. It was the greatest blade ever forged and the last crafted by Thurin the Shaper. Constructing Shadowbane grievously maimed the God of Forge and Craft, Father of the Dwarven race. He could handle the heat of the forge but the intensity from the foul sweltering blood of the dragon was more than even Thurin could withstand. The dragon's blood burned Thurin's left hand to the bone, forcing him to wear a glove to cover the hideousness."

Megildur exclaimed, "And this is the sword you say I am destined to reclaim from the Tree of Life? The same tree of stone that the Traitor pinned the High King Cambruin to?" Zeristan nodded in agreement. Megildur shouted as he stood to his feet across the table from the Wizard. "You expect a mere Aelfborn boy, who has never left his village, to find a missing sword that Knights failed to find and defeat a Terror that even Gods could not?"

Zeristan bellowed, standing toe-to-toe with Megildur, "I expect you to be the man that your father and the All-Father know you are! Your mother and father fought bravely for both you and your sister. I would expect nothing less from the man bearing the mark of the All-Father!" Staring deep into Megildur's eyes, Zeristan placed his hand on the Aelfborn's shoulder. "You must no longer think of yourself as the boy from a small village. You are now a man who has survived multiple abductions, survived the hottest desert in all of Aerynth, and lived to tell the tale." Zeristan now had a grin on his face, embracing Megildur and walking with him out the doorway. "Now, let us go forth and find you a force worthy of engaging the Dar Khelegur and retrieve your sister."

"You never told me, how did you know they took me to the desert?" Megildur inquired.

Zeristan jested, "Who did you think that was hovering over the encampment covering your daring escape?"

Megildur retorted, "Then where were you when the Manticore snuck up behind me? That beast could have made a Knight's feast out of me!"

"Don't be ridiculous Megildur," Zeristan chortled. "That beast was only a cub!"

The two of them walked off laughing toward the gates exiting New Mellissar. Now if only Megildur knew where to find anyone else to help him save his sister, anyone bold enough to face the Elves of the High Mountains. Megildur felt more confident having a mighty Wizard on his side. Now, he just needed an army.

CHAPTER 8: Centaur Cohort

"Where do we go from here?" Megildur asked. He knew they needed help but was unaware of anyone daring enough to challenge the Elven nations.

"We seek a race that hates the Elves, even more than you do right now," Zeristan replied. "We seek the Centaur race, more specifically the Centaur Cohort safehold of Fort Ekarros." Megildur was familiar with this place, since they were neighbors who kept to themselves. Fort Ekarros was just north of his home, Fort Viatrus, but Megildur had never met a Centaur before. He heard tales of the Horse Lords deep hatred for the Elves since the Age of Twilight. The Centaurs rallied behind their Godly Father, Kenaryn the Hunter, against the Dar Khelegur, when the Elves defied the All-Father.

Once they passed through the gates of New Mellissar, Zeristan turned to Megildur. "Now, you will need to travel much faster than you have so far." Zeristan waved his hands and the Aelfborn cringed, fearing he may send him somewhere unpleasant again. Instead, nothing happened. He just stared back at Zeristan. The old man bellowed, "Well, try running around." Megildur was unsure of what Zeristan was up to but he figured he would play along. He began to run, but it was much faster than he had ever travelled before. It felt as if he was running on the clouds and moving faster than a bird. He stopped just short of running the old Wizard over.

Megildur cheered, "This is amazing, what did you do?" He tried to keep his composure, which was difficult at this point.

"I applied a temporary magical enchantment to your boots to give them the speed of the Windlords," Zeristan replied. "Your speed has increased. This will decrease our travel time and make our journey to Fort Ekarros easier." After a few more times of Megildur running in circles, and receiving stares from Zeristan, the two of them continued north on the path toward Fort Ekarros. Megildur felt more at ease having Zeristan with him. His last trip in this direction landed him in the desert and nearly incinerated by a religious cult. They traveled for a short time but covered a great distance. Megildur glanced at their destination ahead of them. He noticed an overturned cart in the road and an arm protruding from it. He began to slow when Zeristan grabbed his shoulder and shook his head, letting him know not to slow down. Zeristan motioned forward with his other hand projecting an energy bolt in front of them. This energy blast knocked the cart from the path and sent the body flying out. Megildur was in shock. He felt they might have been able to save the injured traveler if Zeristan had not blasted the cart. From the corner of his eye, Megildur detected something shiny. He turned his head just in time to see an arrow flying in their direction. Zeristan waved his hand in the direction of the arrow, and it vanished from sight. The old man sent another energy bolt in the direction the arrow traveled from and knocked the assailant to the ground. Zeristan gave Megildur a slight grin. They both continued forward on their journey, but the Aelfborn looked upset.

Soon after, they reached a safehold. Megildur assumed it was Fort Ekarros. Zeristan halted before reaching the entrance.

Megildur scolded, "What happened back there with destroying that cart? We could have helped that person before you hurled them to the winds!"

Zeristan replied, "That was an ambush, my young Aelfborn. You still have much to learn about traveling about in Aerynth. These roads can be treacherous. Marauders would like nothing more than to leave you lifeless on the side of the road. They also would relieve you of your worldly possessions." Zeristan wrapped his arm around Megildur and proceeded toward the gates. It was true the Aelfborn did have much to learn. He never traveled across Aerynth, until now.

When they reached the entry to the safehold, Megildur assumed the pair of guards standing outside were Centaurs. He heard that they possess the upper half of a man and their lower half was that of a horse, and that was exactly what these guards looked like. They stood taller than most beings in Aerynth. Large and majestic creatures they are. Zeristan declared, "Brave and noble Horse Lords. My companion and I seek a meeting with your Ruler."

"Who calls upon the Ruler of the Centaur Cohort?" One of the guards demanded. Both guards drew their weapons and Megildur feared the worst. He was sure Zeristan could handle these two but he was unsure of what adversaries were beyond the gates.

The old Wizard proclaimed, "Zeristan the Wise. I was Wizard and counselor to the late High King Cambruin and ally to the Centaurs." He turned to Megildur and whispered, "I hate boasting about myself, but the Centaurs are meticulous about formalities and presentation.

"It is I whom you seek, oh wise Wizard," a voice came from behind the gates. The large gates opened and the two guards bowed to the one who spoke. He was a tall Centaur donning an armor so bright it was nearly blinding when the sun shone upon it. The Centaur moved out into the open and Zeristan gazed upon their leader as if he recognized him.

"Atreus!" Zeristan cried out. "It's good to look upon you old friend!" He walked up and greeted the leader of the Centaur Cohort. "We must speak to you on an urgent matter." He turned to the Aelfborn and introduced him, "This is Megildur, and it is his quest we need to discuss with you."

"As you wish Zeristan," Atreus replied. "Please enter my home." He guided them past the entryway and into Fort Ekarros. Structures lined the fence perimeter and the center of the safehold was bursting with Centaur villagers. They seemed to be both curious and startled by the new arrivals. This clan of Centaurs did not coexist with other races but they did not persecute other non-Centaur beings. They were a peaceful people, until provoked. Then they could be fierce opponents. Atreus guided the two travelers into a large structure in the safehold and sat them down on a stone structure. "Forgive the accommodations, we do not get many non-Centaur visitors," Atreus admitted.

"There is nothing to forgive," Zeristan replied. "We are just grateful you took us in and allowed us an audience with you." This was the most respectful and humble Megildur had ever seen the old man. It was a side of him he had never witnessed. He was grateful for this side of Zeristan, since his diplomacy may be what saves his sister.

"The honor is mine, old friend," Atreus replied. "Now you mentioned having an urgent matter to discuss?" Both Atreus and Zeristan turned to Megildur, as if they expected him to speak. The thought of having to be diplomatic and request assistance from someone he had never met terrified the Aelfborn. He had a tough enough time speaking with his parents or the elders of his village. His heart began to race and his palms began to sweat. If he did not control his composure soon, fainting in front of both of them would be next. He took a deep breath and steadied his nerves.

Megildur stated, "Yes, Sir. Recently the Dar Khelegur attacked my village just south of here, Fort Viatrus. Both Elves and Minotaurs raged through our village, killing all in sight and destroying all that stood. We can eventually rebuild but they abducted someone close to me, my sister." Megildur's composure began to falter and a single tear rolled down his face. He wiped the tear from his cheek and looked at Atreus who had a look of concern. The Aelfborn continued on, "I plan on going after her and facing the might of the Elven nation but need more allies on my quest. Will you join me?" He stared into the Centaur leader's compassionate eyes trying not to look aggressive but at the same time not too weak.

Atreus took a deep breath and sincerely asked Megildur, "Your intentions are noble, but do you fully understand the quest you are asking us to join you on? The Dar Khelegur will not be easy to defeat and becoming a prisoner to those Elves is a fate worse than death."

With strength and conviction Megildur responded, "That is why we must challenge them. If we do not free the prisoners they now hold and stop their tyranny, they will swarm over all of Aerynth like a plague."

The wise Centaur ruler looked over to Zeristan, who showed a look of confidence in Megildur. He owed the Wizard his life multiple times over and did not wish to doubt the faith of his friend. Seeing the Aelfborn's determination Atreus resounded, "It would honor us to join you against the Dar Khelegur! You can count on the Centaur Cohort to fight at your side. We will save your sister!"

Megildur finally felt confident he could retrieve his sister. He shook hands with Atreus. "Thank you!"

"Now we will need more forces to counter their magical powers," Atreus admitted. This baffled Megildur since he barely had the courage to ask Atreus, let alone another nation all together. "I can call upon our brethren in Greensward Parish. Perhaps even the entire Church of the All-Father nation might join us on this worthy and noble quest. Now come, you two must be weary and you need your strength for the journey to Greensward Parish. It's further than the journey you made today. So eat, drink, and rest for we will leave at first light!"

Atreus bellowed out commands to his people who assembled a feast around the fire. Megildur sat next to the blaze while the Centaur people catered to him, feeding him and making sure his goblet was never empty. Several of the Centaur clan shouted Megildur's name and raised their drinks in his honor. This made the Aelfborn feel welcomed but he still doubted his own abilities and this notion that he was some heir to the High King Cambruin. He also knew nothing of the outcome of his parents; did his father already have his sister and they were safe in their village? Either way, it did not matter. The Deathless Empire needed to pay for attacking his village. Zeristan could see the concerned look on the Aelfborn's face and went to check on his wellbeing.

"What troubles you?" Zeristan asked. "Your goblet is full, the food has no end, and we have found a force large enough to make a formidable campaign against the Elves…once we get more assistance from Greensward Parish. Why do you not rejoice?"

Megildur whispered, "I am not the fierce Warrior they think I am. I cannot lead this clan to victory! I can't even fight one Minotaur without getting crushed to death!" Zeristan could see Megildur was beginning to panic, so he stood with him and they walked to a remote area away from the festivities.

Zeristan reassured, "You must start believing in your abilities; everyone else around you does. Do you think for one moment that the mighty All-Father himself would have given you his mark if he did not know you were the one to reclaim Shadowbane and bring balance to Aerynth?" Megildur shook his head no. "Then you need to act like the man you will become, not the boy you once were. Your father entrusted you to protect the family, and we will help you fulfill the promise you made to him. We will save your sister and rid Aerynth of the Dar Khelegur. A High King must believe in himself in order to rule." Megildur grinned at the wise Wizard and thanked him by placing his hand on his shoulder. Then they both returned to the festivities. All eyes were on them when they returned.

"Attention everyone!" Atreus proclaimed. "I want you to raise your drinks in honor of the brave and courageous Aelfborn. He has chosen to engage the contemptible Dar Khelegur to save his clan and has honored the Centaur Cohort by inviting us to join the battle. So drink to the mighty one, drink to Megildur!" They all cheered his name and applauded. Megildur had never been the focus of such praise and notability before. He began to believe in the faith the Wizard had placed in him. For the first time he felt he would be able to save his sister. Now, as for fulfilling his destiny and reclaiming Shadowbane, he could only handle one quest at a time.

CHAPTER 9: The Road to Greensward Parish

Megildur awoke the next morning and realized he had passed out in a tent after the festivities last night. Fortunately, he was alone. That way nobody could see his agony after a night of revelry. He had no idea the Centaurs were so jovial. He stumbled around the tent, gathered his clothes, and procrastinated getting dressed, to delay going outside to face the others. He had most of his clothes on and reached for his boots, when the tent opened and Zeristan stood before him.

Zeristan remarked, "Good morning, Megildur." He had no idea the Wizard was one of those people who enjoyed the morning. Even as a child growing up in his village, he despised the dawn and tried to stay in bed as long as his mother would let him.

Megildur groaned, "What is good about it? How can you have nights like last night and still wake so alive in the morning?"

The Wizard responded, "It comes from centuries of practice. Now grab your boots and get a move on. The Centaur group is ready to depart." Zeristan turned and left the tent while Megildur pulled up his boots and stood. He swayed for a moment and toppled back to the tent floor. He shook off the feeling, since he knew he must not show weakness so soon in his journey. He stood once again, slightly swayed, but was able to regain his balance this time. He pushed forth into the frigid morning air and continued past a group of tents to see an army of Centaurs. There must have been nearly a hundred of them wearing armor and armed for battle. He could smell the metal in the forges from the blacksmiths sharping blades and hear them pounding out armor. He walked into the crowd of Warriors and could see Atreus and Zeristan talking on the far side. He almost made it to them when Atreus noticed his presence and greeted him.

Atreus thundered, "Good morning, Megildur." Not another morning person, the Aelfborn thought to himself. "I trust you slept well?"

Megildur grumbled, "Sleeping was not the issue. Waking the next morning was." Atreus and Zeristan laughed at the inexperienced Aelfborn. "How can you enjoy yourselves like that at night and then wake so cheerful?"

"Years of practice, my young one," Atreus replied. Zeristan looked at Megildur and grinned. "Now we must prepare for the journey to Greensward Parish. Since you bipedal races are so slow, I have arranged for you to ride with two of my most trusted Warriors." He motioned toward his clan and two Centaurs approached. "I present Bowen, my Master Archer, and Thaddaios my Master Swordsman." Both Centaurs bowed to honor their guests. "Bowen will carry Zeristan and Thaddaios is responsible for Megildur. We will depart soon, so prepare." With that said Atreus nodded to Megildur and walked off to make sure all was ready. Zeristan began talking with Bowen, so Megildur decided to approach Thaddaios.

"It would honor me to transport you to your destination," Thaddaios stated.

"Thank you," Megildur replied. "I am not good at riding horses and until I came here I had never even met a Centaur, so forgive my inexperience." He gave

Thaddaios a slight grin. He was just trying to make friends before entrusting his life to him.

"No need to explain," Thaddaios replied. "It is not often we transport bipedal races, but I have done this before so you should not worry." He explained to the Aelfborn that he would be using a saddle to make the journey easier. They both finished preparing for the trek to Greensward Parish. Megildur tightened the saddle to Thaddaios and he could hear silence befall the Centaurs. He looked up to see Atreus move to the front of the clan.

Atreus bellowed, "Centaurs, we ride to Greensward Parish to gather more forces! Then we will march to the gates of Aelarnost, vanquish the evil within its walls, and rescue the innocent captives! The Dar Khelegur will experience the demise of the Deathless Empire under our hooves!"

The Centaurs roared out a loud battle cry as they advanced onward, beginning the trek to Greensward Parish. Megildur jumped onto the back of Thaddaios so he would not miss his own quest. Since he had never ridden a Centaur before he did not know what to expect, but he knew they would arrive faster than running there on foot. Granted the temporary spell Zeristan placed on their boots did increase their speed; he heard stories of Centaurs incredible endurance at maintaining superior velocity. Megildur held on for dear life while they raced through forests and open plains. He could feel the wind through his hair and the ground tremble with the force of the Centaurs stampeding across Aerynth. When they raced along, he could see other creatures scampering away at the sound created from their thundering hooves. Megildur noticed the shadows cast from the sun were stretching longer and longer, meaning the day would be ending soon. He hoped they would not travel through the night since he could use a break and a chance to stretch his legs. After a short time, he noticed the group beginning to slow and he heard a command to halt coming from up front.

"It appears we are making camp here for the night," Thaddaios said tilting his head back so Megildur could hear him. He proceeded to hop down from the back of Thaddaios, just to find his legs no longer worked. While Megildur tried to regain his balance, Zeristan approached.

Zeristan laughed, "Doing alright, Megildur?" The Aelfborn glared at him.

Megildur resounded, "I will be fine!"

"Glad to hear it," Zeristan replied. "We need to discuss our battle plans for Aelarnost." Zeristan guided Megildur over to a more secluded spot to converse.

Confused by the elderly Wizard, Megildur responded, "But we have no battle plans."

Zeristan jested, "That is what we must discuss. I have advised kings on battle plans before and from what I see at our disposal, we would be best to make a sneak attack. A full out bane would take too long and they may move the prisoners if we give them any advanced notice. Therefore, the first item we need to attend to is finding the building where they hold the prisoners. We will likely find the prison barracks along a perimeter wall. Now, we will need a sneak attack." Megildur attentively listened to Zeristan since the young Aelfborn had never seen battle plans, let alone planned an attack on a safehold. When the Wizard finished, a guard notified Zeristan that Atreus wanted to see him, so he left the Aelfborn.

After absorbing as much information as the wise Wizard was willing to give, Megildur returned to Thaddaios. Unfortunately, he was still pondering

Zeristan's battle plan and did not notice the saddle in front of him. Megildur tripped over the saddle and found himself face down on the ground. Thaddaios responded, "Let me help you." He leaned in to help Megildur and saw his exposed shoulder, revealing the mark of the All-Father. Thaddaios stared at Megildur, who rose to his feet and looked nervously back at the Centaur. "You bear the mark of the All-Father?" Thaddaios began to bow when Megildur halted his movement.

Megildur whispered, "Please do not bow. Just because I have this mark, does not make me better than anyone else. I do not want the others to know."

"As you wish, M'Lord, but His mark upon you does make you better," Thaddaios replied. "It has long been foretold of the one bearing the mark of the All-Father reclaiming the mighty Shadowbane and bringing peace and unity to Aerynth. This tale passed from one swordsman to another for generations."

"Well, I doubt this tale was referring to me. I can barely wield a sword let alone a mighty one," Megildur replied. "Not much need for sword skills when you live in a small village and tend to animals."

"Excuse me for a moment, I need to get something," Thaddaios replied. He went to a nearby cart and pulled out an object covered in cloth. He opened the object to reveal two swords, both with intricate detail and design. He turned to Megildur and presented the swords. "My father gave these to me. He seized them from the Chaos Dark Lords after the War of the Scourge. My father told me the swords required a greater purpose. I can think of none greater than teaching the future High King of Men." He pushed forth both swords, for Megildur to choose. Megildur picked up the one closest to him and held it up to the light, to examine it. "Now if you so choose M'Lord we can begin your lessons."

"I would be most grateful Thaddaios," Megildur replied. "I would also be most grateful if you would stop referring to me as 'Lord'. They have not crowned me, nor have I even retrieved Shadowbane. I am just…"

"The rightful heir to the High King Cambruin," Atreus interjected while he and Zeristan approached. "Also, you are the one who bears the mark of the All-Father to retrieve Shadowbane and bring peace to Aerynth." Megildur glared at Zeristan for publicizing information that the Aelfborn did not want revealed. Atreus noticed the glare and commented. "Please do not chastise Zeristan, I insist on knowing who I am sending my clan off to battle for. I hope you would not deny me this?"

"Of course not," Megildur responded. "You would be foolish not to inquire. Forgive me for keeping this information from you, but this is not something I would expect most to believe."

"It has been foretold, since Cambruin's betrayal. Thus, the Turning began…leading Aerynth into a dark period," Atreus commented. "The heir of the High King would pull Shadowbane from the Stone Tree in Kierhaven. Then you could restore the High Kingdom and bring peace to Aerynth. The Centaurs have always come to the aid of the Gods and obeyed their wishes. We will not fail you, Lord Megildur." Atreus placed his hand on Megildur's shoulder and bowed his head, in honor of the chosen hero of Aerynth. The Aelfborn returned the gesture by also placing his hand on Atreus' shoulder but found that a bit difficult since the Centaur stood nearly a foot taller than him. Regardless, the act was true and it appeared the would-be High King's destiny would be hard to avoid now.

CHAPTER 10: The Plan

Megildur practiced from sunrise to sunset with Thaddaios to become a Master Swordsman. Until he could handle the weight of the broadsword given unto him, they practiced with wooden swords. This was preferable at the time since it hurt less when Megildur missed and Thaddaios countered. The Centaur was an excellent teacher, and Megildur felt more comfortable each day.

It took them almost a week to cover the distance to Greensward Parish, but they finally reached the outer gates. The bluish colored walls of the safehold towered over the travelers. The fortress was Elven in design and the bastions were tall and majestic. This city was both ominous and magnificent simultaneously.

"Lord Megildur," Atreus commented. "We should have only a few people approach the gates. We do not want the High Priest to think we are an attacking force." When Atreus finished his sentence, one of the Centaurs yelled out about an approaching object; it was an arrow. It landed near Atreus' feet. Megildur noticed a piece of parchment attached to the arrow. He knelt down and collected the parchment, opened it, and read the message.

"Well, it appears we are too late for a subtle approach," Megildur said. "The High Priest Maethorion refuses to surrender and prepares for our impending attack. What should we do now?" Megildur looked a bit lost at this time. Diplomacy of any kind baffled Megildur, let alone between great nations.

"The five of us will approach the gates and explain our position," Atreus replied to Megildur, but also looked at Zeristan, Bowen, and Thaddaios. They knew this was a risky move since they would be vulnerable, if the High Priest ordered an attack. However, they would have to take the chance if they were to gain allies to their cause. Megildur could see guards lining the fortress walls, with archers at the ready. He hoped this would end well. They moved forward toward the gates with no weapons drawn but they still carried them. Hopefully the High Priest would not see this as a hostile gesture. When they were close enough to see the eyes of the archers, another arrow landed at their feet.

Someone shouted from the wall, "That is the last warning you will receive before I order the archers to cut you in half Atreus." They stopped their advance since it seemed futile to go further and allow the arrows to skewer them.

"High Priest Maethorion, is that your voice I hear old friend?" Atreus replied.

"Old friend?" The voice behind the wall retorted. "This is Maethorion, ruler of Greensward Parish and High Priest of the Church of the All-Father. However no friend of mine, old or not, would approach with armed forces to my gates. If you are my old friend Atreus, I would suggest leaving before I order the attack. If you are not my friend I can just order the attack now!"

Zeristan whispered to Megildur, "This is getting us nowhere. I can get us before Maethorion if you can convince him of our intentions." Zeristan smirked at Megildur.

"I can agree to those terms," Megildur replied with a smirk. "I assume you intend to teleport us inside the walls?" Zeristan nodded. "You will need to gently disable his guards once we arrive, so I may negotiate with the High Priest." Zeristan nodded once more and proceeded waving his hands to initiate the teleporting. Within moments, the two of them were standing before Maethorion, who had a guard on either side of him. Maethorion was Elven, with brown skin like the trees, indicating he was from the Twathedilion clan, Elves of the Forest. The guards began to draw their swords but were unable to unsheathe them before Zeristan struck them with bolts of energy. The powerful Wizard was able to unleash this power to both guards at the same time and directed accurately on either side of the High Priest. Megildur drew his sword and directed it at Maethorion.

The Aelfborn bellowed, "I am Lord Megildur, rightful heir to the High King Cambruin and chosen by the All-Father himself to reclaim Shadowbane!" The Aelfborn then drew back his shirt to reveal the shimmering mark of the All-Father on his shoulder. Seeing this mark swiftly forced the High Priest to his knee.

The High Priest announced, "Long has your coming been foretold mighty Lord. You will have my obedience and that of my people, Lord Megildur." Megildur was a bit surprised to see this once arrogant leader now bending a knee to him. He began to feel that this mark carried great weight and power.

"I do not want your obedience. I want your allegiance," Megildur said while lowering his sword and extending an open hand to the High Priest. Maethorion raised his head to see the gesture and was in shock. Someone with Megildur's claim to the throne and support of the All-Father asking for allegiance and not obedience was unheard of.

Maethorion extended his arm and allowed the Aelfborn to help him up from the floor.

Maethorion resounded, "You shall have my allegiance then, Lord Megildur!" Maethorion turned to reveal the hundreds of Warriors, servants, and commoners within Greensward Parish. "My people, this is Lord Megildur. He is the rightful heir to the High King Cambruin and chosen by the All-Father to reclaim Shadowbane and restore Aerynth to its once glorious state. They shall be our honored guests. Open the gates and let the Centaur Cohort in!" With one wave of his hand, the guards opened the gates and Atreus led his people inside. While Megildur watched his Centaur companions march inside the gates, he noticed another Elf approaching along the side of the fortress walls. "Lord Megildur, may I present my son Turwaithion."

"Lord Megildur," Turwaithion said while dropping to one knee. "I am Captain of the Guard for the Church of the All-Father. My men and I are at your command." Once again, Megildur extended an open hand and helped Turwaithion to his feet.

"Thank you, Captain Turwaithion," Megildur replied and then turned to Maethorion. "If we can isolate ourselves somewhere I can discuss with you the reason for our visit." Maethorion bowed his head in agreement and escorted Megildur and Zeristan to the courtyard. "I also wish for Atreus and his commanders to join us, if there is no objection?"

"Of course, they would honor us with their presence," Maethorion responded.

Megildur shouted, "Atreus, please join us with Thaddaios and Bowen. We have much to discuss." Atreus nodded in agreement and followed with Bowen and Thaddaios.

Maethorion escorted his visitors to a large regal building with two staircases leading to golden doors. Turwaithion pushed the doors open to reveal a detailed foyer with marble columns holding up a second level to the massive building. The other side of the foyer was a staircase that spiraled upward to the second level. They followed Turwaithion up this staircase. This place impressed Megildur, since the only large building in Fort Viatrus had three levels to it but was a hovel in comparison. The Fort Viatrus building was more like worker's quarters and not meant for noblemen. At the top of this staircase, they found a table grand enough for large gatherings, such as this one. Everyone sat down around the impressive table, everyone except Megildur who stood at the head of the table to unveil the details of his quest to Maethorion and Turwaithion.

"First, I would like to thank you for agreeing to meet with us," Megildur began. "A few weeks ago the Dar Khelegur of the north attacked my village, Fort Viatrus. Both Elves and Minotaurs raged through the village, killing all in sight and destroying all that stood. We will rebuild but they captured several people to use as slaves, including my sister. I need more forces to rally against the Dar Khelegur." Megildur observed Maethorion and Turwaithion look at each other in disbelief and then look back at him. "I know they are powerful, but I have a plan. Do you have a map of their fortress?" Turwaithion stood and walked to the far side of the room and returned with a scroll. The Captain opened the parchment to reveal a map of Aelarnost, the High Court fortress for the Dar Khelegur. "Thank you, this will help. They have most of their common buildings along the northern wall. This will likely be where they are holding their prisoners. The Centaur Cohort will attack the southwest corner. Once they have the Elves attention, the Church of the All-Father will begin an assault from the southeast. This will draw all their forces to the southern half of Aelarnost leaving the common areas desolate. Zeristan and I, along with a few others, will teleport inside the fortress walls and retrieve the slaves. Once we are out, we will signal both forces to withdraw. Does anyone have any questions?"

"It will take us some time to get to Aelarnost with all of our equipment for the bane," Maethorion announced. "I will need to send a Scout ahead of the rest with a Scroll of Summon Bane Circle, to announce the bane. The Scout can setup the bane stone and siege tents just outside their fortress. The trebuchets and ballistas will be difficult to transport through the mountains to the north."

"That is why we will travel through the forest to the south and without siege weapons," Zeristan replied. Shock colored their faces.

"It will be impossible to attack them without siege equipment," Maethorion bellowed. "We will need these weapons if we are to take the…"

"We are not there to take Aelarnost," Megildur interjected. "The battle is a diversion not a full out bane. Our primary concern is with saving the prisoners. If you decide later that you wish to take Aelarnost for yourself, please do so. If we announce ourselves as a bane with the intent of taking their fortress, they will have time to prepare and make sneaking into the back of Aelarnost more difficult. We will also need our Scouts, Huntresses, and Rangers to survey the area before we move in and disable any Scouts they have. Once again if they find out we are coming, it will destroy the element of surprise." Megildur could see the disappointment on the faces of his newfound allies. "I know you were hoping this was the opportunity to destroy the Dar Khelegur and crush their arrogance, but this is not the time. We will have other opportunities. I am sure that one stealth attack will not stop them of their wicked ways and that we will be confronting them again. However, this assault will weaken the Elves." With that said, the morale in the room lifted, and Megildur felt confident once again that they could save his sister. "We depart at first light, prepare the rest of the day, and get a good night rest for tomorrow we leave to attack the Dar Khelegur!" The room exploded with glorious battle cries and conviction. Megildur knew he finally had a worthy force to engage the Elves of the north.

CHAPTER 11: Golden Treasure

Megildur walked out of the massive building and onto the ground within Greensward Parish when the High Priest Maethorion called out to him.

"Lord Megildur, might I have a word with you?" Maethorion requested. "I have something that might interest you. I see you wear leather armor. May I interest you in something more prestigious?" Megildur was curious, but also cautious by this action, because of Maethorion's previous reception and Megildur's earlier mistrust of the Cleansing Flame cult. On guard, he followed Maethorion to an edifice with guards surrounding the entrance. The sentries opened the doors and Megildur could see this was their armory, with more guards positioned within. Inside the next room, Maethorion opened an ornate passage to display his personal stock. Megildur discovered bold and gallant weapons, along with armor selected by the High Priest himself. He guided Megildur over to a suit of armor mounted on the far wall. The armor glistened as bright as the sun with gold and white metal. It was the most magnificent armor he had ever seen; even knights did not have armor of this magnitude. "Here," Maethorion said. "Feel the weight of the helm." He placed the golden helm in Megildur's hands. The headpiece was incredibly light, considering it was solid metal.

"It feels too light to deflect the blow from a sword," Megildur commented. Maethorion respectfully took back the helm and placed it on a stone block. He unsheathed a broadsword from his collection and swung the sword with all his might, striking the golden helm. He placed the sword back in its scabBard, picked up the helm, and gave it back to Megildur to examine. The Aelfborn was in shock to see the helm without any damage upon the exterior where the High Priest struck it. "I stand corrected, it can withstand a blow from a sword," Megildur replied with an astonished look upon his face. He placed the golden helm back upon the stone.

"The armorists originally designed and forged this suit for the Elven King Sillestor," Maethorion remarked. "He had ordered it just before his treacherous act of betrayal to the All-Father himself. The All-Father had engaged in battle with one of the Beast Lords. Beast Lords are false Gods the Dar Khelegur worshipped at the time. Sillestor attempted to strike the All-Father from behind using Shadowbane. It was due to Thurin's rapid act of bravery that Shadowbane's blow met with the maimed hand of the sword's creator. After Thurin stopped Sillestor from his attempt of betrayal, he then squeezed the breath from him stopping just before death. Thurin took Shadowbane from the ground where Sillestor had dropped the sword and with one swing he took the Elven King's head from his deceitful body." Megildur had a look of horror on his face. He had no idea of the magnificence and tragedy surrounding the mighty weapon. Maethorion continued, "After his execution Sillestor obviously had no need for the completed armor. It passed from one ruler to another within the Dar Khelegur until someone decided the cursed armor did not belong in Aelarnost. The opportunity to acquire the armor arose and I knew that one day it could serve another Warrior chosen by the All-Father to right the wrongs in Aerynth. I know now that chosen Warrior is you,"

Maethorion said as he once again picked up the helm and placed it in Megildur's hands.

Megildur paused for a moment, uncertain if he was worthy of such noble armor. He remembered Zeristan's words that a High King must believe in himself in order to rule. "I accept your offer, Maethorion. I vow to be a better man than the original intended for this armor," Megildur said as he kindly looked at the High Priest. Even though Maethorion was an Elf, Megildur did not have any animosity toward him or his people. After all, his mother was an Elf, which meant Elven blood flowed through his veins. "I will don this armor at first light, before we leave for Aelarnost."

Megildur and Maethorion proceeded outside into the courtyard to find Turwaithion bellowing out orders. He had most of the inhabitants of Greensward Parish scurrying around preparing for something. Megildur asked Maethorion, "Is this in preparation for our journey tomorrow?"

Maethorion chuckled, "Oh no. With living in Aerynth, war is inevitable. Inhabitants always expect conflict. Turwaithion is preparing a feast for our guests before we head off for battle. Now follow me, I will show you your quarters where you can change before the festivities." Maethorion escorted Megildur to an extravagant tent, which stood taller than any of the other tents around. "These quarters are for our honored guests. If you have any needs, please ring this bell on the table and your personal valet will see to your every need. I will have someone bring the armor to your tent." Maethorion exited the tent and left Megildur to change.

His gear from the journey was already inside the tent, unpacked and laid out for him. He removed his shirt and the sleeve caught the edge of the tent, causing him to stumble backwards into a table, which knocked the bell to the ground. He reached for the bell when a young attractive human female entered the tent. Her black hair flowed like silk and she had pale skin that shown like moonlight glistening on the water. She observed Megildur was half-dressed so she proceeded to remove her shirt without saying a word.

Megildur blurted, "What are you doing?" This caused her to pause with a confused look upon her face. She now stood over him wearing only a revealing undergarment over her chest. With haste, he handed her shirt back while carefully trying to help cover her body.

She responded, "Forgive me M'Lord. My orders are to accommodate your every need, and I presumed you desired intimacy. If I am not to your liking I can fetch another handmaiden."

Megildur's eyes widened and he began stumbling on his own words. "No, you are to my liking...I mean I do not desire any physical affection. No wait that did not sound right! Oh All-Father, save me from this mess!" He sat down on the edge of a chair by the table. This confused her even further. Megildur, seeing the bewildered look on her face, motioned for her to sit down on the edge of the bed just opposite of him. "I am sorry. I was not calling you into my tent for anything, let alone that! Not that you are not desirable...oh I am making this worse!" He took a deep breath and decided to ask a simple question that might break the tense moment. "What is your name?"

"I am Marie, M'Lord," she replied with a quick curtsy. She remained in that position until given the command to sit back down, which did not occur to

Megildur for a short time. He never commanded servants before now.

Megildur replied with an irritated tone, "Please sit down and do not address me as Lord." Marie sat down on the edge of the bed once more. Her face scrunched up and hesitation filled her eyes, but she fought her instinct to remain silent and spoke.

"Forgive my insolence M'Lo…" Marie stopped herself before calling him Lord again. "Forgive me, Sir, but they told me you are Lord Megildur, heir to the High King Cambruin and chosen champion by the All-Father himself to retrieve Shadowbane."

Megildur sighed, "Yes, I am. But just a few weeks ago I was just an inadequate peasant who could not even protect his village from marauders."

Marie whispered as she leaned over and placed her hand on Megildur's leg, "You do not appear inadequate to me, Sir." This made him uncomfortable and he sprang from the chair and walked to other side of the tent. "My apologies, Sir, I did not mean to offend you?" Marie bowed her head and proceeded to exit the tent. She felt she had disgraced herself before Megildur.

Megildur blurted out, "Wait. Do not leave. Your actions have not offended me. You are beautiful. I just have not been able to stop thinking of…" Megildur paused unsure if he should be talking to Marie about this.

"You are in love with another?" Marie interjected. Megildur dipped his head in agreement. "Is she from your village?"

"No. She helped me escape when the Temple of the Cleansing Flame in the desert captured me," Megildur responded. "Her name is Zabrina but she is all I can think of, dream of, or desire to be with." Megildur looked at Marie with lovesick eyes. "I am sorry, but I have no feelings for you in that way." Marie stood from the bed, walked to where the bell still laid on the ground, picked it up, and placed it on the table. She stopped just before exiting the tent.

Marie murmured, "She is very lucky. If there is anything you need from me just ring the bell, Sir." Marie walked out of the tent leaving the half-dressed Aelfborn sitting in his chair.

Megildur finished changing after a short time of thinking of his Desert Flower, Zabrina. He opened the tent flap to see that Turwaithion had prepared a great feast. There was a roaring bonfire in the middle of the courtyard and food as far as the eye could see. The others were already enjoying the drink, especially Maethorion who had joined Turwaithion, Zeristan, and Atreus in singing battle songs. Megildur knew he must put on a happy face and join the festivities, even though all he could think of was Zabrina. He took a deep breath and walked out into the courtyard.

As Megildur walked across the safehold, he noticed all the different races of Greensward Parish intermingling peacefully. There were Humans, Elves, and even his own race, Aelfborn. He halted when he stumbled across a rather large shadow laid before his path. He glanced up to find a Half Giant wielding a mug of ale in each fist. The sizeable brute glared at the tiny Aelfborn, smiled, and went on enjoying the festivities. Megildur moved aside, allowing the Half Giant a wide passage.

Before he made it to the bonfire, a Bard for the Greensward Parish spotted him entering and announced his presence to everyone. They all cheered and surrounded the Aelfborn. Megildur knew this would be a long night and an even longer journey ahead of him.

CHAPTER 12: First Kill

Megildur heard no sounds of birds chirping, nor did he hear the sound of his little sister running across the floor. Instead, he awoke to the sounds of Warriors preparing for battle. Noise emanated though his tent of metal armor and weapons clanging together while they loaded them into the wagons. Marie had already prepared his clothes for the next day while he slept. He slipped on his undergarments and then started on the armor. He had never put on cumbersome armor like this before. Until now, the most he wore was leather coverings. The boots and leggings were easy enough to handle, but the breastplate was difficult. He knew he would need help so he decided to ring the bell, this time on purpose. It took Marie a few moments to arrive.

"You called for me, Sir?" Marie asked, entering the room and curtsying. She could see he was having issues putting on his armor. "Allow me to assist you with that, Sir." Marie went to work helping Megildur with his armor.

"You laid out my clothes and brought over the armor for me?" Megildur asked Marie. She nodded that she had done so. "Thank you for doing that. I can bet the armor was not an easy task. Even though it is lighter than steel, it must have been a chore carrying it clear across the compound."

"That is my job, Sir," Marie replied. "Besides, the armor is easy as long as you only take one piece at a time." She gave a slight smile to Megildur, who let out a chuckle at her comment. She finished with the breastplate, armguards and gauntlets and when

Megildur turned to face her, she handed him the helm to his new suit of armor. "You are ready for battle, Sir!"

"Thank you, Marie," Megildur replied. "Well I need to get outside and see where I can help." He gave a quick look to Marie and left the tent. He walked just a short distance to the courtyard to see they were all waiting for him and had prepared everything. They even had a horse saddled and ready for him.

"Lord Megildur, this horse is one of the finest in our stables. It would be an honor for you to ride him," Turwaithion said while bowing at the side of the stallion.

Megildur replied, "Thank you, Turwaithion; I am honored to accept." He pulled himself upon the horse, which was taller and larger than any horse he had ever ridden before.

Zeristan advised, "Good morning, Lord Megildur. You should say something to the soldiers before we depart, since after all this is your quest." Zeristan grinned at the boy knowing he had little experience speaking in front of a large group, let alone hundreds of Warriors. He was confident that the young Aelfborn could do it anyway. Megildur rode his horse to the front and the group fell silent. He took one deep breath and decided to recall some of the stories that his father and Zeristan told him of past battles in Aerynth.

"Today we ride out to stop a malevolent force that has terrorized our world for too long," Megildur bellowed. Even the blacksmith's helpers in the far reaches of the crowd could hear his words. "The Dar Khelegur's first act of treachery was when they accepted a gift from the Gods only to turn on them by destroying the temples and worshipping false Gods.

Then the wicked Sillestor committed the vilest act of betrayal by turning Shadowbane against the All-Father himself." By this time, the Warriors were roaring with anger and hatred toward the Elves of the north. "I wear this suit of armor, which was intended for Sillestor, to show the Deathless Empire that they are not superior. We will take back what is ours, destroy what is theirs, and when I am standing in Aelarnost with the High Elf Lord on his knees before me, I shall take his head!" The Warriors screamed out with a cry for vengeance since all of them had suffered in one way or another to the Elf Lords of the north. While they were still motivated from the speech, Megildur raised his sword and shouted out, "Ride to victory!" The group started out on the long journey to Aelarnost with Megildur taking the lead. In addition, Maethorion, Turwaithion, and Atreus rode alongside him but Zeristan was nowhere in sight.

They traveled southwest, below the bay, to avoid the cold and treacherous northern mountains. This path would be longer but easier to travel as there were no mountains south of the bay and the temperatures were much warmer than the icy capped peaks. With a large group of Warriors, blacksmiths, and servants, it would take longer than if Megildur and Zeristan traveled alone. However, this would be unwise. The Dar Khelegur had a massive and more powerful force than the two alone could handle.

After traveling most of the day, Megildur could see the edge of the bay. Both Maethorion and Atreus agreed they should make camp here for the first night. Most of the group started to unload the tents. Maethorion and Atreus sent out Scouts, Rangers, and Huntresses to survey the land and check for any unwanted guests in the area. Megildur decided to move closer to the bay to see the water, so he rode his horse in that direction. It felt like an eternity since he went to the sea to watch his sister play. He sat on his horse staring at the bay and remembered a simpler time. Zeristan approached on his horse.

"Greetings Megildur," Zeristan said, stopping his horse alongside Megildur and joined him while he stared into the bay.

Megildur huffed, "Zeristan, are you forgetting my title of Lord? I am the heir to the High Throne, am I not?"

Zeristan countered, "Yes, you have that title because of your ancestor! However, just because the All-Father chose you, it does not prove you are worthy! I will use the title when you deserve it!" This last statement drew Megildur's attention away from the bay. "I had the honor of counseling many kings over my lifetime. I have seen many who have risen to power and many fall from the throne." Zeristan looked straight at Megildur with a serious yet concerned demeanor. "Your speech was bold and motivating but being a King means more than just destroying and conquering. Besides having to be bold and motivating, a King must also be compassionate and merciful or he is just a cruel dictator."

Megildur thundered, "Compassion and mercy are for the weak! It was those same qualities that cost Cambruin his life!" Megildur was fuming at this point that Zeristan was challenging him.

Zeristan replied in a more stern voice than before, "Remember Megildur, I was there for the fall of the High King. Mercy did not kill him. Betrayal killed him, betrayal from one of his own with his own blade. That same type of treacherous act has befallen both cruel and compassionate kings alike." By this point, Zeristan was also fuming but it was due to Megildur's insolence and misunderstanding of what it means to be a good ruler. "Remember the outcome of the one whose armor you now wear. He also ruled without compassion, without mercy, and once he was without his head, his rule ended. With that in mind, I will take my leave of you now, Lord Megildur."

Zeristan rode back to the camp and dread now replaced Megildur's fuming emotion, over the thought of the outcome of the late Elf King Sillestor. Even though Megildur was young and unproven, the thought of being as cruel as the late founder of the Dar Khelegur sickened him. His mother had told him stories of how the merciless acts of Sillestor broke apart the great nation of Elves and why her people, the Gwaridorn, turned to the seas to escape his tyranny. If Megildur was to reclaim Shadowbane and restore peace to the war torn world, he knew he would need to be a better ruler than Sillestor ever was.

Megildur sat staring out to the bay for a bit longer, contemplating Zeristan's words. He eventually turned his stallion around and went back to the camp. By that time the Scouts, Rangers, and Huntresses had returned from surveying the surrounding areas and found no threats. His tent was already standing, so he went inside to remove his armor. After removing most of the dust and dirt from a long days ride, he decided to join his companions around the bonfire. He tried to forget about duties and responsibilities for a while. Megildur found Bowen, Thaddaios, Turwaithion, and a few other men he did not recognize sitting near the fire enjoying some ale. When he approached the group, Thaddaios offered the Aelfborn Lord a mug, which he accepted while sitting down. He was not one to partake in strong drink, but he figured refusing at this time would be rude. He needed both their allegiance as well as their friendship.

One of the men slurred, "S-sooo whhhy arrre wee attaaakin t-thee Elves tooo ta nurth nooow?"

"They kidnapped Lord Megildur's sister and we are using the assault to sneak in and retrieve her," Thaddaios replied.

The drunken Warrior blurted out, trying poorly to contain his own self-amusement. "I-iss yuuur seestuur aan attraaacteev weeench oor dooes shhe reesemmmble aan Orc?" Megildur scowled and reached for his dagger.

Turwaithion lashed out at the drunken Warrior, "She is a youngling, and you will hold your tongue before I let Lord Megildur remove it from your insolent mouth!" He placed his hand over Megildur's sheath preventing him from taking action.

The drunk conceded, "Foorgiiive mee Loords, I meeaant noo o-offense by me words."

Megildur made sure to keep his distance from him though. He found the drunk annoying and the massive amounts of ale he consumed did not improve his arrogance. Megildur, still on his first mug of ale, lost count of how many the drunken Warrior had finished off. He looked into his empty mug and considered retiring for the evening when a familiar voice murmured.

"Allow me to fill your mug, Sir." It was Marie, his personal servant. Megildur was shocked to see her there.

Megildur asked with a bit of surprise in his voice, "Marie, what are you doing here?"

Marie teased, "Refilling your drink, Sir." After filling Megildur's mug, she proceeded in filling the mugs of the other Warriors around the fire.

The drunken Warrior hollered out, grabbing Marie by the waist and pulling her onto his lap. "Weeell if yee do noot waaant thiis weench, I'll have herrr!" She dropped the pitcher of ale. The shocked look on her face alerted Megildur that she would prefer to be anywhere but in the arms of this drunk.

Megildur demanded, rising to his feet, "Release her at once!" The drunk released her and Marie scurried away to a nearby cart. The drunk stumbled to rise and face Megildur. The excessive amounts of ale had clouded the Warrior's judgment and the drunk unsheathed his sword.

The Warrior shouted, "I grooow tirrred of yeer worrrds boy! Let meee shooow yooou thheee powerrr of a truue warrrrior!" Numerous Warriors drew their weapons and advanced toward the drunk.

Megildur commanded, "Stay your weapons!" The Aelfborn turned to the drunk, knowing he must deal with him directly if he was to earn the respect of the others. "I will teach you to respect women, you insolent pig!" That insult aggravated the drunken Warrior further, causing him to thrust his sword at Megildur. He dodged the advance with ease allowing the drunk to fall into the fire. The Warrior scampered from the flames, but was unable to feel the full effect of the burn due to his saturation of ale. The only weapon Megildur possessed was a dagger his father had given him, but he felt it would be sufficient against this oaf. The Warrior stood, faced Megildur, and swung his sword, completely missing the Aelfborn. Fortunately the rest of the crowd pulled back giving the two room to engage each other. By this time, Megildur had unsheathed his dagger and stood ready for the next attack. After two strikes that failed to land on Megildur, the drunken Warrior let out a death-curdling yell. He charged the

Aelfborn, tackling him to the ground. The two struggled for dominance for a moment until a gasp emanated and both stopped struggling. Blood oozed from the area of the skirmish but only Megildur moved. He pushed the lifeless drunk off him and stood triumphant from the encounter. His dagger still plunged into the chest of the now dead Warrior. He pulled out his dagger and wiped it off on the Warrior's shirt before placing it back in his sheath.

"Behold the champion, Lord Megildur!" Thaddaios cheered, holding up Megildur's hand after his victorious battle against the drunk. The crowd began to cheer.

Megildur shouted, "No!" He pulled back his hand from Thaddaios. "This wasn't a noble victory! This was a drunken fool who consumed too much ale and disrespected women." The cheering from the crowd dissipated. "He had no respect for anyone including himself and my act of ending his life proved that fact. Just because another person's responsibility is that of servitude does not mean they deserve any less respect." Megildur glanced at Marie when saying this. "The All-Father created all of us equal. It is the cruelty of people like those we go to battle with now that makes slaves of us all." Megildur panned over the crowd to see all had stopped their festivities and were hanging on every word he spoke. He turned to Marie, made a motion for her to follow and he made one last comment to Turwaithion. "I think they all have had enough for this night."

Megildur walked back to his tent with Marie close behind. He threw open the tent flap and stormed inside while the commotion of Turwaithion's dismissal of all Warriors commenced. Once inside he turned to face Marie. "I apologize for his behavior…" He could not finish his sentence since

Marie had wrapped her arms around him with the biggest embrace he had ever received.

Marie exclaimed, "Thank you, Sir! I will forever appreciate the act of kindness you showed for me this night. No one has ever protected me against such maliciousness nor has anyone ever demanded such respect for a person like me." She finally pulled back and looked him in the eye. "You are trembling, Sir. Are you alright?" Megildur withdrew to the other side of the tent. "You have never killed a man before, have you?"

Megildur responded, "Today was the first time. I never went far away from my village before a few weeks ago."

"If you had not stopped him he would have violated me," Marie countered. "Worse yet, his stupidity and arrogance would have resulted in the death of others in your group. He was a reckless drunk. I am sure after his arrival back in Greensward Parish he will still be a pig!"

"Thank you, Marie, but I think I would like to be alone for now."

Marie murmured, "Yes, Sir. I will be nearby in case you need anything. Just remember I am eternally grateful for what you have done this night." Marie walked out of the tent and Megildur changed before going to sleep. While he lay there, he knew what he did was best for the well-being of people like Marie and Zabrina. However, he did not know how the others would feel about his actions tomorrow. He confronted the drunk on his own to earn the respect of the Warriors, but that action may have the opposite effect. He would have to face that dilemma in the morning.

CHAPTER 13: Shaded

Megildur made his way from the tent, expecting to find many glaring at him in disgust. Instead, everyone greeted him with "Good morning, M'Lord." This came as a shock to the young Lord. He thought killing one of his own would have created contempt for him, not exuberance.

"Good morning, Sir," Marie said as she approached Megildur from behind. "Here is your breakfast." Marie had once again fetched his meal as she normally did. Now he expected exuberance from her, but he needed to inquire about everyone else.

"Marie, why is everyone cheerful this morning? I expect them to want my head for my actions last night," Megildur asked with a bit of confusion. "I thought after killing one of my own allies, this would have driven everyone to hate me?"

Marie whispered, "The man you killed was cruel and malevolent to all, both kin and enemy alike. Many were glad to see his lifeless body at the fire last night." Megildur looked shocked to hear this.

"She is correct, Lord Megildur," Zeristan interjected while he approached from nearby. Marie bowed to Zeristan and stepped back in respect of his arrival. "Not all deaths arrive unwelcomed, especially his. Even his own brother killed him once just to stop his excessive arrogance." Zeristan chuckled at the thought. "Remember that the All-Father closed the gates to Heaven and Hell to all of us. His death just means he will go back to his Tree Of Life. Of course, with his insolence and lack of love from his own family they probably unbound him from their Tree Of

Life and left him errant. His type will end up in Sea Dog's Rest wallowing in the filth." This lifted Megildur's spirits and allowed him to hold his head high again. "Now, let's get our horses. We have another long journey ahead of us and the sooner we start the better." Zeristan and Megildur proceeded to the front of the group to meet with Maethorion, Turwaithion, and Atreus.

Maethorion bellowed, "Lord Megildur, glad to see you are doing well this morning." He put his arm around the young Lord and isolated him from the others. He muttered, "I apologize for the actions of my Warrior last night. I hear he was insolent, rude, and deserved his outcome. I promise to limit the ale for the duration of our journey, to keep the men in line."

Megildur replied, "Let's just save some of the drinking for when we defeat the Dar Khelegur!" The two of them laughed while they rejoined the others with their horses. After a brief check on the troops, Maethorion signaled Megildur that all were ready. Megildur gave them the, "Let's move out" command.

They were going to follow along the southern shore of the bay and reach the edge of the river they must cross by nightfall. At that time, they will camp along the shores and brave the crossing of the river for next light. While they rode, Megildur still could not stop thinking of the man he killed the night before. Yes, everyone did say his death was a welcomed one, and he was sure the drunk returned somewhere in Aerynth, but it did not stop Megildur from weighing heavy upon his actions. Someday death will mean the end to existence on Aerynth and the gates to Heaven and Hell will be open for those souls, but not today. They rode for most of the morning, while Megildur stayed isolated in thought.

They finally stopped around midday to water the horses and feed everyone. Megildur stayed in isolation and found a rock overlooking the bay to relax. He sat there for a short time until Marie approached with a plate of food for the young Lord.

"Here is your food, Sir," Marie smiled and asked, "Can I fetch anything else for you, Sir?"

"Thank you for the food, Marie," Megildur replied. "Please sit down and stay awhile. I do not wish to be alone anymore." He gazed back out to the bay again, while nibbling on the food she brought. "This spot reminds me of the place I used to bring my little sister to swim. She loves the water. I suppose she received that appreciation for the sea from our mother, she was from the Gwaridorn Elf tribes, the 'Masters of the Sea'." Concern filled Megildur's face when he thought of his sister.

"You two are close?" Marie inquired.

Megildur replied with a bit of laughter in his response, "No, we had the usual sibling rivalries." Then the amusement vanished from his face and he replied, "But I love my sister, even with her bratty attitude. Also, I promised my father I would protect her and I will not stop until I have freed her." He continued to gaze out onto the water for a bit and handed the plate back to Marie, having touched very little of the food on the plate. "Thank you for the food, I will be back at the campsite in just a bit." Marie bowed her head, collected the plate, and went back to the camp. Megildur knew by this time the others were finished tending to the horses and that they must continue the journey, so he got up and proceeded back.

"Lord Megildur," Zeristan said. "We are ready to move on when you are. Everything alright?" Zeristan could see the young Lord lost in thought.

Megildur retorted, "Yes, everything is fine. Let's move out!" He wanted to avoid any conversations about his feelings. The Aelfborn knew Zeristan meant well, but he felt cowardly admitting he had remorse for killing the drunken Warrior the night before. Dismayed that life and death did not carry much weight anymore in Aerynth; Megildur rode quietly near the head of the group with Maethorion leading the way. They rode for several hours until Maethorion slowed the pace. Up ahead Megildur could see a river flowing south across their path; this would be the river they must cross.

Maethorion bellowed, "Make camp here. Turwaithion, setup sentry points and send out the scouting parties to search the surrounding areas." Turwaithion bowed his head and went off to perform his orders. Maethorion turned to Megildur, "Many Thieves and bandits roam along the riverbanks, so we must be alert." Megildur agreed since they had encountered a few even on the road to the Centaur Cohort. Since the beginning of the Age of Strife, Thieves, bandits, and mercenaries have run rampant. The only law and order that existed anymore was pure survival. The High King Cambruin was the last ruler to care about the wellbeing of those living in Aerynth.

Megildur decided to advance down to the river to survey the waterway for the crossing tomorrow morning. He could spot a low point in the river downstream just a bit where they could cross. The water came to their knees but the wagons could traverse that height. Megildur stood on the riverbank. He felt uneasy, as if he was not alone. He examined his surrounds carefully but could not spot anyone, or anything else, around him. Still the feeling grew more prominent the longer he stood there. Finally, he spotted a reflection of light on his left side and then an arrow was visible. He reached for his sword only to realize his weapon was missing from his side. The arrow flew right past his shoulder, narrowly missing him. Apparently, the arrow did strike its intended target. Megildur heard someone yell out in agony. When the Aelfborn looked to his right side, he observed someone appear out of thin air with an arrow in his arm. He followed the path of the arrow back to its origin, where one of his own Scouts stood with a bow. Megildur bowed his head in appreciation for the well-placed arrow that saved him from the Thief. Upon further inspection of the Thief, Megildur realized he was the one who had relieved him of his sword.

"On your feet!" Megildur commanded, grabbing the Thief. He retrieved his sword and the Scout bound the Thief's hands. More of the scouting party arrived to disclose the Thief's identity. One of the Rangers removed the Thief's hood, revealing his face. The Thief had pale pasty gray skin and sunken inward black eyes, black as coal. He was also lacking hair, on either his head or his face. He did not even have eyebrows.

"A Shade!" The Ranger snarled, pulling out a blade and held it to the Thief's throat.

The Shade snickered, "Go ahead Ranger, I am sure your mother would enjoy some more time with me!" This caused the Ranger to press the blade deeper into the Shade's neck. The force against his neck made him wince in pain. The Shade grumbled under his breath, "Not back to my Tree of Life again." The Ranger, void of sympathy, was about to begin slicing.

Megildur commanded, "Stay your weapon. I want this one alive for questioning." The Ranger just stared at Megildur and finally withdrew his blade from the neck of the Thief.

The Ranger resounded, "As you command, Lord Megildur." He yanked the Thief forward and escorted him back to the camp.

Megildur followed close behind, while the Ranger dragged the Shade into a tent off to the side of the encampment. Many of the other servants and Warriors watched the Ranger heave the freakish looking Thief into the tent. "Fetch a healer," Megildur commanded one of the servants nearby when he entered the tent. The servant bowed and exited the tent to carry out the Aelfborn Lord's order. The servant returned with a Priest, as Lord Megildur commanded.

The Priest scoffed, "What do you wish done with this, abomination, Lord Megildur?"

"Remove the arrow from his arm and heal his wound," Megildur instructed the Priest. The Priest, Ranger, and Thief all looked at Megildur in disbelief at his request.

The Priest gibed, "M'Lord, this, thing, is an unholy abomination and unworthy of saving. His kind does not even believe in the All-Father nor do they pay homage to Him."

"I did not ask for you to convert his faith," Megildur countered, with a growing irritation in his voice. "I commanded you to remove the arrow and heal his wound! If you are unable, or unwilling, to do so then I will replace you with someone nobler who will carry out my commands!" Megildur's defiance shocked the Priest. Most normally do not argue with Priests.

The Priest conceded, "My deepest apologies for my insolence, Lord Megildur. I will proceed in healing this…individual." The Priest turned to his patient and broke off the tip of the arrow. He pulled out the arrow and the Shade winched. Once the Priest removed the arrow, he began to wave his hands and focus on the hole in the Shade's arm. Megildur watched the wound vanish in amazement. He had heard of the healing process before, but he had never seen it with his own eyes. The Priest stood, turned to Megildur, and bowed. "I have healed his arm. May I be of any other service, Lord Megildur?"

The Shade jested, "I don't suppose you would like to dance for us, would you?" The Priest leered at the Shade and returned his attention to Megildur.

"Thank you for your services," Megildur replied. "You're dismissed." With that said, the Priest exited. Megildur turned to the Ranger and commanded, "Leave us."

The Ranger replied in astonishment, "M'Lord, you cannot trust this Thief."

Megildur replied, "I did not say I trusted him, I just commanded you to leave us." The Ranger bowed and left, leaving the Shade Thief and Megildur alone. The Aelfborn Lord turned to face the Thief, who just stared back unsure of his intentions. "So, why were you trying to steal my sword?"

The Thief countered, "Because a Chaos sword like that could fetch a hefty price in Sea Dog's Rest, and I need all the gold I can get."

In a puzzled tone Megildur inquired, "I have never seen your race before. I heard the Ranger call you a Shade, is that true?" The Thief nodded but did not reveal any more details. Megildur, wanting to know more about this race, asked for more information. "So where did your race originate from?" The Thief said nothing, so the Aelfborn attempted another approach. "What's your name and why are you so hesitant to return to your Tree of

Life?" Megildur inquired. The Shade Thief glared at him, not wanting to give out any more knowledge. "You know I could always turn you over to the others. I am sure my Warriors would love to rip apart a Thief." Megildur grinned at the Shade, knowing his interrogation was preferable than torture at the hands of his army.

Reluctant, the Thief admitted, "The Tree of Life where I'm still bound is the one where my birth parents abandoned me as an infant. Maelstrom Isle is worse than this place. I was traveling to the Carloon Outpost where they accept 'my kind'. You just happened to be along the way and I had not eaten in some time. As for Shades, they call us the Pales Ones, for obvious physical traits." The Thief raised one of his shackled hands to display his pale skin tone. "Our race emerged after the Turning. We are the offspring of normal Human parents. Nobody knows where we came from." The Shade was even more perturbed than when he first arrived. "Oh, and my name is Gaal. There, are you satisfied now?"

"Carloon Outpost? I have heard of that place," Megildur responded. "They also refer to it as the Thieves' Den, correct?" The Shade Thief nodded. "Well, I guess that is all I needed to know about you. Guard!"

Gaal exclaimed, "Oh I see how it is! First I tell you what you want under the terms of not giving me to your Warriors and then you betray me by handing me over!" The Shade Thief looked terrified when the same Ranger, who dragged him there, now entered the tent.

"You are to replace the prisoner's bindings with a leg shackle so he may move about the tent," Megildur instructed. "Then, have some bedding placed inside to make his stay comfortable. I will send my personal servant over later to bring him some food but she is the only person allowed to see the prisoner." The Ranger agreed that he would carry out the instructions. Megildur turned to Gaal, "We will care for you but leave you in shackles, until I know I can trust you."

Gaal shrugged his shoulders in disbelief. Megildur left and went straight to his tent.

CHAPTER 14: The Crossing

As the new day began, Megildur walked outside to see Maethorion, Atreus, and Zeristan strategizing how to cross the river. Atreus wanted to cross near the neck of the river where it attached to the bay but Maethorion found this part to be too treacherous. Maethorion wanted to cross further downstream at a low point but Atreus was thinking this would be too far away. As for Zeristan, Megildur thought he would most likely just hover over the river and not get wet at all.

"Alright. Let's calm down and discuss what is best for all," Megildur interjected before the two leaders went at each other's throats. "For the sake of the wagons and servants, we need to cross at the low point downstream." He turned to Atreus and said, "It's not too far away. Now, let's finish getting packed and head for the river." Both leaders bowed and went off to prepare for the crossing.

"Nice diplomacy, Lord Megildur," Zeristan responded, placing a hand on the young Aelfborn's shoulder. "With tactics like that I can see why the All-Father chose you." He started to walk away but Megildur grabbed his arm before he got too far.

"Zeristan, why did you not take control back there?" Megildur inquired. "With your experience and wisdom you could have made them cross wherever you wanted."

"While it's true that experience and wisdom go hand in hand, so does knowing when to stay out of the way. This is not my fight," Zeristan explained with a grin. "Besides, it was the perfect opportunity for you to gain some wisdom through experience." Zeristan wandered over to the horses and prepared to cross the river, Megildur followed close behind. The Aelfborn looked at Maethorion and Atreus who both signaled they were ready.

"Let's go!" Megildur bellowed and the entire army advanced forward. Since the river was already within view of the camp, they reached the river in a matter of moments. Megildur led them straight to the spot where he wanted everyone to cross. He stopped the troops and turned to address Maethorion and Atreus. "You two lead the army forward, across the river, while Turwaithion and Thaddaios cover the midsection. Zeristan, Bowen, and I will cover up the rear making sure everyone gets across." Everyone agreed and took their positions.

Maethorion and Atreus went into the river first and found the current was a bit strong, but nothing those two could not handle. Some of the Warriors slipped on the rocks below the waterline but still nothing too treacherous so far. By the midsection, with Turwaithion and Thaddaios, the support groups began to enter the water. Megildur worried most about them, since the wagons gave more resistance to the river's currents. Also, the support personnel were not as strong as the Warriors, but they were handling themselves just fine. The front of the pack was finally emerging from the river on the other side just as the last of them entered. Megildur could see Gaal was not too happy with having to cross the waterway. Shackled to the back of one of the wagons did not improve his disposition. While Megildur was watching Gaal act like a beast getting an unwanted bath, the Shade distracted him from the wagon directly in front, which had stopped suddenly. The last wagon collided with the afore mentioned wagon forcing everyone forward. Megildur quickly scanned the wreckage only to find Marie was missing. She plunged head first into the rapids.

The backside of the wagon collapsed on Gaal, pushing him down river also. Megildur did not hesitate but he knew he could not save them both. He shouted to Zeristan, "Get Gaal, I will save Marie!" She managed to grab onto a log protruding from the water but Megildur knew this would not hold. He dove in, risking his own life, and battled the raging current to reach Marie. He wrapped his arm around Marie but she slipped from his grasp. Knowing he only had one chance left to save her, before being dragged out to sea, the Aelfborn Lord clenched the back of her cape and swam with all of his might back to the river's edge.

Gaal yelled, "Get me out of here!" He reached for a nearby rock but was unable to hang on. The Thief felt an arm reach into the water and lift him up. Zeristan hovered above the river with the Thief dangling by his boots. Gaal's bald head skimmed the water like a skipping stone. Zeristan dropped the drenched Shade on the riverbank and turned to check on Megildur, who by now was ashore as well.

Marie exclaimed trying to catch her breath, "Thank you, Sir! I thought I would drown in that river since I never learned to swim." Marie gave Megildur a quick embrace.

All he could muster, at the moment, was a half-smile. He escorted her back upriver to see that the rest of the Warriors had fished the wagon out of the water. The lead blacksmith arrived to assess the situation.

"It will take a few hours to repair, M'Lord, but we can fix it," the blacksmith advised Megildur.

"Very well, please start right away." The blacksmith summoned over his assistants to start with repairs. Megildur turned his attention to Maethorion. "We will rest here awhile to give the blacksmith enough time." Maethorion agreed and tended to the troops while Megildur tended to Marie. He motioned to some handmaidens to assist her. "Help her change out of her wet clothes and have her sit by a fire to recover." He turned to a few of the male servants not helping with the wagon repairs. "Start the fire for our drowning victims and take this wet sack with you," he commented with a smirk while patting Gaal on the back to follow the servants.

Gaal managed to let out a small "Thank you" under his breath to Megildur and Zeristan. He gathered what little remaining composure he had left and cleared his throat. "I despise being indebted to anyone, so my life is yours...until I can repay the debt I owe you." He turned to follow the servants and sit by the fire.

"So much for no honor among Thieves," Zeristan beamed while he joined Megildur to check on the rest of the army.

Maethorion already had Turwaithion checking on the rest of the wagons for any stress from the crossing but they found no more damage. After a few hours, the blacksmith completed the repairs and everyone loaded the wagons and got back on the road to Aelarnost. They traveled along the southern shores of the bay. The weather was pleasant, but getting colder with every turn north toward the Elven fortress. They lost a lot of time at the river with the accident, so they all decided to make camp early and make one more push tomorrow for Aelarnost. Megildur was eager to get some rest. The day exhausted Megildur, with the mishap and all the traveling they had endured. The most he had traveled before this whole quest began was to New Mellissar for supplies with his father.

While the others setup the tents, Megildur decided to take one last visit to the bay, since he knew after tomorrow they would be out of sight from the calming shores. He found a spot to sit down and stare out into the bay. He found this relaxing, until his mind began wondering about saving Aranel. The Aelfborn's thoughts next shifted to his rescuer, the Desert Flower, Zabrina. With just one thought, he could smell her sweet scent. He could sit there for hours, and he did.

Marie whispered when she approached Megildur, "Am I disturbing you Sir? I can leave if you would prefer."

"No need to run off, sit down a while," Megildur insisted since Marie was leaving to respect his solitude. "How are you feeling after your little swim in the river today?" Megildur made the sarcastic comment with a slight smirk.

Marie answered, "Better, thanks to you, Sir. You had no reservations about jumping in to save me, I will always be eternally grateful for your bravery." She blushed, turning from Megildur to look out into the bay.

"Brave? It terrified me to jump in that water," Megildur replied. This shocked Marie and she stared at Megildur in disbelief.

"If you were so terrified, why did you jump in the water?" Marie asked. "You could have ordered one of your Warriors into the water to rescue me."

Megildur admitted, "Honestly I did not even think about it, I just jumped down from my horse and dove in."

"That is what makes you brave. That must be the reason the All-Father chose you as his champion," Marie proclaimed, standing up and placing her hand on Megildur's shoulder. She smiled and went back to the camp.

Megildur sat there thinking of what she said. Marie was not the first one to mention a reason for the All-Father choosing him. He just hoped he could live up to everyone's expectations of him, or that he even lived long enough to save his sister.

CHAPTER 15: The Aracoix

Megildur awoke to the sound of birds chirping. However, the longer he sat there listening the more he noticed the light chirping sound changed into more of a shriek. He emerged from his tent to find nobody remaining in the camp. In fact, he could not detect any evidence that anyone ever existed in the camp. Megildur could see a few trees off in the distance with birds flying around them and he felt compelled to investigate. The closer he got to the trees, the louder the birds squawked. Getting louder and louder until the noise was so intense Megildur covered his ears and dropped to his knees. The birds continued their deafening assent to the point where Megildur thought he might lose consciousness, and then it ceased, leaving him in silence. He stood up and examined the area but all the trees were void of any birds.

"M'Lord! Sir, you must come with me now!" Megildur was in shock. He turned to see the voice was not that of a person but of a beautiful sparrow on a branch. He leaned in closer and the bird's mouth opened wide enough to fit his entire head inside. The bird screamed "Megildur!" He awoke to see Marie standing over him and he was on the floor.

Marie pleaded, "Sir, we must flee to safety." Even though Megildur struggled back into reality, he managed to scrambled to his feet, hastily put on his armor, grab his sword, and dash outside. He could see that the noise was not from ordinary birds but from giant birds, in the form of men, flying through the sky. Each appeared Human in shape from the shoulders down; however, above the neck, they possessed the head of a bird. In addition, feathers covered their bodies. "Aracoix," the Aelfborn Lord thought to himself. Megildur's father told him tales of when they first appeared in Aerynth around fifty years after the fall of Cambruin. It took several years to contain their infestation. This took less time than most threats, such as when the Dark Chaos Lords invaded Aerynth during the Age of Days. Even the Gods themselves had a difficult time casting them back into the Void from which they came.

"Look out!" Marie screamed when an Aracoix Warrior dropped from the sky in front of Megildur. The Aracoix raised his sword and swung at Megildur, who was able to deflect the blow with his sword.

"Take cover under that wagon over there," Megildur motioned to Marie to hide under a nearby wagon to avoid the attackers. Trying to protect Marie distracted the Aelfborn Lord. The Aracoix disarmed him and knocked him to the ground. After he felt Megildur was no longer a threat, the bird Warrior turned his attention to Marie and approached her while she lay under the wagon. He raised his sword to her but was unable to strike since Megildur jumped onto his back and plunged a dagger deep into his neck. The Aracoix Warrior flailed so hard from the wound that he threw Megildur from his back and pulled out the dagger. This attack served its purpose. The birdman now turned his attention back to Megildur. He remembered his training from Thaddaios and jumped to his feet, retrieved his sword, and engaged the Aracoix. Megildur was able to parry most of the Aracoix Warrior's attacks but one landed on his armor and knocked him back. Megildur lowered his sword for just a moment and the Warrior took this time to advance against him. He spun around, as if he was going to run, but followed through with the turn until he came full circle. With his blade up high, he struck for the neck of the Aracoix and his sword hit its intended target. Megildur managed to lop off the head of the bird Warrior. The decapitated Aracoix's body slumped to the ground. Megildur had his first engagement on the battlefield and he emerged victorious. His rejoicing would have to wait though, since they were still in danger from the Aracoix attack. He motioned to Marie to stay under the wagon and he turned to join his comrades in battle.

Turwaithion cried out, "Lord Megildur! Over here!" Megildur could see that Turwaithion, Maethorion, Bowen, and Thaddaios were deep in the battle. They vanquished several Aracoix themselves, but the battle was not over yet. He also could see they lost a few Warriors during this conflict. "The Aracoix safehold must be nearby!" Turwaithion roared, slamming another bird Warrior to the ground.

Megildur knew they could not stand to lose any more before getting to Aelarnost. He yelled out while leaving the group, "Watch my back. I mean to end this now!" Megildur ran out to the first Aracoix he could find on the ground, tackled him and held a dagger to the bird Warrior's throat. "You tell your Master that we are not coming after the Aracoix, we mean to attack the Dar Khelegur to the north. However, if we see another Aracoix before reaching our intended target, I will turn my forces to your safehold when we finish with the Elves. Do you understand me?" The birdman nodded that he understood and once Megildur released him, the Aracoix flew straight into the sky and seemed focused on a distant target. A few moments later, the Aracoix shrieked out to the other bird Warriors, bowed his head in Megildur's direction, and flew off. The other Aracoix attackers disengaged and pursued the first one Megildur threatened. Zeristan, Turwaithion, Maethorion, Bowen, and Thaddaios all gathered around Megildur to find out what happened.

"What did you say to that Aracoix?" Zeristan requested from Megildur.

"I told him that if I saw another Aracoix between here and Aelarnost that we would attack his safehold after we finish with the Elves," Megildur replied with a sinister sneer on his face. Zeristan and the others loved his threat and all laughed about it. When the laughter diminished, Megildur asked, "So how many did we lose to the Aracoix?"

"Just a few, but I am having our healers summon them back as quick as possible," Maethorion responded. "By the time Turwaithion has the rest of the army ready to travel this morning, we will have our lost Warriors back."

"That is an impressive recovery," Megildur replied. "What did you mean by saying the healers will summon them back?"

"Healers have the power to summon people across Aerynth," Zeristan interjected. "Think of it as teleporting someone without being next to them." Zeristan grinned since he knew Megildur would remember his first teleporting incident, which landed him in the livestock's hay.

Megildur exclaimed, "Marie!" He remembered she hid under the wagon during the attack. He went back to find her unharmed and peering out from the wagon when she spotted Megildur.

Marie burst out, "Thank you for stopping that Aracoix!" She grasped Megildur and only stopped when she realized how uncomfortable Megildur felt during the embrace. "Excuse me for the outburst, Sir."

She brushed off her dress, bowed her head, and turned her attention on preparing to move out.

Megildur cleared his throat, took a deep breath to relieve his tension, and went to Maethorion, Atreus, and Zeristan who were all discussing the attack from the Aracoix.

"What provoked the Aracoix into attacking us?" Megildur asked the group.

"The Aracoix have a strong dislike for all other races," Atreus replied. "With the exception of a few who have joined mercenary or Thief guilds, they affiliate only with other Aracoix. They also despise magic and renounce all Gods. Nobody even knows where these birdmen came from. They just appeared in Aerynth during the Age of Strife."

"What was that focusing the Aracoix did before departing?" Megildur inquired.

"The Aracoix have the ability to communicate with each other using telepathy," Zeristan educated the Aelfborn Lord. "When they first arrived nobody knew how to converse with them, but some began to understand their mental form of telecommunication."

"I assume they did not like us approaching their borders and felt we were a formidable threat," Maethorion added. "Their safehold is to the southwest of here and I am sure they were tracking us through the night."

Megildur resounded, climbing upon his horse, "I am sure they will not interfere with us during our journey. Maethorion, are we ready?" Maethorion gestured to move once again. Megildur sat bold in his saddle and addressed his army. "We will continue to Aelarnost and arrive in time to attack during nightfall. Let's move out!" The Aelfborn Lord was even more confident after his newfound victory over the Aracoix.

They started their turn northwest, pulling away from the bay, and heading into the frozen mountains. They avoided these icy peaks as long as possible, but now they must enter them in order to reach the Elven fortress. The weather was still sunny but getting colder as they ascended toward Aelarnost. Their plan to attack Aelarnost was a simple one. They would stop just outside the tracking range of the Elven fortress and send out scouting parties. Their function would be to eliminate any Scouts outside the fortress that could alert enemy forces of their arrival. Atreus would have his troops cause a distraction near the front of Aelarnost. Megildur would use this diversion to slip in undetected and rescue his sister. Also, he was unsure if his parents were still trying to free his sister or if they had succeeded and were already back home in Fort Viatrus. He would have to find out after their rescue attempt. They would soon be at Aelarnost and he would have his answers, one way or another.

CHAPTER 16: Assault on Aelarnost

Maethorion signaled Megildur that they had finally arrived just beyond Aelarnost's tracking range. Megildur halted the troops and signaled for the scouting party. Between the two great factions, the Centaur Cohort and the Church of the All-Father, they had nearly a dozen qualified soldiers for the job, comprised of Scouts, Huntresses, and Rangers. Megildur was confident in their skills and had already seen their abilities after the one Scout saved him from the Thief, Gaal.

"I want you to split into groups to isolate all Scouts and sentries around Aelarnost," Megildur instructed the reconnaissance party. "Be sure to take them alive, because if you kill them and they return to the Tree of Life inside Aelarnost, they will know we are here before we are ready. Now, Turwaithion will divide you into groups and may the All-Father guide you in your mission." Turwaithion divided them into four separate units, one for each direction. It was not long before the first group appeared dragging along a Scout from the Dar Khelegur. Turwaithion had the Scouts bound to trees in the south and guarded. They had six Elven Scouts tied to the trees and all of the groups, but one, reported no more Scouts in their search path. The final group came back dragging one suspected Scout, but the man was not Elven. He appeared to be Human. The Ranger and Scout dragged him before Megildur, Zeristan, and Maethorion.

"Lord Megildur, we found this man trying to sneak into Aelarnost," the Centaur Ranger proclaimed. "He said he was trying to get back in for his family." The Ranger lifted the half-conscious man's head and Megildur could see it was his father, Aedan.

Megildur exclaimed, "Father! Release him at once!"

"Yes, M'Lord," the Ranger and Scout both replied while they carefully laid Aedan on the ground.

"Father, are you injured?" Megildur inquired as he knelt down next to his father to assess his health. Aedan was not bleeding from any injuries, just a bit shaken from the blow to his head during his scuffle with the Ranger and Scout.

Aedan cried out. "Megildur, is that really you boy?" Even before Megildur could reply, Aedan embraced his son. Aedan became fully aware of his surroundings and that confused him a bit. He pulled Megildur back to ask, "Why does this army follow your command and whose armor are you wearing?" Before Megildur could reply, Turwaithion approached with news.

"Lord Megildur," Turwaithion announced. "The scouting parties are all in and no more Scouts or sentries remain outside the perimeter of Aelarnost." Aedan gawked at Turwaithion and then back at his son.

Megildur commanded, "Very well. Atreus and Maethorion, prepare your forces for the diversionary front. Zeristan get Bowen, Thaddaios, and two Rangers. I will join you soon." The three men nodded, knowing Megildur needed to be alone with his father, and they departed to prepare for the pending attack.

Aedan demanded when he rose to his feet, "Lord Megildur? What is going on son? Who are these people and why are they calling you Lord?"

Megildur countered, "Father, I can explain everything to you, but I must first get inside Aelarnost and rescue Aranel."

Aedan divulged, "It's not only your sister inside, but your mother as well. Your mother and I returned to New Mellissar after the Dar Khelegur forces killed us both. We rushed back to Fort Viatrus, to find you were both gone. We assumed they took you both back to Aelarnost for slave labor, so we made the long journey here together only to find your sister once we slipped inside the safehold. They inadvertently killed me during my torturing. They meant my suffering to be an example to other slaves of what would happen for disobedience. I just recently made it back and was looking for a way in, when your Centaur friend clubbed me over the head and dragged me here." Aedan was rubbing the newly formed knot on his skull.

"Let's go rescue them together," Megildur replied, holding out his hand to his father. Aedan shook his hand and pulled him in to embrace his son. "It's good to see you are well, Father."

"Likewise," Aedan responded. "But do not think this lets you off the hook. I still expect an explanation as to what is going on, Lord Megildur." Aedan gave his son a slight smirk.

Megildur agreed, "Yes Sir, I will explain everything once we free Mother and Aranel." He knew his father would hold him to this promise. How was he going to be able to explain that when he died in Fort Viatrus from that Minotaur attack that he met the All-Father? The All-Father then selected Megildur as His champion to recover Shadowbane and bring peace to Aerynth. He experienced it first hand and still found it unbelievable.

Megildur and his father moved closer to Aelarnost to find Zeristan talking with Maethorion and Atreus. "Are we all set?" Megildur asked. All three replied they were ready. "This is my father, Aedan. He will be joining my stealth group coming in from the back of the safehold." Each of the three shook Aedan's hand.

"Your son has performed admirably, you should be proud of him," Zeristan commented. "You raised him well."

"Thank you. I look forward to hearing how he performed after we rescue the others," Aedan replied while looking at Megildur. He did not have a look of disappointment or disgust, but more of curiosity. He knew his son must have done something noble and worthy to earn the armor he wore, not to mention his command over two great factions.

"Maethorion, Atreus, begin the diversion," Megildur commanded. "Once you have the majority of their forces to the front of the safehold, I will lead my group to the opposite side and search for the captives." Maethorion and Atreus agreed. They gathered their forces to the southwestern corner of the safehold. Once the massive groups of nearly a hundred soldiers were in position, Maethorion ordered his Channelers into the air above the southwestern corner. Channelers were powerful magicians who have learned to channel the major elements within Aerynth...Earth, Fire, Air, and Water. Maethorion now had several of these powerful magicians in the air creating a violent and destructive lightshow over the heads of the Dar Khelegur. One Channeler would cast a spell of lightning, while the other two bomBarded the safehold with fire and ice. This assault not only caused a diversion but also eliminated much of the Deathless Empire forces.

Atreus positioned his troops at the southeast corner of the safehold and began his assault. Most began pounding on the walls, shaking loose the stone structure. This gathered the remaining armies within Aelarnost to that corner of the compound. The inhabitants attacked with arrows and a barrage of magical spells to sway the Centaurs. However, this only strengthened their resolve and they retaliated with arrows and spears. It appeared to the Aelfborn Lord that the diversion was a success.

"Alright, let's move to the northeast side," Megildur instructed. Megildur, Aedan, Zeristan, Bowen, Thaddaios, and two Rangers moved into position. The walls around Aelarnost were similar to Greensward Parish, in that they were Elven in design and tall. At least archers did not line these walls, thanks to the diversion led by Atreus and Maethorion on the opposite side. Now it was Zeristan's turn to sneak them inside Aelarnost. Megildur glanced at the Wizard, who took that for his signal to levitate above the top of the perimeter wall and survey the compound. After a moment of checking for enemy forces, Zeristan descended to report his findings.

"There are no guards in sight," Zeristan stated. "I can translocate us just beyond this wall and next to some buildings. I do not know which building they use for their slaves. Ready?" Zeristan looked at the other six members of his group and since nobody protested, he waved his hands in a circular motion and sent the entire group into the enemy's compound. Once materialized, Megildur noticed the buildings Zeristan spoke of. Since nobody was certain which of the numerous buildings the slaves resided, they split into several groups to shorten their search.

Zeristan and Maethorion paired up and searched a building together. The Wizard opened the door and peeked inside, only to find rows of beds. He presumed this was the barracks for the troops.

Megildur, along with Aedan, came across a small hut. Although they found no prisoners in the hut, it had shackles against a wall and torture devices on a table near the door. Aedan winced after getting a whiff of the room. The smell of rotting flesh and dried blood was overwhelming. "They had me blindfolded when the guards dragged me out of the barracks, but this smells like the place where they beat me." Aedan pulled back from the hut and noticed a building with waste flowing from under the floorboards. "This looks like the place they held us, it also lacked proper plumbing." It did indeed resemble slave barracks, but the lock on the door did not appear easily circumvented.

Zeristan boasted while walking up behind Megildur, "I will handle this." With a quick spell, he was able to melt the hinges off the door. The massive metal door then toppled over to the ground, allowing Megildur and the others access inside.

Vanya cried out, "Megildur, we are over here!" Megildur could see that both his sister and mother dwelled in a separate cell for the women.

"Mother!" Megildur replied. "Zeristan, help me with this door. Bowen and Thaddaios take the Rangers and free the men." Megildur watched Zeristan work his magic again and melt the hinges away. When the door fell, Megildur and his father moved it aside to let all of the slaves out. Megildur went straight to his mother and sister, when the path was clear. "Mother, I am so happy to see you again." He embraced his mother and did not want to let go. He pulled back and looked down at his little sister. He was unsure if she would be happy to see him or angry with her brother for not saving her from the Elves' first attack on their village.

Aranel shrieked out as she ran for her brother, "Megildur, you rescued me!" She fastened herself to her brother's side and kept repeating, "You rescued me, you rescued me." He let her hang on to him for a few moments and finally he pulled her back and knelt down to her.

Megildur assured, "I promised Father I would protect you. I am sorry it took me so long though." His sister did not care. Having her entire family back together overjoyed the young Aelfborn.

"I am proud of you Megildur," Vanya said and then looked at Aedan. "We both are proud of the man you have become, but how did you convince anyone to follow you?"

"He convinced two factions to assist in his quest," Aedan interjected. "Plus, they call him Lord Megildur, for which he has not given a reason yet." His father and mother both looked at him with confusion in their eyes. The entire conversation even puzzled Aranel.

"I promise, I can explain everything," Megildur replied. "But I prefer to discuss this once we're far away from Aelarnost."

"That would be preferable, but not possible it seems," Zeristan interrupted, gesturing outside the doorway at the substantial group of Minotaurs converging on the slave barracks. They formed a barricade outside the building but for no foreseeable reason they stopped their advancement several yards away. They remained huddled, as if they awaited further commands.

Megildur whispered, "Zeristan, can you transport us outside the fortress walls?" He was unsure if Zeristan could transport all the slaves, since there were now several dozen of them that they rescued.

A sinister voice hissed nearby, "You could try half-breed, but it will cost you this little wench's head!" Megildur could see no one, except their group and the large group of Minotaurs. This voice did not come from the enemy blocking their escape but from within their own group. Aranel gasped. Megildur turned to her to see his sister's head yanked back by someone or something, but no attacker was visible to him. A blade materialized at his sister's throat. When he followed the blade up, he could now see an Elven Assassin wielded it. Certain rogues, such as Assassins, Scouts, and Thieves, possess the ability to vanish from sight completely. This invisibility makes them hard to detect and even harder to fight. Aedan advanced on the Elf, but this only increased his grip on Aranel. This caused her to wince in pain from the now increasing tension of the blade upon her throat.

The Elf snarled, "Another step Human, and you will have the cursed blood of this half-breed sprayed upon you! My thralls will decimate all of you, if I so command. Did you think your foolish little light show outside would distract us while you saved these worthless slaves? All you have accomplished is helping me increase my slave count for the day." The Elf began to chuckle since he knew he had the advantage. "Drop your weapons or suffer a fate worse than death!" Megildur dared not challenge him, since he feared the Elf would hurt his sister. Even if he did manage to save her, the Minotaurs would stop them from leaving. The Aelfborn Lord was unsure how he would handle this dilemma but no options other than slavery were present at this time.

CHAPTER 17: The Dar Khelegur Disaster

Megildur stood there helpless against the Elf, who had his sister by the throat, and the horde of Minotaurs breathing down his neck. He did not want to place his family or his troops under the tyranny of the Deathless Empire, but he also did not want to cause them any ill fate either. If, in this day and age, there were a fate worse than death, the Dar Khelegur would know of it. Megildur motioned for the others to lower their weapons while he began to lower his sword.

The Elf sneered, "A wise choice half-breed! If you didn't surrender I would have…!" The Elf's reprimand ceased when his scornful tone turned to a gurgling sound. Megildur felt a hot liquid spray across him and he noticed this liquid, was blood. The Aelfborn Lord looked up, fearing the blood was from his sister, and found the source of the blood was from the Elf. Their fortunes had improved but this confused Megildur, along with the rest of his group. He noticed the blood originated from the Elf's neck, which now had a sizable gap in it. Megildur wondered how this injury could have occurred. A blade then appeared near the wound. Megildur followed the blade back to the wielder. It shocked him to see Gaal, the Shade Thief, materialize behind the incapacitated Elf.

Gaal exclaimed, "I thought he would never shut up! Why are Elves so arrogant?" Obviously pleased to see him, Megildur smiled at Gaal.

Megildur wanted to know how he escaped and was able to sneak inside, but that would have to wait.

He picked his sword back up from the ground and stared at the immense group of Minotaurs, just waiting to disembowel them. The giant bull-like Warriors grew increasingly agitated, now that their commander was dead. With nobody to command the thralls, they did not advance but somehow knew they must kill the intruders. As both groups considered their next move, an Elf ascended into the air from behind the Minotaurs.

"Destroy the Wethrinaerea!" The Elf commanded the Minotaurs, pointing at Megildur. The Elf wore a crown and dressed majestically, but Megildur did not know who he was.

Gaal whispered to Megildur, "That is Dar Thaelostor Caunion. He's ruler of the Deathless Empire, and a cruel one."

"How in Aerynth would you know who that is?" Megildur replied, staring back at Gaal.

"Any good Thief knows thy enemy," Gaal smirked at the Aelfborn Lord. "And I believe he just called us the deceitful ones."

Megildur now knew his enemy, but had no idea how to stop him. The Minotaur horde began to claw at the ground, looking just like any beast before they charge. Waiting for the Minotaurs to attack, Megildur noticed a lone soldier running toward the enemy group, one of Maethorion's men. He was wearing heavy armor from head to toe but did not appear to be a match for the Minotaur horde. He reached the middle of the herd and began waving his hands in the same manner Zeristan would when conjuring a spell. The Minotaur Warriors started beating down on him but the soldier did not stop. A bright light shown down from the sky, almost as if the Heavens had opened up and the All-Father himself created the light. The beam filled the herd of Minotaurs and the

Elven ruler dropped to the ground and attempted to flee, but it was too late. For this was no ordinary light, it was a beam of pure energy the soldier conjured. The soldier raised his arms and released an energy blast more powerful than anything Megildur had ever witnessed. The blast threw everyone nearby to the ground. This included all the Minotaurs, the Elven ruler, and even the soldier who initiated the explosion. The blast of energy nearly blinded all others. After checking on his group, making sure all was well, Megildur moved in to evaluate the damage. Minotaur Warriors lay motionless on the ground and the soldier, who saved them all, was lying in a newly formed crater because of his blast.

"He is a Sentinel," Maethorion commented, approaching from the southern half of the safehold. "We call the energy blast you witnessed the Divine Word of Binding. It's powerful but unfortunately it also affects those who cast it."

"He gave his life for us?" Megildur inquired, looking upon the Sentinel.

Maethorion responded, "Do not fret M'Lord. Remember, nobody in Aerynth dies since the Turning. He will return to Greensward Parish, maybe a bit charred, but he will live."

Megildur stood over the Sentinel for a moment but a noise distracted him in the distance. It was Caunion, crawling away like a snake. The blast did not deprive him of life, but Megildur planned to change that. He walked over to the Elf Lord, unsheathed his sword, and placed his weapon at the base of the Elf Lord's skull.

Megildur commanded, "Get on your knees coward!" Caunion stopped crawling and turned to face him. The Elf Lord decided to stand rather than kneel before Megildur, but the Aelfborn Lord kept his sword trained on Caunion's head.

Caunion scoffed, "Why should I bend a knee to a half-breed like you?"

Megildur roared, "I am Lord Megildur, rightful heir to the High King Cambruin and chosen by the All-Father himself to reclaim Shadowbane! You will bend a knee to me or I will cut you down where you stand!"

Caunion countered, "You're Cambruin's heir?" The Elf spit on the ground near Megildur's feet. "That carries little weight to an Elf. The fool deserved his outcome. I only wish the All-Father would receive the same fate. As for Shadowbane, that sword carries a curse since Wethrinaerea stole it from the rightful owners, the Elves."

Filled with rage over Caunion's comments Megildur hit the Elf Lord in the gut with the hilt of his sword, finally causing him to drop to his knees. He placed his sword at Caunion's throat when the Elf Lord looked up.

Megildur lashed out, "Thurin gave Shadowbane to your people, as a gift! Afterwards, the Elves turned their backs on the Gods and placed their beliefs in false Gods! Finally, Sillestor made the greatest betrayal of all time! He turned Shadowbane upon the All-Father and attempted to stab him in the back!" By this time, Megildur was fuming while he stood over the Elf Lord, his sword still focused on Caunion. Megildur glanced up to see most of his army, and family, gathered around watching his confrontation with Caunion. "You deserve a worse fate than Cambruin, and you shall receive it!" Megildur raised his sword and began to swing it down with all his might. Caunion closed his eyes and winced, but the sword stopped just short of the Elf Lord's throat.

"Your fate will be nothing less than what you have done to others, oppression." Megildur sneered at Caunion and kicked the Elf Lord to the ground. "Bind him and prepare him for travel back to Greensward Parish. He will make a nice addition to the community, as a slave. There your arrogance shall be stripped from you." Several Warriors dragged Caunion off for binding.

Caunion shouted, "I will release my vengeance upon you half-breed! You will rue the day you did not kill me!"

"Let us remove ourselves from here." Megildur said while turning to face his army and family. "I prefer not to be here when these Minotaurs return." He regrouped with the others and all of them went out the front gates with no opposition. Aelarnost was an empty shell, due to Megildur and his allies. He succeeded against the might of the Dar Khelegur, now to face an even greater adversary, his parents.

CHAPTER 18: Separation Anxiety

Megildur's army and his family returned to the camp they made prior to the attack. It was south of Aelarnost and just outside of their tracking range, in case the Elves decided to retrieve Caunion. Once Megildur tended to the troops, assuring their losses were not too great, he turned his attention to a more pressing matter, talking to his mother and father. Megildur entered his tent and found Marie tending to his family's needs. His mother, father, and sister had just finished their morning meal and they all turned their attention to Megildur.

Marie announced, "I will bring your food immediately, Sir." She turned to exit but Megildur stopped her.

"Do not bring me any food, I need to talk with my family," Megildur replied.

Marie murmured, "As you wish, Sir." She slightly bowed and left the tent.

Aedan spoke, "Well, Lord Megildur, where do we begin?" Megildur's new leadership role had them all puzzled. "Last memory I have of you was a scared boy promising his father to protect the family. Now you lead an army, formed by multiple guilds, and carry the title of Lord." Aedan stood from the chair he was sitting in and placed an arm on Megildur's shoulder. "It's quite a dramatic change from the boy who hated doing chores to become the Lordly ruler who conquered the Deathless Empire." Aedan smiled at his son, grinning ear to ear with pride at the man he had become.

"Megildur, what happened to you in Fort Viatrus?" Vanya inquired. "When I saw you last that Minotaur had just impaled me with a sword from behind. What happened after that moment?"

"Well the Minotaur who stabbed you did not stop there," Megildur explained, removing his armor. "Afterward, the beast turned his attention to me. I was no match for him. So once I annoyed him with a scratch from my dagger, he crushed me with his hoof." Megildur began to pace inside his tent, telling the tale of his journey so far. "I died and instead of returning right away, my spirit went elsewhere. I floated in a misty haze listening to multiple voices talking all at once. I found the event maddening. I called out after the noise stopped and a voice told me to have no fear. At that same time, someone touched me on the shoulder and I received this mark." Megildur exposed his shoulder to show his family the glowing mark he received.

Aedan exclaimed, "That is the mark of the All-Father!"

"Yes, it is. Zeristan told me that the All-Father chose me to reclaim Shadowbane and that I was the rightful heir to the High King Cambruin." This news widened Aedan's eyes. Aedan stared at Vanya, then he began to pace around the room.

"Zeristan the Wise is with you?" Aedan questioned his son. Megildur nodded. "It has been a legend passed down from Father to Son for several generations in our family. I should have told you before now. We wanted to shelter you and Aranel from the cruelty of Aerynth. I guess the All-Father decided it was time you knew. We suspected someday the All-Father would call upon us to retrieve the mighty sword forged by Thurin and reclaim our heritage. We just did not know when or who the All-Father would choose."

"You knew?" Megildur exclaimed. The Aelfborn's blood began to boil, but he knew his family suffered enough at the hands of the Elves. Megildur took a deep breath and calmed his thoughts. "So you know why I must leave to begin my quest for Shadowbane."

"No you will not!" Vanya interjected. "We just put our family back together and I will not let you tear us apart!" She took on the role of the protective mother, clutching both Megildur and Aranel. Letting the motherly embrace continue for some time, Aedan placed his hand on Vanya's arm.

"We cannot stand in the way of Megildur's destiny." Aedan responded. "The All-Father gave him this quest." Vanya looked up from her children and released her grip on both of them. "Besides, Megildur reached the age of maturity. The All-Father just laid out his path before him." Aedan gave Megildur a proud smile but he knew deep down that this would not be an easy quest. Even experienced knights had set out to find Shadowbane and come back empty handed. Some unfortunate souls never came back.

"Thank you both for understanding," Megildur sighed. He was not looking forward to leaving his family, but he knew the significance of this quest. "I will call a meeting right away with Maethorion and Atreus to advise them that I am departing." Megildur turned to leave the tent but someone blindsided him, a slightly smaller Aelfborn girl who attempted to stop his departure.

Aranel squealed, "I will not let you leave, big brother!" She blocked Megildur from moving, or at least tried. Aranel pushed against him until she exhausted herself and slumped to the floor crying.

"You have nothing to fear," Megildur responded, kneeling down to comfort his sister. "I have rallied armies behind my cause before and I have the support of the All-Father." Megildur raised his sister's head to look into his eyes. She could see the confidence in his eyes and that helped her to stop crying.

Aranel wailed at her older brother, "But we just got our family back together! Who is going to take me down to the sea when Father is gone? I will have nobody to tease. I love running into your room and waking you early in the morning. Who will I torment now?"

"I love you teasing me in the mornings," Megildur replied. That was a lie but he figured it would make his sister happy to hear that. "I must complete this quest, for our family, and for Aerynth. We have all lived in fear of guilds like the Dar Khelegur and the Temple of the Cleansing Flame. We need Shadowbane to bring peace to our shattered world. Even though I am not with you at Fort Viatrus, I will always be with you in spirit. Besides, I hear your voice in my head even when you are not around." Megildur smiled at Aranel. She jumped into his arms and hugged her brother.

Aranel exclaimed, "I love you, brother!"

"I love you too, Aranel," Megildur admitted, returning his sister's embrace. He then heard applause coming from just outside the tent. He stood up and pulled back the tent flap to find Marie, Maethorion, Atreus, Zeristan and the rest of his army. Embarrassed, Megildur walked outside with his family close behind him.

"We apologize for listening into your private conversation, Lord Megildur," Maethorion said once the troops quieted down. "We heard your sister cry out. We thought you were in danger, until we heard why she wept." Maethorion separated himself from the rest to talk with Megildur. "So, it's true that you plan to set out on the rest of your quest now?" By this time Marie, Atreus, and Zeristan joined the conversation.

"Yes, it's true. However, I must continue without an army. I am unsure what obstacles I will face but I am certain the All-Father wishes for me to draw as little attention as possible on this quest." Megildur bowed his head and with sincerity spoke his next words. "I would like to thank all of you for helping me rescue my family. I couldn't have accomplished that part of my quest without you." Megildur turned to address certain individuals. "Maethorion, please take our new guest, Caunion, back to Greensward Parish. I am certain Aerynth will be better off with him in your custody."

"Certainly, Lord Megildur," Maethorion said while bowing.

"Atreus, if you would be kind enough to escort my family as far as the Centaur Cohort?" Megildur requested.

"It would be my honor to take them all the way to Fort Viatrus, My Lord," Atreus concurred. Megildur bowed his head to the mighty Centaur ruler in gratitude.

Marie interjected, "I will prepare a travel pack for you, Sir!" She scurried away. Megildur noticed her agitated demeanor, but was unsure what provoked it.

Turwaithion declared, "It would be an honor to join you on this quest."

"I appreciate your offer Turwaithion, but this is a mission of stealth," Megildur replied. "Unlike the attack on Aelarnost, this quest requires gathering information and sneakiness. Something tells me you prefer a straightforward fight as opposed to stalking in the night." Megildur chuckled, placing his hand on Turwaithion's shoulder.

Gaal boasted, "Basically, he needs my skills." The Thief materialized next to the Elven Captain. He placed his arm atop of Turwaithion's other shoulder.

Turwaithion bellowed, "You abomination, I should have executed you when we first captured you!" He brushed the Thief's arm off his shoulder. Megildur laughed.

"To be blunt, yes, I do need your sordid talents," Megildur countered. "Less attention we draw to this quest the better our chances. We will also need someone who knows the tale of Shadowbane, so we might know where to start looking."

"It would appear you need the talents of a Bard, Lord Megildur," Zeristan stated. "Not only do they know melodies to sooth the savage beast but they are also masters of the chronicles of Aerynth."

"I am sure we can find one in Thieves' Den," Gaal replied.

"Then that will be our first stop," Megildur announced. "Gaal, see about some provisions and I will meet you back here soon." Gaal agreed and departed. Megildur returned to his tent to collect his supplies.

Megildur entered his tent to see Marie flinging his items into a bag. He knew from experience never to confront his mother or sister when they were this upset but he had no choice, he needed his belongings.

Megildur inquired, "Are you alright Marie?" He knew the answer to that question was no, but he did not know another question to ask.

Marie retorted, "No I am not alright, Sir!" She finished packing and turned to face Megildur. "Everyone knows it's a mistake to seek Shadowbane, except you. Death and disaster have always surrounded that sword and you want to run right out into the same fate as many other knights…just like him!" Marie knew she had said too much and burst into tears, spinning to leave the tent. Megildur grabbed her arm before she made it to the opening.

"Who are you referring to?" Megildur asked. Her actions and references puzzled the Aelfborn Lord. He sat down with Marie.

Marie looked at Megildur. "You are very much like him, my father that is," Marie admitted once she finally stopped crying. "He was a Warrior who dreamed of following the Knights of Cambruin to find Shadowbane. One day he heard the sword might be in the Dwarf safehold and he went off to find it, leaving Mother and I." Marie started to tear up again. "He never came back, either with or without that damn sword!" She stood up from the chair with mixed emotions. She loved her father and missed him but also hated him for leaving.

"I am going on this journey at the All-Father's request," Megildur replied. "I am uncertain of the journey ahead and I know it may lead to failure, or worse." Megildur took a deep gulp at the thought of what else might happen. "I am certain, with the backing of the All-Father, I will prevail." Of course, Megildur's confidence about the journey was mainly for the sake of his family and for Marie. Personally, he was terrified. Megildur lifted Marie's chin and looked her in the eyes. "I will also investigate what happened to your father." That put a smile on her face. He picked up the bag Marie packed for him and collected his armor. He knew he would need it.

Megildur walked out of the tent, met with Gaal, and said his final farewells. His mother and sister wept when he walked away but his father stood strong, with a look of pride in his son. Aedan knew what Megildur faced, which increased his pride knowing that he still was willing to meet the challenge. He only wished for his son's safe return.

CHAPTER 19: A New Journey

Megildur and Gaal walked for several hours without seeing any signs of life. Finally, some form of civilization appeared when they came over the next hill, a safehold. Inhabitants were not visible. However, they did see an object rise from the center of the safehold and start moving in their direction. It was flying, which was an unusual occurrence in Aerynth. While the object drew closer, their dread grew deeper. At last, the object was close enough to see what it was, an Aracoix Scout. The traveling companions remembered the last encounter with these birdmen, on the way to Aelarnost. It would be more treacherous for Megildur and Gaal if they had to battle more Aracoix alone. The two travelers unsheathed their weapons and prepared for the worst. The Aracoix Scout stopped before reaching them and appeared to be thinking of his next course of action. It stared at them and let out a single shriek before turning around and flying back to his point of origin.

"I have never seen an Aracoix turn and flee from a conflict." Gaal remarked with a baffled look on his face.

"I guess our last encounter deterred them from wanting to fight," Megildur replied with a grin. He did not expect the Aracoix to be so reluctant to face him again but it pleased him, especially since he lacked an army this time.

The lucky pair continued in their southeastern direction toward Thieves' Den. They knew they would not make it to the safehold during the daytime but they kept moving so long as the sunlight remained. Megildur did not like all the walking they must endure but he was ecstatic it was not through the hot deserts of Aerynth. By sundown, they reached the same river they had crossed before when journeying to Aelarnost.

Gaal moaned, "Oh wonderful, this river again. I almost drown crossing the last time."

Megildur laughed, "At least this time you're not bound to a wagon." Gaal glared at him. "Besides, it's nearly nightfall. We will make camp here and cross in the morning. Resting shall make the crossing easier." Gaal agreed and the two made camp.

Megildur lay on the ground gazing up at the stars. Observing the sky, he wondered if the All-Father had made the right choice with him. After all, it would have been wiser to choose his father since he is a cunning leader. These thoughts plagued the young Aelfborn until sleep caught up with him.

Megildur heard a noise and opened his eyes, but Gaal did not stir. The Aelfborn did not recognize the sound, but he noticed a glowing orb of light approaching.

"Who's there? I can hear you, now show yourself!" He grew a bit impatient since the situation was making him nervous. The light engulfed Megildur's being, calming him. He remained still as the orb began to speak.

"Hello again, my young Aelfborn champion," the voice called out. Megildur hesitated. He recognized the voice but it concerned him to not know from where. "Why do I disturb you so, my child?"

Megildur implied, "It might put my mind at ease if I could see who I am speaking with."

The voice affirmed, "If that will bring you peace, I think I can grant your request." An elderly man with a silvery gray beard emerged before Megildur. He was taller than Megildur and wore a robe made of golden silk. It surprised Megildur to see a material of this type shimmer so bright on such a dark night, and with no light shining on it.

"Are you the All-Father?" Megildur asked the man.

"I am," He replied to a doubtful Megildur. "Why do you question what you can see with your own eyes? Do you think I would look more gallant in armor?" He waved his hand and bright heavy armor now covered all of his body, except for his head. "Or would I be more cunning and wear leather?" With another wave of his hand, he now wore a suit of leather armor, much like the type a rogue would wear. "The outward appearance we project does not change who we are within." The All-Father walked next to Megildur wearing the golden robe once again. He placed his arm over Megildur's shoulder and guided him to walk along the newly formed stone path before them. "What bothers you on such a peaceful night?"

"I do not mean to question your decisions, but are you sure..." Megildur paused, uncertain if wanting to question a God. He did create Aerynth and most of the creatures on it.

"Am I sure you are the right one to reclaim Shadowbane and bring peace to Aerynth?" The All-Father interrupted. He stopped walking to glance down at Megildur. "Let me tell you of another quest I offered to a king. In his darkest hour, I told him of a weapon so powerful; it could bring hope to the hopeless. He was not able to leave his men during their massive battle, so he sent one man in his place to recover the weapon. Now this bold knight, who went on the quest for his king, had the most humble of beginnings. He was the son of a blacksmith, who took up his father's trade when he was seven. The boy never wanted to pursue blacksmithing. Instead, he yearned for knighthood. Being the son of a blacksmith lacked the nobility to warrant such a title. Therefore, the boy left home at the age of twelve. He met another knight who told him in order to be a knight he must defeat fifty foes in battle. So that is exactly what this blacksmith's son did before going to see the king, who was so impressed he bestowed the title of knight upon him."

"You speak of Sir Caeric Blackhammer," Megildur added. "He was one of High King Cambruin's champions. My father told me of his tale but I never heard of his lowly beginnings."

"Many of the men you admire start out as nothing more than peasants," the All-Father replied, smiling at Megildur. "It's not how you begin your life that matters, but how you live it." Hearing this caused Megildur to beam back at the All-Father.

"About time you woke up you lazy worg," Gaal said to Megildur when his eyes opened. "Help me with this fire before we freeze to death. How can the temperature smolder during the day and freeze at night?" Gaal was shivering while he gathered some logs and kindling for a fire. "Why are you smiling?"

"I awaken with a warm heart and a renewed conviction," Megildur beamed. "The All-Father visited me in my dream." Gaal stopped gathering kindling to stare at Megildur.

Gaal mocked, "There is no All-Father! If there was he would not let his champion freeze!" Without warning, the fire burst in intensity sending Gaal stumbling back in fear. The flame turned blue and a massive hand emerged from the embers, as if to strike down the insolent Shade. As swift as it appeared, the fire returned to its normal yellowish-orange color, this time with no hand. The intensity of the fire did decrease but not to the same meager level that it was before Gaal spoke so arrogantly.

"Do you believe in the All-Father now?" Megildur queried the almost charred Thief. "How is that lack of faith holding up for you?"

Gaal vowed, "I believe in Him! I will believe in anything He demands as long as I am allowed to live…in one undercooked piece preferably!"

Megildur laughed as Gaal attempted to check his body for any fire damage. Megildur did not want to eat this morning. He was still marveling in the confidence the All-Father expressed in his abilities to recover Shadowbane.

"This should be easy enough," Megildur commented, looking at the river they must traverse. "I will cross first and make sure it's safe for you." Gaal seemed a bit perturbed by the coddling from Megildur. If the Shade remained unbound during their last crossing, he would not have nearly drowned. Megildur went into the river and discovered it was a couple of feet deep, hardly a challenge for him. He continued without any issues until he reached the middle of the river. He felt something tug at his ankle and before he could look down, it dragged him into the water. It kept the Aelfborn Lord fully submerged, pulling him upriver. Then, abruptly, his motion stopped. He lifted his head from the water to find Gaal standing over him. He tried to pull Megildur from the river but something was yanking Megildur back down.

Gaal exclaimed, "What happened?" No sooner did the Shade ask when he heard a shrieking sound. He turned around to see a red wormlike creature lunge out of the river toward him. He let go of

Megildur to pull his dagger out. He placed his arms over his face to shield himself from the creature and inadvertently filleted the worm.

Gaal turned back to help his companion by stabbing the red worm wrapped around his leg. Megildur muttered while Gaal helped him to his feet, "Thanks. That is the one thing I hate about the water. You never know what is in it!"

Gaal boasted, "See, I am not so clumsy without a wagon attached to me." He sneered at Megildur while the two finished crossing the river.

"Indeed you are not clumsy," Megildur admitted, sitting down at the river's edge for a few minutes. He removed his boots to dump the excess water and to eliminate anything hiding inside. His feet were wrinkly, like one of his pigs back home.

"What's this monster?" Gaal asked, examining the remains he dragged ashore.

"My mother told me of red worms her people, the Gwaridorn Elves, encountered at sea," Megildur replied. "They called them Delgaran Worms. Translated it means red horror." Gaal looked at the gutted worm with disgust and threw it back into the river.

Gaal inquired, "If they are from the sea, why did we find them in the river?"

"This river lets out into the sea just south of here, I guess they traveled upriver looking for food," Megildur surmised.

Gaal scoffed, "I'll say, they found us! Personally I would prefer not to be some worms feast!"

Megildur stood up, "We should keep moving if we are to make it to Thieves' Den by nightfall." Gaal agreed and the two got back on their journey.

CHAPTER 20: *Mellissar*

Now that Megildur and Gaal were well on their way and the remaining armies were packing up, Zeristan decided to prepare for the Aelfborn's pending victory. He went to Megildur's family to say goodbye before leaving for Mellissar, the old capital for the Kingdom of Men and Cambruin's last residence.

"Am I intruding?" Zeristan asked, pulling back the tent flap where Aedan, Vanya, and Aranel were sitting.

"Not at all, please come in," Aedan replied. He stood to greet the Wizard. "So you are the mighty Wizard who counseled both my son and my...great-grandfather? I think that is right. The High King Cambruin was dead long before my birth."

Zeristan responded, "I've had the honor of advising many great rulers, including Cambruin and the soon to be High King Megildur."

Aranel interrupted the Wizard to ask, "Are you a demon?"

Vanya retorted, "Aranel, do not be rude!" She pulled her daughter back and addressed Zeristan, "I am sorry, she can be a bit impish at times."

Zeristan chuckled, "That is quite alright." He knelt down next to the young Aelfborn child. "Why would you suspect I am a demon?"

"Cause my brother said that only demons and Elves have been alive that long, and you don't look like an Elf," Aranel replied.

"Actually, the All-Father himself created my kind just before he created the Human race," Zeristan admitted. "That was when time began on Aerynth, at the dawn of the Age of Days."

Aedan exclaimed, "That would make you, over five thousand years old!"

"Yes," Zeristan affirmed. "However, I did not come here to spout off about my historical knowledge of Aerynth. I am off to Mellissar, to prepare for Megildur's coronation."

"You mean my son is really going to be the next High King of Men?" Vanya inquired. "Since the Age of Strife began, over one hundred years ago, no one in Aerynth respects or acknowledges royal bloodlines anymore."

"He is the rightful heir of Cambruin and chosen champion by the All-Father to retrieve Shadowbane," Zeristan responded. "It's only logical that he would take up the throne in Mellissar and rule the ten Kingdoms of Men."

Aedan gasped, "I am still in shock over the news. My son, the High King?"

"Well, Megildur is special, since he has the blood of multiple royal lines," Zeristan announced while looking at Vanya. "However, there is another reason I want to proceed to Mellissar. I feel Sir Adelard, the Steward of the High Throne in Mellissar, will not step down to just anyone who claims title to the High Throne. Also, there's the matter of Queen Bronwyn."

"Cambruin's widow?" Vanya asked. "What about Queen Bronwyn?"

"About fifty years after the death of her husband, the Queen returned to Mellissar. She demanded Sir Adelard ordain her High Queen," Zeristan educated Aedan and Vanya. "Chaos erupted between Queen Bronwyn, Sir Adelard, and the remaining Knights of Cambruin. At one point a knight even tried to take control of the city and claim himself ruler, but I helped put a stop to that and Sir Adelard remained the Steward."

Vanya exclaimed, "Well that settles it! We will accompany you to Mellissar! I will not let my son go from one dangerous quest to an even more dangerous town!" Vanya began gathering her belongings and preparing Aranel for travel.

Zeristan warned, "Are you sure that is wise? I do not think this is the type of family trip you would want."

"Oh, she wasn't asking to join you," Aedan interjected. "She was telling you she is going to Mellissar."

Zeristan grinned and replied, "We will teleport to the nearest runegate, and I will open the portal to the runegate near Mellissar, when you are ready."

Aranel looked worried, "We will tele what? Will it hurt?" She looked to her mother for comfort.

Zeristan reassured, "No, my little one, it does not hurt. It's the way that mages, such as myself, travel great distances in a short time."

Aranel, not knowing if she could trust the old man yet, looked up at her mother who patted her on the head and whispered, "You will be just fine, Aranel." The young Aelfborn beamed and followed her mother, father, and the Wizard outside.

Once clear of other people, Zeristan began to wave his hands and a bubble enveloped the four of them. He sent all of them to the nearest runegate, where the Wizard stood upon the platform and again waved his hands to open a portal on the runegate. It opened and he stood back, gesturing for the others to step onto the portal. One by one, they walked onto the platform and vanished. At last, all four of them stood on the runegate platform closest to Mellissar.

"It's this direction," Zeristan guided Megildur's family. "I am unsure of who will be in the capital. I haven't returned in some time." Vanya and Aedan looked at Zeristan, and then each other. They were unsure of how Sir Adelard would receive them, since one of them was a descendant of Cambruin and the other an Elf. Relations between the Elven and Human races have been volatile ever since the All-Father created Men, but even more so since the War of Tears. This war pitted Elves against Men for nearly two hundred years.

The unlikely foursome traveled for several hours before reaching the outer walls of Mellissar. When they arrived, nobody expected the once majestic capital to appear in such shambles. Vines and foliage riddled the towering walls. The gates to the main entrance appeared rusted and dilapidated. It looked more like an ancient ruin, instead of the glorious thriving city it once was.

A voice shouted from within the walls, "Halt! Who approaches Mellissar?"

The Wizard announced, "Zeristan the Wise, Wizard and Counselor to the late High King Cambruin. I come with word of good tidings soon to come!"

A weary voice replied while opening the main gate, "Well, that would be a good change, my old friend." An elderly man stood before the travelers wearing tattered leather armor, with a bow slung across his back.

Zeristan exclaimed, "Sir Adelard! Is that you?" He approached the knight, who was acting as a guard. He greeted his old friend. "What are you doing at the front gate?"

Sir Adelard sighed, "All of the original Knights of Cambruin have left, and even the widow, Queen

Bronwyn, has given up her fight for the High Throne. Come in, come in." The old knight guided Zeristan, Vanya, Aedan, and Aranel inside. "An Elf and an Aelfborn? You sure travel with different company these days Zeristan."

"These people are good, but it's because of their son that I am here," Zeristan responded.

The Wizard sat down on a nearby bench with the Steward of Mellissar and explained everything to him. He told him that not only was Megildur the heir to Cambruin, but the All-Father chose Megildur to retrieve Shadowbane. Even though Sir Adelard always thought this day would come, the news surprised him.

"I must send word out to the other Kingdoms of Men," Sir Adelard replied. "I am not sure this will please all of them, but I must notify everyone." He rose from the bench where they sat and walked toward the castle. He stopped before reaching the doors and turned back around. "I am also uncertain of how Queen Bronwyn will react. She gave up her fight for the High Throne some time ago, but news of an heir coming to reclaim the title may fuel her cause again." This news startled Vanya and Aedan since it would be their son dealing with the repercussions.

The travelers followed Sir Adelard when he stepped into the foyer of the castle. Beyond the main hall, they could see two large doors, which looked as if they were inoperable for some time. It appeared that the steward did most of his work in the foyer since there was a cluttered desk with maps and books scattered across it. The steward grabbed some parchment from a drawer and a quill from an inkwell on the desk and began feverishly writing. When he finished writing the letters to the other kingdoms, he glanced past his shoulder to see Aranel staring at his desk.

Sir Adelard admitted, "I know it's a mess in here, but I thought I would have to find the heir of Cambruin. I never suspected anyone would guide him to me."

The elderly man stood from his desk. He walked back out the main doors and over to a stable. The doors were open, but it was so dark just past the doorway nothing inside was visible, until they got closer. When the steward approached, a large furry beast stirred just past the doors. It appeared in the doorway and took up the entire opening to the stable. It was enormous and a bit overwhelming for Aranel, since the young Aelfborn froze in her tracks. Sir Adelard saw her reaction to the beast and turned to reassure her, "Do not fret little one, this great big wolf is my friend. He will not hurt you." He took Aranel by the hand and walked her over to the giant wolf. The beast's stature was so great that Aranel could play beneath his underbelly without ducking at all. The beast bowed his head and let the Aelfborn child pet him. The cautious Aranel did this for a moment, smiled at the wolf, and scurried back to her mother's side.

Aranel whispered into her mother's ear, "I like that wolf. He is soft." Vanya smiled at her daughter, and the cautious Aedan released the grip on his sword. His daughter petting a wolf unsettled him.

Sir Adelard slipped the letters into a pouch around the wolf's neck, whispered something into its ear, and stepped back. The wolf bound out of the stable and through the dilapidated gates.

"My friend is fast," Sir Adelard advised the others. "He will get word to the ten Kingdoms of Men soon. We'll have to wait to see what form of response we get." The old knight started walking back to the castle. "You are welcome to stay in the guest wing of the castle. I will show you the way."

Aedan and Vanya did not like the idea of waiting to see how the other kingdoms received the news that the heir to the High Throne has returned. Nor did they like idea that some may have disdain toward their child but for now, they had to wait.

CHAPTER 21: Thieves' Den

Megildur and Gaal had been walking for several days without seeing any signs of life. Early one morning, they found what they were seeking.

"Is that Thieves' Den?" Megildur asked Gaal.

"Yes, that's it," Gaal replied. "Now, let me give you a few words of advice. Keep your head down and make sure you don't let anyone know who you are."

"Why do I need to hide who I am?" Megildur replied. "Everyone in Aerynth knows me as a half-breed, not a Lord."

Gaal countered, "Honor and nobility do not exist here! For the most part they are all Thieves, cutthroats, and bandits." Gaal looked a little concerned about Megildur going in too headstrong and getting them killed. "Now we should hide our packs out here somewhere, especially that armor of yours too." Megildur now looked a bit concerned but figured one Thief should know the tactics of another. He followed Gaal's advice and hid his belongings in some brush nearby and the two walked to the front gates.

"Will they accept Aelfborn in this safehold?" Megildur now asked since he knew some safeholds only accepted certain races.

"Aye, they accept many races here," Gaal replied. "So stay on your toes and keep a watchful eye on your possessions. Otherwise they just might walk away." Gaal smirked at Megildur since stealing from others was his profession.

As Gaal promised, the guards let both of them in without question. Once Megildur was past the gates, what he saw amazed him. The safehold was full of almost every race in Aerynth. He observed people on a daily basis like Aelfborn and Human but Megildur saw others all too familiar. There were Aracoix, the dreaded bird men, Elves and Irekei. Unfortunately, one Irekei walked past Megildur and spit on the ground before Megildur's feet. The red-skinned man then muttered something in his language, which he did not understand.

Megildur exclaimed to Gaal, "What did I do now?"

"He didn't like your tattoos," Gaal answered, pointing to Megildur's exposed mystical tattoos on his face. "He called you 'Hru bhi', which if I remember their language means 'very ugly'." The Aelfborn Lord remembered what Zeristan told him before about Irekei hating any markings on the body. He would have to avoid other Irekei, or cover his body, if he wanted to avoid other detestable fluids projected at him. Gaal reached over to a nearby table and temporarily relieved someone of their cloak. "Here, this cloak should help for now." Megildur swung the cloak over his shoulders and pulled the hood forward, concealing most of his face.

Looking up, Megildur spotted a race he had never seen before. The individual did not walk but instead hovered across the ground. Without any warning, the female stopped and made contact with the ground. She turned her head toward Megildur and Gaal. He could see glowing red eyes when the female began to hover again, toward Megildur.

She asked in a soft but sinister voice, "What are you staring at boy?" Her skin looked hard and pale white. Her hair was bright red, like the color of blood, and he could see two of her teeth came to a point like daggers. Her touch was like ice. Megildur discovered this when she caressed his face with her decrepit hand.

"I did not mean to stare," Megildur replied trying not to shiver from either her cold hand or his fear of this creature. "And I am not a boy!"

She bellowed, "You are to me, half-breed! My existence started long before any man, or boy!" She glared once more at Megildur, which he could feel deep into his heart. She turned back on her original course. "We will meet again, boy!" She vowed when her back was to both of them.

"What was that atrocity?" Megildur asked Gaal. He took a deep sigh of relief that she was gone.

"That was a Vampire," Gaal commented. He also sighed after the Vampire disappeared. "They are dark and ominous creatures of the Void, who drink the blood of others to sustain their contemptible lives." Gaal shivered at his last comment. Apparently, he did not like them much either.

"Let's find a Bard to help us and get out of here," Megildur stated, trying to regain his composure after his first encounter with an undead being. They both went to the local tavern, everyone in the safehold gathered there. Megildur hoped this visit to a tavern fared better than his last one. His stopover at the tavern in Sea Dog's Rest was not a pleasant one. They stood in the doorway and it was just as Megildur dreaded. It smelled as the stables back home do, before he cleaned them. There was also a strong aroma of ale, making the place horrendous. They barely made it past the doorway when the trouble began.

"There you are, Thief!" An enormous Half Giant bellowed, grabbing Gaal by the shirt and swinging him around to the wall. "Where's my gold?"

"I'm sorry, do I know you?" Gaal winced, since the brute intensified the pressure against him.

The brute lashed out, "You remember me. I'm the one you and your last friend had the nerve to steal from. Perhaps I will just kill you and call it a day!"

"Look, I told you before as I will tell you again! I didn't know that other Thief!" Gaal argued with the enormous brute but only managed to increase his anger. The Half Giant raised Gaal off the ground so high his feet were dangling in the air.

Megildur intervened, trying to see if he could save Gaal from a beating. "We just walked in here, how could he have stolen anything from you?"

"This is not his first time in Thieves' Den," the brute countered. "Now go away half-breed or you will get a thrashing after I'm done with this abomination." The Half Giant increased the tension of his grip, causing Gaal severe pain.

Megildur scanned the room to look for help, but nobody even raised their head to see what transpired. He knew it was up to him to help Gaal, or this brute would crush his companion. Megildur picked up a nearby empty pitcher and smashed it over the brute's head.

"So you want your thrashing now?" The Half Giant responded after dropping Gaal and brushing off the remnants of the broken pitcher. He approached Megildur, emitting an evil laugh. He now wielded an enormous battle-axe. The brute raised the axe above his head to strike Megildur but before he could swing he found himself surrounded by rings of light. The Half Giant looked confused, since he was unable to move or deliver his deadly blow. Megildur could hear a melody strumming from an instrument but had never heard such a tune. He turned to see a female playing a small harp behind him near the doorway.

"We had better move, that spell will only hold the brute for a short time," the whimsical lass advised Megildur and Gaal.

Megildur admitted, giving a hand to Gaal and raising him from the floor. "I see no advantage to waiting around here for a beating." The three of them fled the tavern and subsequently Thieves' Den. None of them wanted to slow their pace for some time after leaving the safehold, since they knew the brute would catch them. Eventually their stamina diminished and they all needed to rest. "So who do we thank for rescuing us from that brute in the tavern?" Megildur asked their rescuer when all of them sat down together.

"My name is Honoria," she replied. "I am a Bard and I hate seeing bullies like that one back there pick on others."

"Thank you, Honoria. Fortune has smiled upon us as we were in Thieves' Den looking for a Bard," Megildur chuckled. "My pale companion is Gaal and I am Megildur. We were seeking anyone in Thieves' Den who knows the tale of Shadowbane. We heard one rumor that it may still reside at Stormvald inside Korvambar."

"You are Lord Megildur, of Fort Viatrus?" Honoria inquired, startling both Megildur and Gaal. "And are you the same Lord Megildur who rallied multiple guilds to bane Aelarnost and captured Dar Thaelostor Caunion?"

Megildur queried, "Have we met before? How do you know about that bane?"

"M'Lord, everyone in Aerynth knows of the Aelfborn Lord who defeated the Deathless Empire and of your treacherous journey across the desert after escaping from the Temple of the Cleansing Flame." Honoria continued her tale of Megildur's journey, as if he had not lived it. "The Bard's communication network is vast across Aerynth, although nobody knows of Lord Megildur's journey prior to the attack on Fort Viatrus by the Dar Khelegur." Honoria looked puzzled at Gaal wondering if he knew why this is so, which of course he had no idea.

"That is because my journey didn't begin until my death in Fort Viatrus," Megildur replied. Honoria listened attentively hoping he would elaborate, that way she could complete his epic tale. "After the Minotaur crushed me with his hoof, I died but instead of reappearing at any Tree of Life I returned somewhere else. It was a misty place where all I heard were voices talking over one another until it drove me insane, then all of them silenced at once. I heard a voice tell me to have no fear and that person placed their hand on my shoulder and left His mark upon me." Megildur exposed his right shoulder showing the three interlocking circles.

Honoria gasped, "That is the mark of the All-Father! So, it's true! The All-Father has chosen his champion to recover Shadowbane and restore peace to Aerynth?" She first gazed at Megildur and then her eyes moved to Gaal.

"Don't look at me to doubt him," Gaal retorted. "The last time I questioned the All-Father, He almost roasted me...literally! No way will I doubt Him again. I am a believer in Lord Megildur's claim that the All-Father chose him." Gaal mumbled more under his breath, "Although I doubt one person made all that exists."

"I know, it was difficult for me to accept at first too," Megildur responded. "Recently the All-Father came to me in a dream and I now understand why he chose me. For one reason I am the rightful heir to the High King Cambruin and secondly, He has picked other champions who come from meager beginnings such as mine."

Honoria conceded, "I too have heard rumors of the Dwarves guarding Shadowbane. It would honor me M'Lord if you would allow me to guide you to Korvambar. I would also be able to scribe your journey so that all of Aerynth will know of your deed! I know someone in Fort Irsadeng, along the east coast. Her people could ferry us to the isle of Stormvald."

Megildur responded, "Well I am not so sure about the writing of our journey, but we could use a guide to Korvambar. It's getting dark, so we should make camp here and set out at first light for Fort Irsadeng." Megildur turned to Gaal, "Could you find some firewood while I start a small fire with this kindling we have here?" Gaal agreed and departed to gather wood, none of them wanted to freeze in the night air. Megildur and Gaal started a roaring fire and the three of them enjoyed some music provided by Honoria. For the sake of all in Aerynth, Megildur hoped they could recover Shadowbane.

CHAPTER 22: *Nightly Disturbance*

They talked well past sundown and Honoria even told the tale of the creation of Shadowbane by Thurin, back in the Age of Twilight. She told them how the God of Forge and Craft created the sword from the rarest minerals in Aerynth. She also told them the tale of Sillestor's treachery against the All-Father. How after Thurin vanquished the Elf Lord, He returned the sword to the center of Aerynth to his children, the Dwarves, to protect. Honoria proved how valuable her knowledge would be on this journey.

"Well we should get some sleep," Megildur admitted after many hours of tales from their newfound Bard. "Tomorrow we will begin our quest for Fort Irsadeng."

Honoria declared with conviction, "I am sure my friend there can help us. She joined my side for many quests, before settling in one safehold."

"That would be a welcomed sight, a safehold that is not trying to kill us for once," Gaal retorted. Megildur laughed since the last few safeholds they entered did end with fighting, although Megildur started the fight in Aelarnost.

"Good night all," Megildur said before bedding down for the evening. He still longed for a real bed to sleep in, but that would have to wait until he possessed Shadowbane. Honoria and Gaal also would have preferred staying at an inn but knew the journey would be difficult. Nevertheless, for now they all made the best with what they had, as all three of them laid in the dirt around the campfire.

Unfortunately, their peaceful slumber did not last the night. An unfamiliar noise awakened Megildur. He also had an uneasy feeling just before the noise that they were not alone but he thought that was another dream. The noise occurred again and Megildur knew someone, or something, was in the surrounding area. He reached for his sword but did not make it before someone grabbed him from behind. The assailant lifted him soaring into the night sky, twice the height of a normal man. His feet were dangling and he was unable to speak because the assailant had him by the throat and proceeded in choking the life out of him.

An all too familiar voice whispered, "I told you we would meet again, boy!" Megildur could see a pale white arm materialize below his chin and knew this was the Vampire from Thieves' Den choking him. He could feel her hardened icy hand around his face when she pushed his head back, exposing his neck. She leaned in with her frozen breath blowing on his flesh and pressed her sharp teeth against his neck. All Megildur could do was flail his legs about, but escape was impossible for him.

Gaal shouted, "Release him, you vile succubus!" He threw whatever he could find from the ground, in an attempt to stop the Vampire's attack. However, nothing could penetrate her cold hardened flesh.

The Vampire Assassin hissed, "You incompetent fool! You have no chance against me!"

"But I do!" Another voice emanated from behind the Vampire Assassin. Everyone, including the Assassin, turned to see a winged creature materialize behind the Vampire. The creature's skin had snakelike scales and was bright red, like blood with hair to match. In addition, three horns protruded from its skull. It held a flaming torch and swept the flame near the Vampire's head, causing the Assassin to drop Megildur. The Aelfborn Lord plummeted to the ground, unharmed. Gaal helped him back to his feet. The bloodsucking Assassin turned to face the winged creature, but withdrew from the torch used against her. The Vampire unsheathed a dagger and thrust the weapon at the flying creature. The winged beast dodged the attack and retaliated by cramming the flaming torch down the throat of the Assassin. The Vampire dropped to the ground and let out an awful noise, as best she could with a torch in her mouth. The creature of the night now lay there, lifeless. At that time, Megildur and Gaal realized Honoria was nowhere in sight.

Megildur screamed out, "Honoria, where are you?" Gaal began to scour the area looking for any sign of her.

"I am here, M'Lord," the winged creature spoke. Megildur and Gaal froze and stared at the creature in disbelief, which now was descending from the sky. Megildur suddenly recognized the leather armor the creature was wearing was the same as Honoria's armor, when last he saw her. He looked closely at the creature, but kept his distance. He was still cautious about the creature's claim. The creature began waiving its arms, casting a spell of transformation into the Human form they knew as Honoria. She timidly glanced at both of them.

"H-how...I mean what...um, who are you?" Megildur stumbled to find the right words but the entire occurrence dumbfounded him. He tried to gather his composure until he realized, he was not the only one confused by what just happened. Gaal was still standing there with his mouth wide open in awe. Megildur pushed upward on Gaal's jaw to close his mouth, after he realized how childish they were behaving. "Sorry to react this way, but I have never seen anything like that before," he admitted.

Gaal yelled out, "Neither have I! That was awesome! I loved the way you..." Gaal noticed Megildur was glaring at him to be silent. He wanted to find out with whom they now traveled. Once Gaal restrained his excitement Megildur turned his attention to Honoria, who was now sitting down with the rest of the group in her Human form.

"I am a Nephilim," Honoria stated. "Our race emerged on Aerynth after the murder of your High King Cambruin, during the Age of Strife. Many of us live among humans and other races using a spell, Mundane Eidolon. It transforms our bodies to mimic Human traits, as you can see." She stood up, did a slight twirl, and sat back down across from a bewildered Megildur and Gaal.

"I've heard Nephilims live in Maelstrom and worship Dark Chaos Lords," Megildur commented, trying not to offend Honoria. "Isn't this true?"

"That is true," Honoria responded. Gaal had a shocked and dismayed look on his face. "However, there are many of us who do not follow the Dark Chaos Lords and choose to live among the other races of Aerynth." She looked at the two of them to see if they could accept her or not. "Is this knowledge something you can tolerate or should I depart now?"

Megildur countered, "Please do not leave. Forgive us for our ignorance about your race, but the full lore of the Nephilim race is not common knowledge. I would hate to lose such a strong champion due to our inability to accept an unknown race. Besides, you bested a Vampire who was about to turn me into mutton, thanks." He extended his hand in friendship, hoping Honoria would consent and stay with them.

"Thank you for understanding," Honoria replied, accepting his hand in friendship with a smile. She turned to face Gaal for his decision, acceptance, or refusal.

"Hey, you do not need to look to me for acceptance," Gaal replied. "I am considered an abomination by most races and most people, plus my profession as a Thief, nobody looks kindly upon us." Gaal smirked back at Honoria. "Besides, I thought you were on fire when fighting that Vampire! Or she was on fire! Either way, you were great!"

Megildur jested, "Alright, now that we have decided to keep our newfound friend we all need some sleep. However, it is painfully apparent we need to sleep in shifts so we always have someone on guard. I will take first watch and check the perimeter for any other marauders while you two get some rest. Gaal, I will wake you in a few hours for your shift." Gaal nodded his head in agreement and both of them attempted to get some rest. Megildur patrolled the nearby foliage.

A few sweeps of the surrounding area, Megildur discovered he was too agitated after the assault from the Vampire Assassin. He decided to pace near the campfire and considered their next move, come first light. He was so wide-awake, and Gaal slept deep enough to snore like a hellhound, Megildur decided not to wake him. Nobody in all of Aerynth had seen Shadowbane since Kierhaven vanished from this world. Megildur thought of only one place it might be. The one place the Gods would entrust with the sword was with the Dwarves who helped forge it, deep under Korvambar. It was the Dwarves that Thurin entrusted with Shadowbane before, when Sillestor betrayed the All-Father. It remained with the Dwarves until Beregund crept into the Halls of

Haganduur, the Dwarf armory deep under Korvambar, and brought Shadowbane back into the world.

"You never woke me for my shift," Gaal commented while rubbing his eyes. At that time, Megildur noticed the sun was beginning to peek over the trees. Morning had arrived.

"I was unable to rest, so I figured I would remain on guard and let you sleep," Megildur admitted. "If you get wood for the fire, I will prepare the food for breakfast. We need something to eat before we start for Fort Irsadeng."

"Sounds good," Gaal replied and began his search for wood. "Well, look who decided to wake. Good morning, Honoria." Gaal gave her a quick smirk and departed to find kindling for the fire.

"Good morning, Gaal," Honoria responded. Gaal was nearly to the trees by the time she replied to his greeting. She noticed Megildur was searching his pack for food, but was just able to find dried meats and some beans.

"Good morning, Honoria," Megildur said. "I would offer you some good food, but in our haste to depart Thieves' Den I was unable to restock our supplies." He continued searching through his pack but he found nothing more.

"Will this do?" Honoria asked. She pulled out some fresh meat and bread from her pack. "I was already planning on leaving the safehold before I stumbled upon you two."

"Oh, real food!" Gaal exclaimed upon returning to the campsite. He dropped his firewood and rushed to Honoria.

Megildur scolded Gaal, "Gaal quit ruining our meal!" He snatched the food from Honoria before Gaal drooled on it. "This will be great, thank you."

Megildur grinned at Honoria and turned to Gaal with a frown. "It hasn't been that long since we had real food. Try not to act like a beast for once and get that fire going or you will be eating your meat raw."

Gaal did not seem to mind the idea of raw meat, but he started the fire regardless. Megildur cooked and Honoria split the food among the three travelers. Nobody trusted Gaal to hand out the food evenly in his starved condition. They finished the meal, packed up, and started out for Fort Irsadeng. None of them knew what danger awaited them on the path to the safehold.

CHAPTER 23: Bane Crashing

Megildur found some large trees and Gaal pulled out his water, first drinking some and then dumped a bit of the water over his bare pale scalp. The group traveled all day without rest. Due to severe exhaustion, they decided to sleep for the night and forgo their usual evening meal. With the trio unable to sleep in a few nights, they all felt a bit fatigued. Gaal took first watch.

Megildur opened his eyes; he was not asleep for long. He was unsure if he actually heard something, or if paranoia took over due to what occurred with the Vampire assault earlier. He lay there, mentally arguing with himself. He began to hear crashing sounds in the distance. Megildur sat up, examined the area without rising from his seated position, and noticed a section of sky between the trees, brighter than the rest. He also noticed Gaal was missing from the camp.

"You hear it too," Honoria mentioned. She too arose from her resting position. "I thought I was dreaming the noises."

Megildur whispered, "As did I. Where is Gaal? He's supposed to be watching the camp while we sleep!" From between the two of them, Gaal materialized, causing both of them to fall backwards.

Gaal chuckled, "Whoa, you guys almost scared me. Now if you want to see something scary, follow me."

Megildur whispered, "Alright, but you really need to stop sneaking around invisible like that."

"That is what Thieves do best," Gaal smirked. "Now crawl on the ground to the top of this next ridge and watch the show."

Both Honoria and Megildur did just that and they did indeed find the exhibition before them daunting. Right before Megilder's eyes, a battle erupted. The massive bane stone came down in front of towering city walls and planted itself in the ground. The stone was a large obelisk with circular swirl markings on the surface. Approximately twenty feet tall and five feet in diameter. All their eyes widened in awe as a magical barrier surrounded the stone. It was circular in shape with mystical markings along the outer ring. A war was about to begin, and the three friends had front row seats.

Both sides began placing siege tents, bulwarks, ballistas, and trebuchets. It was a colossal undertaking that shockingly did not take long. Soon both sides were ready for battle. One guild trying to breach the city walls and take down the Tree of Life that sits in the defending city's center. The defending guild must demolish the bane stone planted just outside their city walls. This could prove to be difficult and dangerous for the defending guild because by attacking the bane stone, the defending guild must leave the security of their city walls to assault this giant obelisk. But, if the defending guild destroys the bane stone, everything goes back to how it was before they proclaimed the bane.

Commands flew through the air like weapons. Two guilds of different races attacking each other with all their might and powers they wielded. Aelfborn, Aracoix, Half Giants, Humans, and Shades against Centaurs, Half Giants, and Humans. The factions contained several classes like Assassins, Bards, Priests, Scouts, Thieves, Warlocks, and

Warriors...the other with Bards, Priests, Scouts, Warlocks, Warriors, and Wizards. Aracoix flying and swooping down on their victims, while the Wizards were conjuring spells to take them down. Shrieks pierced the skies above as Half Giants and Centaurs clashed in heavy hand-to-hand combat on the ground. Trebuchets rocketed boulders to their marks crashing into fortified walls, making them explode into dust.

Gaal found it impossible to look away, almost entranced by the whole ordeal. Honoria found herself sickened by all the bloodshed and noise. The three just froze with mouths open for several minutes just watching the onslaught of combat. Not one of them uttered a word. Unsure if they even took a breath if not for their hearts pounding in their chests. Megildur was taking the whole event in as a learning experience and did not want to miss a beat. Even though Megildur did not understand all the validities of a bane, he knew protecting one's Tree of Life was of the upmost importance. If the attacking guild forces its way through the city walls and annihilates the Tree of Life, everything changes. A new Tree of Life spawns. The ownership of the new Tree of Life, and all city assets, transfer to the individual who initiated the bane.

Just as the trio was deep into being spectators at the incredible site, nobody even noticed the Scouts and Assassins who just materialized behind them on the hill. The assailants grabbed all three of the spectators and bound them with rope. The aggressors easily subdued the trio and escorted them to the battle. Megildur could see an enormous man at the front of the group, another Half Giant. They were sometimes in the New Mellissar safehold as well, but everyone avoided them because of their short tempers and incredible strength. At their last encounter with one, in Thieves' Den, Megildur understood why everybody shunned them.

"So what did we capture tonight, boys?" The brute asked the Scouts and Assassins, who detained them before the Half Giant. "A half-breed, an abomination, and a wench! What a pathetic scouting party!"

"We are not…" Gaal interrupted but the brute silenced him by putting his sword to the Shade's throat.

The brute bellowed an insult, "One more word from this pasty abomination and I will gut him like a pig, cook him, and serve him to my men!" His arrogant laughter at the trio was no longer contained. "And what are you looking at, filthy half-breed? If your whore of a mother could have kept her legs closed I would not have to look at you right now!" A Scout shoved Megildur into the large brute, who wrapped his oversized arm around the Aelfborn's head. The stench from his unwashed armpit made Megildur nearly pass out. The Aelfborn knew he did not stand a chance against the brute's sheer size, strength, nor odor so he had one option left, insults.

Megildur taunted, "You know, you really should stop talking. Every time you open your mouth, you prove your lack of intelligence! In fact, you should just end your miserable existence now since you also prove your incompetence with every action you take!"

The brute was so mad, he took his right arm, pulled it back, and swung with all his might at the insolent half-breed's head. Megildur used this opportunity to work his way loose from the brute's grip, and his bindings. He dropped to the ground. He grabbed the brute's own sword and aimed it straight for the Half Giant. Using the brute's weight against him, and to his own advantage, Megildur plunged the sword deep into the Half Giant's chest. The brute looked into Megildur's eyes, the Aelfborn snarled at him. The Half Giant toppled to the ground with his own sword protruding from his chest. Megildur twisted around to face two other Warriors, who drew their swords on him, but they halted upon orders from their leader.

"Wait! Do not kill them yet!" The leader commanded. He walked up behind the Warriors. "So, you bested one of my Captains? No loss there, I never did like his constant use of the term 'half-breed'." Megildur could see that the leader was also an Aelfborn. "Of course, you are not one of mine, so I can't let your actions against one of my men go unpunished." Another Aelfborn ran up to the leader and whispered in his ear, pointing at Megildur. The Aelfborn Lord now wondered how much worse this night could get. "Are you sure?" The leader looked in shock at the other Aelfborn and turned his attention to Megildur, as if to examine him from afar. "Lower your weapons and kindly escort our guests to my siege tent," the leader commanded. He turned around and walked to a large red tent off to the side of the battlegrounds.

"Megildur, what is going on?" Gaal asked.

Megildur whispered to Gaal, "I am unsure, but stay alert. We may need to escape, fast." Megildur was a bit uneasy about this Aelfborn leader, but he figured he could have killed him by now if he pleased. Only time would tell if he was a trusted ally.

CHAPTER 24: Friend or Foe

They escorted the three of them to a large tent, filled lavishly with furniture and servants to attend to the leader's needs.

"Release them and remove their bindings," the leader commanded his men. "You're dismissed," he told the Scouts and Assassins after they cut the rope from Gaal and Honoria. "Forgive me Lord Megildur, I did not recognize you. I am afraid your deeds travel faster among Bards than your description," he smiled at Megildur. He handed him a goblet his servant just filled with a drink, possibly wine. Megildur looked into the drink in disbelief, wondering if the leader poisoned his beverage. "Oh I assure you, we would not poison your drink. If I wanted you dead I would have let my men gut you outside." The leader grinned at Megildur while the servants tended to the needs of Gaal and Honoria. "I am Commander Nostarion, ruler of Mercenary Company from Fort Leontar, just north of here. You arrived just as we were in the midst of a bane against a nearby safehold, Erkesh Point."

"What is the quarrel between your two factions?" Megildur inquired as he took a drink and set the goblet down.

Nostarion laughed, "Just the same as everyone in Aerynth. We struggle for land and power." He motioned for more refreshments for his new guests. "I must admit, your assault on Aelarnost was most impressive. It takes a lot to confront and defeat the Dar Khelegur."

"Thank you. Apparently it takes two factions to defeat them," Megildur admitted. "I am still amazed they followed me on such a risky endeavor."

"I would not be too surprised," Nostarion replied. "Many of us are still loyal to the All-Father and would follow his champion into battle without question." He raised his eyebrow at Megildur and the Aelfborn Lord knew his past was now common knowledge to the commander.

"I see the Bards have allowed all of my past to become common knowledge across Aerynth," Megildur said, scowling at Honoria.

"Do not look down upon the Bards," Nostarion replied. "It's their role in life to record the tales of everything in our world. Without them we would have no knowledge of our past, or our present." He placed a gentle hand on Honoria's shoulder, to reassure her of a Bard's responsibilities. "Now, Lord Megildur, I know your journey is long and strenuous. How may I ease your burdens?"

"We could use more provisions, ours have run a bit short as of late," Megildur requested.

"Done, I shall have my Steward attend to that need," Nostarion motioned to one of his men to assist Gaal in that task. Gaal and the Steward left for food and supplies. "Now, I will send for your belongings from your campsite." Nostarion motioned for another servant to handle the task. "Please enjoy yourselves here. My people will tend to your needs. I must excuse myself to check on the progress of my bane." Nostarion nodded his head and left.

Honoria squealed, "I am going to talk with their Bards!" She scurried away. "I have so much to tell them." Megildur stood there rolling his eyes. He still considered the Bards to be no more than storytellers for children. Although, Honoria vanquishing Vampires is an advantage.

After Megildur relaxed for several hours, as best he could with the sounds of trebuchets off in the distance, he decided to go find Gaal and Honoria. He stepped outside to find the Aelfborn who informed Nostarion of Megildur's royal identity. This Aelfborn was shirtless and proudly displaying his mystical tattoos, which all Aelfborn must have. He was watching the battle continue.

"Mesmerizing, isn't it?" The Aelfborn asked when Megildur walked up beside him.

"Yes," Megildur replied. "I have never seen a battle like it. How did this happen?"

"Banes like this are quite common in Aerynth," the Aelfborn responded. "Nostarion wanted this territory so he unfurled a bane scroll outside Erkesh Point. While waiting for the opposing city's response, we place our siege equipment."

"Bane scroll?" Megildur inquired. "What exactly is a bane scroll?"

"It is a declaration of war," the Aelfborn replied. "The leader of a guild, or one of their Inner Council, will purchase the enchanted parchment from a magic sage. Once the leader, or Council member, activates the scroll, they will pin it to the front gates of the city they are declaring the bane against. This is how we wage war in Aerynth. The defending city can then decide if they wish to surrender, or fight."

"Do you really have to wait for an official time to fight?" Megildur inquired.

The Aelfborn chuckled. "People in Aerynth are always fighting, but without an official bane the Tree of Life and all city assets are protected from damage. Sometimes guilds will sneak inside another guild's city and campout within the city walls, just to wreak havoc. You know, kind of like what you did in Aelarnost." The Aelfborn smiled at Megildur.

"Do guilds ever surrender without a fight?" Megildur asked.

"It is rare, but some have," the Aelfborn replied. "Most prefer to fight and some smaller guilds will join a larger nation if they are outnumbered by the attacking guild."

Megildur was so fascinated with the art of war in Aerynth, that he did not notice the two servants tasked with collecting their belongings were walking in his direction.

"M'Lord, here are your possessions. Where would you like us to place them?" The larger servant asked.

"You may leave them right here. Thank you," Megildur replied. The servants placed the items near his feet, bowed, and left. Just after, Megildur observed Gaal walking back with a cart in tow full of food, water, and blankets. "What did you do, empty their stores?"

Gaal exclaimed, salivating over the thought of eating all of this food. "Nostarion said we could have anything we wanted!"

"True, but we need to be able to carry the provisions," Megildur replied. "Are you going to be our beast of burden?" Megildur glared at Gaal. The Shade realized they would not be able to carry it all, but his desire for food conquered him. "Alright, pack what you can into our bags and we will leave soon. I need to find Honoria." Gaal sneered back at Megildur and began feverishly packing their bags.

Megildur began his search for their companion but was unable to track her down. Eventually, one servant was able to point him in the right direction. Near the outskirts of the fighting, he found several

Bards huddled around, eagerly listening to Honoria. As he approached, he could hear her tale.

"As the fiendish bloodsucker began to drink the Aelfborn Lord's essence, he worked his way loose of her grip, grabbed the flaming torch, and rammed it down her gullet, vanquishing the foe!" Honoria detailed the escapades of Megildur to the wide-eyed Bards. She noticed Megildur standing near the group listening. "Speaking of our hero, here he is." She pointed out Megildur to the group. They all cheered at the sight of the honored hero.

Megildur responded, "Thank you all. Honoria, we must leave now." He gave a slight wave to the group and turned to depart, before his embarrassment vanquished him. The two of them walked away and Megildur whispered to her, "Why did you tell them I killed the vampire? Remember, you were the one who saved us all."

"M'Lord, I am a Bard. I am no hero, nor do I want to be," Honoria replied. She stopped to address Megildur face to face. "Aerynth needs a savior, now more than ever during these dark days. The All-Father chose you, and you alone, to be the savior and champion of Aerynth. It is my role in life to record and distribute your heroic tale of how you defeat foes and recover Shadowbane. Nobody wants to hear the tale of a Bard who slayed a vampire. They want to hear how the future High King saved the world." She smiled at Megildur, who after listening to all the praise from Honoria was a bit red faced.

"Thank you for your praise," Megildur replied. He placed his hand on her shoulder. "However you are wrong about one thing, you are a hero. More than you will ever admit to, but still a hero." He grinned back at her. "Of course, let's keep stretching the truth to a minimum." They continued to meet Gaal, who by now finished packing.

"Alright, I am ready," Gaal announced. He slung his overstuffed pack onto his back, nearly toppling over.

"How did you fit all of those provisions into the packs?" Megildur asked, noticing the cart was empty. He looked down and found his answer. The other two packs are also bulging beyond capacity and the seams looked like they wound rip at any moment. "How do you expect us to carry those packs? That will break Honoria's back!" She looked at Megildur, turned to the packs, slung hers onto her back with ease and reached back down to grab Megildur's pack.

"You 'boys' ready?" Honoria boasted. Megildur and Gaal stood there in amazement. She could see they were in shock and wondered how she was able to not only lift her own hefty pack but also carry Megildur's pack. "Remember, I am a Nephilim. We are naturally stronger than other races." She beamed at both of them and turned to depart the bane. "Don't let the curves fool you," Honoria said with a sultry voice, walking away.

"Indeed she is strong!" Gaal replied with an enormous grin on his face as he eagerly followed Honoria. Gaal and Honoria passed Commander Nostarion. He was coming back from checking on the status of his bane.

"I see you are ready to depart, Lord Megildur," Nostarion commented while Megildur grabbed the last of his gear. "It's a shame we were not able to fight side by side in battle, M'Lord. It would've been glorious."

"Perhaps we will someday, Commander. Aerynth is not at peace yet," Megildur replied with a grin at his fellow Aelfborn. "I do have one last request of you.

Can you get word to my family that I am well and on my way to Fort Irsadeng? My mother is Vanya and my father is Aedan; you can find them at Fort Viatrus."

Nostarion warned, "Fort Irsadeng, Lord Megildur? That is the Amazon safehold. They do not allow male travelers."

"Our Bard has a friend there who can help us cross the sea to Stormvald," Megildur reassured the concerned Nostarion.

"I will dispatch my fastest Scout to deliver the message, M'Lord," Nostarion responded, extending his hand to Megildur. "May your journey be swift and your conquests grand, Lord Megildur."

"Farewell Commander Nostarion," Megildur replied. He shook Nostarion's hand. "Thank you once again for your gracious hospitality, and I wish you success on your bane."

Megildur turned to follow his companions. He quickly caught up with both of them. "Thank you, but I can carry my own bag," Megildur commented, taking the pack from Honoria. He stumbled a bit when swinging it onto his back and trying to manage the weight. He glared at Gaal once he realized just how heavy his pack was. That would be the last time he trusted that Thief to pack for him. They were once again on their way and hopefully without any more distractions...except for heavy packs.

Trudging through the lush meadows and ample forests on their way to Fort Irsadeng, Megildur reminisced of his own homestead in Fort Viatrus. This region was vastly superior to the scorching wastelands of the desert to the south or bitter cold of the frozen mountains to the north. Megildur definitely preferred green grass and blossoming flowers. Gaal on the other hand seemed to enjoy anything but the flourishing fauna, made apparent by the vicious sneezing attack produced by the pale Thief.

"Blessings of the All-Father upon you," Megildur wished upon his companion.

"He can bless me by placing me in a dank dingy tavern, with a tall pint of ale and a voluptuous Irekei maiden," Gaal countered with a smile across his pollen-infested facade.

"Must you be so crude?" Honoria snapped. The Bard halted, causing the others to pause as well.

"Hey, you don't know what it was like growing up as the 'abomination' with my human parents!" Gaal rebuked. "The villagers abused me verbally and physically...when they were not busy plotting my demise. Even my own mother and father were involved in a ruse to sacrifice me to whatever god those zealots worshipped!"

"You think my family was any better?" Honoria retorted. "All they cared about was worshipping the Dark Lords of Chaos. They conspired to rekindle the War of the Scourge and 'cleanse' Aerynth. They cared about nothing else, even when the Temple of the Cleansing Flame cultists attacked our settlement...they left me to fend for myself!" Tears began to well up inside her eyes. "I can still hear the screams from the younglings when I close my eyes. The smell..." Honoria plunged her face into her hands and burst out crying, the resilient Nephilim could contain her composure no more.

Megildur placed a hand upon Honoria's shoulder. "I'm sorry for your pain. I have only experienced a brief encounter with the Temple of the Cleansing Flame and that still haunts me." He reached for Gaal, only for the Shade to pull away before Megildur could console him.

"I'm fine!" Gaal grunted as he continued toward Fort Irsadeng. "Let's just find this friend of yours and get on our way." Megildur and Honoria glanced at one another before following their pale friend.

The Aelfborn hoped tonight would actually be a time to get some sleep. No banes, no killing, and no surprises. He pondered if they would ever retrieve Shadowbane. Megildur's thoughts wondered back to Nostarion's unsettling reaction when he told him where they were going. He prayed Honoria was right about her friend, because they do not stand a chance against an entire guild of women who hate men.

CHAPTER 25: Reunion in Mellissar

Day after day, night after night, Zeristan, Aedan, Vanya, and Aranel desperately awaited news from Sir Adelard's messenger, the giant wolf. The boredom was so intense, they decided to help with cleaning up the ancient castle. All but the elderly Steward abandoned the capital over a century ago and apparently, cleanliness was not his forte. The four of them started with the exterior walls and the dilapidated gate. Vanya showed her skill with a blade by chopping down the unsightly vegetation. Each lash of her weapon more precise than the last. Aedan repaired the entrance, displaying his strength by raising the massive stones from the ground and placing them back into the barrier. Even little Aranel proved her worth by vigorously sweeping and cleaning wherever she could find a mess, which was currently everywhere. The Wizard proved he could not only battle foes with his magic, but could also repair stone. He used spells to heal the structures and strengthen the stone where it was weak, or broken. Blocks floated in the air with each graceful swipe of his boney hand. Aranel was in awe of the power and beauty behind each stroke of Zeristan's fingers. The colorful lightshow emanating from his fingertips dazzled her, until she could stand no more and she perched herself against a fallen boulder.

Aedan watched his daughter's fascination as he continued to work on the front gate. The burly man was so entranced himself that he did not notice the next block to lift was furrier than the last. He looked down, after sensing the change in texture. He just seized ahold of a rather large furry paw. Aedan stumbled back and tripped over one of the fallen stones. Gazing up, he discovered Sir Adelard's messenger...the giant wolf. The giant wolf lowered his head and licked Aedan.

"Oh, Orc crap! I feel like a worg's plaything!" Aedan bellowed. Vanya laughed at her husband's demise. He flicked some slobber in her general direction.

Sir Adelard, who rushed over to investigate the commotion, greeted his friend and walked him back to the stable. Sir Adelard returned after a bit to Zeristan and the others, who were still working. All turned to address the troubled Steward.

"I assume my wolf made it through all ten kingdoms. However, this parchment only has a handful of signatures." The Steward of Mellissar fretted, holding up the scroll he sent out with his wolf. "I am not sure why?"

A voice quavered from behind Sir Adelard, near the gates, "You might have a better understanding why if you ever left Mellissar to see what Aerynth has become since the Turning."

Sir Adelard turned to see an elderly man standing in armor just inside the gates. His armor distressed and tattered, much like the man who donned it. Around his neck, the aging man wore a ring of drake's teeth, most likely gathered from successful kills.

Rejoiced to see the man, Sir Adelard exclaimed, "Sir Mardiock Wyrmslayer, you old drake slayer! How are you doing? Where have you been hiding? Come with me, I have a lot to tell you and we must prepare." The two elderly knights walked off together to discuss the arrival of the new High King and to reminisce about the old days.

Aranel approached her mother and father with a confused look on her face. "Mother, what was the Turning the old man spoke of?"

"Well little one," Vanya replied, sitting down on a bench with her daughter. "On the day when the High King Cambruin died, the Turning began. One of Cambruin's own knights betrayed his High King and pinned him to the first Tree of Life. This betrayal angered the All-Father so much that He made the sky darken and Aerynth shook so hard it fragmented the world. At that time, the All-Father also closed the doors to Heaven and Hell. Nobody has heard from the All-Father since that day."

"You mean until Megildur?" Aranel questioned her mother's statement.

"That is correct," Vanya replied.

"Megildur said before he left something about being 'the hair to High King Cambruin'?" Aranel inquired. "What did he mean?"

Aedan chuckled at his daughter's mistaken understanding of royalty and explained, "He said that he is the 'heir' to High King Cambruin. That means Megildur is a blood relative of Cambruin and is the rightful successor to the High Throne over the Kingdoms of Men."

Aranel squeaked, "So if he is a King, does that make me a Princess?"

Vanya laughed with a smile at her eager daughter, "Once he receives the crown, yes it does."

Aranel darted off, yelling back toward her mother, "Then I am off to make myself a crown!" The young Aelfborn Princess bound off to look for supplies to fashion her crown.

Over the next several days, other knights would arrive, along with their entourage. With each arrival, Sir Mardiock Wyrmslayer would educate his old friend, Sir Adelard. Since he was the Steward of the High Throne, Sir Adelard needed to know each of the new arrivals. Of course, Aedan and Vanya used this opportunity to their advantage by listening in as Sir Mardiock Wyrmslayer mentioned the name and history behind each person. Sir Mardiock elaborated on the description since he knew the others were also listening.

"Now that is Sir Malorn. He goes by the title of Saint since the Temple of the Cleansing Flame canonized him nearly fifty years ago. Rumor has it, he still holds onto Cambruin's crown. Although I doubt he, or his cult, would release it to an Aelfborn. They still blame Sir Sesherin, all other Aelfborn, and Shades for the demise of Cambruin."

"The unscrupulous character entering now is Sir Eric Essengal. They call him Eric the Drake, most likely due to his hotheaded nature. He never liked Queen Bronwyn since she seduced Cambruin into marrying her. This action broke the engagement between Cambruin and Sir Eric's sister, Lady Essenmay. After the Queen attempted to have herself crowned High Queen over Mellissar, Sir Eric made an unsuccessful attempt to take over the capital. Subsequently, Sir Eric went back to some of the fragmented kingdoms and made himself warlord over the lands. He turned his back on the knight's code and became a Dark Knight on that day."

"Ah. Here comes Sir Sesherin. He is the Aelfborn that Malorn accused of being the Traitor to Cambruin." The Aelfborn knight proudly walked in displaying the signature body tattoos that all Aelfborn wear, although only his face markings were visible now. "Malorn and his followers captured Sir Sesherin, and then they proceeded with torturing him. They tried for years to get him to admit to the crime, but the brave knight refused. Never did find out how he escaped the Temple of the Cleansing Flame."

"Finally, we have Sir Hurrigan the Huntsman. He renounced his calling as a Ranger to ride under the High King's banner. Many thought Sir Hurrigan might be the Traitor since this knight feared Cambruin would turn on the Rangers. You see, many Elves outside the Dar Khelegur were Rangers and Sir Hurrigan called them brothers, even though he was helping Cambruin destroy the Deathless Empire."

Sir Mardiock's lessons on the knights helped Aedan and Vanya know what challenges their son would face upon his arrival. Now if only they could get them all to agree to Megildur being the next High King.

Vanya peered down to Aranel and noticed she was examining her arms and face. Inquisitively Vanya asked her daughter, "What are you looking for?"

"That one knight had markings on his face, just like Megildur and I do," Aranel replied. "I thought we were the only ones with them?"

Vanya confessed, "All Aelfborn have them, my sweet one. They are mystical markings I put on both of you to help calm those wild feelings."

The next morning, the meeting commenced. Everyone within Mellissar gathered below the steps of the castle to hear the speech. Sir Adelard pronounced, "Brave Knights. Since the tragic day of our High King's betrayal, Aerynth has been in turmoil. We have seen brutal attacks against our neighbors and devastation at every turn. Even the All-Father turned his back on this world because of our actions." The crowd's agitation level seemed to elevate at the Steward's remarks. "However, the day has finally arrived when the All-Father has chosen a champion to bring peace and unity back to Aerynth!"

Sir Eric bellowed, "There is no peace you fool! Cambruin is dead and his descendants are worthless! Only power decides who should rule, the power to crush the lower beings into submission! We do not need Cambruin's heir, and we have prospered just fine without the All-Father as well."

Sir Malorn scolded, "You blasphemous fool! You dare spite the All-Father? You abandoned the knight's code in favor of being a Dark Knight and rule your lands as a warlord!"

Sir Eric countered, "At least I have not proclaimed myself a Saint and pretended to be a God by cleansing the unworthy!"

This accusation angered Sir Malorn, who drew his flaming sword and advanced toward Sir Eric. However, a bolt of energy in between the two enemies halted his attack. The energy bolt once again came from Zeristan, who was not going to let them scuffle. His power forced both of the knights to the ground in opposite directions, along with portions of the ground into the air. When the dust settled, the crowd witnessed another visitor had arrived in Mellissar, Queen Bronwyn. Cambruin's widow strode past the two knights, as they picked themselves up off the ground. She walked up the stairs to confront Sir Adelard directly.

Queen Bronwyn demanded, "Why have you called the remaining Kingdoms of Men and why was I alone not notified, personally? They do not deserve to be here! I am the rightful heir to the High Throne!"

The crowd grew more and more agitated with every bit of malice spewed from Queen Bronwyn. More importantly, the sky began to darken, even though it was midday.

Sir Adelard affirmed, "Your Majesty, I did send out a messenger. I don't understand why my wolf did not find you."

Queen Bronwyn bellowed, "You do not send a filthy beast to notify royalty! I demand notification from the Steward of the High Throne directly! My guards dismissed your mongrel!" The ground started to rumble by now and the entire sky was now black as night. "Why have you summoned these people to the capital?"

"The All-Father chose a new champion and successor to the High Throne, your Majesty," Sir Adelard replied.

Queen Bronwyn snapped, "Do not spout off about that false God! Where was the All-Father when they betrayed my husband?" Thunder emanated throughout all of Aerynth by that time. "Damn that old fool, I am the rightful ruler of Aerynth!"

Silence fell upon all of Mellissar when a single bolt of lightning charged from the Heavens and struck Queen Bronwyn. The force not only shook the ground, but also knocked all of the inhabitants of the capital back several yards. When the crowd rose to their feet, they discovered that nothing remained of Queen Bronwyn except a pile of ash and her crown. Even when someone died, since the Turning, a body normally remained for some time after death, but not in this case.

Sir Adelard exclaimed, "By the All-Father! What happened?" He stood over the remains of the now-deceased Queen.

"I believe you just said what happened to her," Zeristan replied with a smirk. "It's not wise to spat blasphemous remarks upon the All-Father."

Sir Adelard gasped, "Agreed!"

The other knights formed around Sir Adelard, Zeristan, and the newly formed pile of ashes...along with a new hole in the steps. The once smug knights appeared more humble in the presence of the All-Father's wrath. Sir Malorn approached Sir Adelard and withdrew an object from a satchel. It was Cambruin's crown. Now that the clouds had dissipated, the gold shown bright and the marks of the All-Father were visible on the front.

"In light of current events it seems wise to support the claim of this new champion," Sir Malorn stated, handing the crown to Sir Adelard. "Who may I ask is the heir?"

Aedan boasted, stepping up alongside Zeristan with Vanya behind him, "Our son, Megildur." Malorn looked at Aedan with suspicion, then with despise at Vanya and little Aranel, who of course displayed the mystical tattoos revealing her race.

Sir Malorn chided, "An Aelfborn is the new High King?" He looked up into the sky and mumbled under his breath, "Why, All-Father, why?" Looking back down with contempt at Aedan, Vanya, and Aranel the would-be Saint grumbled, "We will see!" He turned toward the gates and departed shouting, "Send word when you set the time for the coronation of the new High King! This one I have to see!"

Many of the other guests chatted with the High Steward Adelard and hastily left Mellissar. The capital cleared out. A single young Elf made his way through the departing crowds to find Vanya. The young Elf had a slight green complexion, meaning he was from Vanya's tribe, the Gwaridorn Elves.

The young Elf gasped, since he was out of breath from running. "M'Lady, word has spread throughout the Bard network. We received a report that your son, Megildur, is heading toward the Amazon guild."

Vanya and Aedan stared at each other in horror. "We have assembled several groups aboard ships to assist. They await your arrival. They are at the nearest port to the east."

Vanya tugged Aedan aside, "I have to help him. I know the Amazon guild and they will not take kindly to Megildur, or his Shade companion."

"You go. I will stay with Aranel and Zeristan," Aedan replied. "We will prepare for Megildur and the coronation." Aedan hugged Vanya and whispered, "Get our son out of there and back on his way."

Vanya whispered back, "I will." She turned to face the Elven messenger and commanded, "Lead the way to the ship!" The two Elves departed for the ships, Aedan held his daughter close.

"Father, are Mother and Megildur going to be alright?" Aranel asked.

In a comforting voice Aedan replied, rubbing Aranel's back. "They will be fine. They will be fine." He picked up his daughter and hugged her, but Zeristan could tell Aedan was worried about his wife and son, and rightfully so.

CHAPTER 26: The Amazon Encounter

By now, the sun had set and the companions walked in total darkness. They were pressing on, ever so vigilant. Even the moon was not visible tonight, making travel much more difficult. The air was getting cold and damp as they neared another river but they continued traveling east nonetheless. The three knew they were getting close by the sounds of the rushing water.

"Honoria, how much further to the Amazon boundary?" Megildur asked. "I am surprised we made it this far without..." Megildur froze. He had an uneasy feeling they were not alone. The deafening cricket sound fell silent. Megildur slowly reached for his weapon. Neither Gaal nor Honoria had time to react, but it was too late anyway.

A voice commanded, "Move and we will kill you!" Several assailants emerged from the surrounding forest, perfectly camouflaged within the terrain. Megildur panned the area to observe numerous women now visible, and heavily armed. Many of the female Warriors wielding bows only possessed one breast. Megildur heard stories of how Amazon women would remove one to improve their skills with a bow. Standing before him was a female Half Giant pointing a spear at him, and she did not look pleased to see him.

"Scyleia, where are you?" Honoria shouted. Hoping her friend was amongst the Warriors.

A voice resounded, "Honoria, what are you doing with these men?" Scyleia emerged from the Warrior clan. She approached, with her weapon still in hand. At the last second, Scyleia sheathed her weapon and embraced her friend Honoria. Scyleia appeared small in stature, but Human female Bards did not require formidable size or strength. Her protection spells were enough to deem her a valuable asset to the Amazon guild.

"Allow me to introduce my friends. This is Gaal," Honoria said, introducing her traveling companions. "And this is Lord Megildur."

Scyleia whispered, "This is him?" Honoria nodded. Scyleia turned to Megildur, "M'Lord, I have heard a great deal about you across the Bard's network."

"Apparently everyone in Aerynth is aware of my doings lately," Megildur responded. He greeted Scyleia. "We were hoping…"

The large Half Giant commanded, "Silence peasant!" She thrust her spear near Megildur's throat. "We will take you before Queen Andromache! She will decide your fate!"

With that last command, the rest of the Amazon Warriors corralled the three travelers and forced them toward the river. Gaal noticed several women carried chains with someone, or something, restrained on the end of their leashes. Upon further inspection, he deduced they were men…or what remained of them. The males wore metal collars around their necks and crawled on all fours, like beasts. They did not wear any clothes and were filthy. On one of the Warriors, Gaal spied an unusual piece of jewelry around her neck. It was a leathery sack containing two round objects within. He looked back down at the male on the chain and realized where the unusual jewelry came from; they were the male's testicles.

"Keep moving or I will add yours to my collection!" The Amazon Warrior shoved the Shade forward, who now looked more green than pale.

Megildur noticed a footbridge used for crossing the waterway. It swayed side to side as the long line of Warriors navigated the narrow walkway. Crossing the footbridge, Megildur surveyed his surroundings and realized the Amazons were on an island or peninsula. The Warriors must have chosen the location for its strategic vantage point. They had to cross another bridge before they could see the light from Fort Irsadeng, the Amazon safehold.

The gates loomed over the menacing fortress. Immense timbers fortified the walls and the bones of their enemies decorated the barriers. The guards pushed Honoria, Megildur, and Gaal into a building that contained small animal-like cages. The smell was enough to make even Gaal's stomach upheave. They were prisoners for sure.

Megildur commanded, "I demand to see your leader!" His guard shoved him into the metal cage like an animal. "I am..."

The Half Giant bellowed, "You are a worthless man who will get to see the Queen when she is ready, not when you demand naive!" The guards slammed the door shut and once again, the three of them were hostages of another barbaric faction. A guild who hated men, that news did not sit well with Megildur or Gaal. The Half Giant oppressor, and the rest of her group, exited the building leaving Scyleia inside and two guards just outside the building entrance.

"Scyleia, what is going on and why have your people enslaved us here?" Honoria pleaded with her friend. "I thought we were friends?"

Scyleia whispered, "We are friends, Honoria," She did not want the others to hear her compassion.

"But my people don't take well to outsiders, especially males." She glanced at Megildur and Gaal, who obviously took offense by the comment. "Why did you bring men here? Now the Queen is going to consider you a traitor to our gender and condemn you as well. She will enslave you all. You will spend the rest of your lives being tortured and existing only as their shackled beasts! They will certainly castrate the males and for you who brought them here...I shudder to think of the consequences."

Honoria grumbled, "Some friend!" She said this loud enough for Scyleia to hear. This caused Scyleia to pause when she reached the door. Turning her head, she looked remorseful, closing the door behind her.

The Half Giant Warrior grunted. "Your compassion for the prisoners is pointless." She approached Scyleia as she left the barracks. "The Queen will decree their fate, as she rightfully should."

"She happens to be my friend!" Scyleia countered the brute's heartless comment. She wanted to cry for her friend but knew an emotional outburst in the Amazon guild would be a sign of weakness. Weakness around these Warriors would lead to her demise. Instead, she turned her sadness to anger with the last statement from the callous brute. This had little effect on the Half Giant, who scowled at Scyleia and walked away.

Preservation took over. Running to the barracks, Scyleia grabbed a travel pack, a bow, and went to an opening on the far side of the safehold. Finding a collection of loose boards, Scyleia managed to push them aside, just far enough to escape. The singular hope now for Megildur, Gaal, and Honoria was for Scyleia to use the Bard network to get help. She wasted no time.

Stranded in the Amazon prison, the three companions looked for a way out. Even Honoria's Nephilim strength was no match for the cage bars, forged from truesteel. It was the toughest metal in all of Aerynth, next to obsidian of course. Regardless, Honoria kept pounding away at the cell trying to escape until exhaustion subdued her and she had to rest.

Honoria gasped, "This is all my fault, I walked us right into a trap." She sat down to gather more breath. "I thought Scyleia was my friend."

"I am just as much to blame," Megildur admitted, causing Honoria and Gaal to both stare at him with confused expressions on their faces. "I ignored the warning from Commander Nostarion about the Amazon guild. I passed it off as paranoia from one guild about another, when I should've weighed it heavily." Megildur turned to Honoria. "We will share this burden together and whatever may come." Honoria took little comfort in Megildur's words, as for Gaal, he took no comfort at all. He still worried for his genitals.

All three worked throughout the night, mulling over escape plans. They looked for weaknesses in their enslavement bindings. None of which worked. Honoria even attempted magic spells on the cages, but this proved futile. Gaal could only fade in and out, which was a useless skill for the situation. Megildur wished Zeristan was with them, he would know a way out...or create his own. He knew wishing would get him nowhere. Night turned to morning faster than they had anticipated. Megildur knew this meant trouble for all three of them.

The Half Giant bellowed, "On your feet pigs!" She rattled the cage door. One of the guards opened the cage with a key. Megildur and his exhausted companions wearily stood to face what came next. The guard motioned for the prisoners to hurry out of the cage, past the Half Giant.

Gaal blurted out, "What, you are not going to even feed us before the execution?" A backhanded motion from the brute followed his outburst, hitting Gaal in the side of the head. Gaal stumbled but managed to stay on his feet, leaving Megildur to believe this was not the Thieves' first backhand from an insult.

"Move outside!" The brute commanded, forcing all three of them through the barracks door. Once outside, the guards took them down a path to an arena full of Amazon women. The atmosphere filled with disdain toward the captives. This was evident by the numerous vulgar comments and items thrown upon them. Once they reached the center of the arena, they saw a woman sitting on a throne. She appeared Human with long black hair, but larger than most. She stood nearly the height of a Half Giant and almost as muscular. The skimpily covered Warrior donned jewels of high rank. The woman only wielded a jewel encrusted gold spear and her people heavily guarded her. Not that she needed to be. They assumed this was the Amazonian Queen.

The Queen demanded an answer from the captives, "Who dares trespass into Amazon territory?" She stood from her throne and pointed at Honoria. "You, female, I should disembowel you for bringing this vile refuse into my kingdom, but I demand to hear what pathetic excuse you have. Speak now!"

"I speak for us," Megildur interjected. "I am..." One of her guards struck him, knocking the Aelfborn to the ground. Megildur gasped for air.

The queen lashed back at Megildur, "Hold your tongue buffoon, or next time you speak I will remove your insolent tongue! I am Queen Andromache, ruler of the Amazon nation, and you will not speak unless I command you to!"

Honoria interjected, "Your Majesty, I am Honoria. I am a Bard accompanying Lord Megildur on his quest given to him by the All-Father. My other companion is Gaal, and we meant no harm. We were just seeking passage to Stormvald."

Queen Andromache taunted, "So you are the mighty Lord Megildur my Bards spoke of?" She descended from her throne to confront Megildur, who was now on his knees before the Queen, subdued by the guards. "I heard of an Aelfborn 'boy' who toppled the Dar Khelegur, with the help of other guilds of course. I also heard of your pointless quest from a fallen God to recover a mythical sword that does not exist." She scoffed at Megildur. "Your pathetic All-Father has no power here, peasant! We worship the true Goddess, Vashteera, the Dark Prowler and Mother of Cats."

Megildur jeered, "If you feel we are worthless travelers on a pointless quest, then why not just release us and send us on our way?" The Queen glared at him, reached down, and lifted him by the throat.

Queen Andromache growled, "I warned you if you spoke again without my command it would be your last time! Cut out his insolent tongue!" The Amazon Warrior restraining Megildur pulled out her dagger and held it to his face. The Queen pulled open his shirt, exposing his chest. "I always hated these filthy Aelfborn tattoos." Queen Andromache proceeded in using her spear to slice into Megildur's flesh, just deep enough to sever the mystical designs and inflict extreme pain upon the Aelfborn Lord. Megildur cringed and writhed due to the intense pain, but that only increased the Warrior's grip. What passed as moments to the world, seemed like hours to Megildur. The Amazonian leader lowered her spear and nodded to one of her immense guards.

The Half Giant brute now stood before him and forced his mouth open, to gain access to the Aelfborn Lord's tongue. Megildur struggled by thrashing his head side to side but the brute overpowered him and pulled his tongue past his teeth. Honoria and Gaal were helpless to stop the persecution, since they too were hostages of the Amazon guards. The second guard holding Megildur from behind moved her blade into position to sever his tongue, but dropped the dagger. Next, the guard herself dropped to the ground alongside her weapon. The Half Giant Warrior released Megildur's tongue, with a shocked look on her face. Megildur was now free. The brute did not stare at the Aelfborn but just past him. Megildur turned to see a female Elf standing atop one of the buildings, holding a bow, but he could not determine whom she was. He looked down at the guard that was restraining him to realize she had an arrow in her back, from the Elf archer perched on the roof. He looked past the building to see an army of Elves charging toward him. Their skin was pale green. They were from the Gwaridorn tribe.

The Elf with the bow yelled, "Megildur, run!" He did not know how she knew his name, but he knew another chance to escape would not come again.

Megildur grabbed the dagger off the ground and turned to face the Half Giant, only to find she had already departed to confront the Elven army. He held the dagger to the guard holding Gaal and she released him at once. He was going to repeat the same action with the guard holding Honoria, but she already worked her way loose of her restraints and subdued her captor. With all three of them now freed, they ran toward the Elven invaders. Megildur assumed that if the Gwaridorn Elves helped him escape then he could trust them, for now.

The Elven archer yelled out again, "Megildur, over here!" Megildur could see her over by a newly formed opening in the perimeter fence. It looked like the Elven army made a considerable hole in the safehold to get their forces inside. Megildur followed the Elven archer through the opening just to get a surprising embrace on the other side. Megildur pulled back to identify who his liberator was.

Megildur exclaimed, "Mother, is that you?" He was in shock at the sight of his mother as an Elven Scout. His mother led a humble home life, not the life of a deadly archer. His mother was not wearing her usual attire but instead wore dusky leather armor with a dark violet hue about it. At some points, when she moved, it almost helped her vanish into her surroundings.

"Hurry, this way! We must get to the ships! The Gwaridorn will distract the Amazons!" Vanya commanded, trying to move Megildur and his companions along. "I shall explain everything once we are aboard." They all agreed, since they did not feel welcomed at Fort Irsadeng.

The four of them vacated the area; the green-skinned Elven army continued their assault upon the Amazon safehold. By taking the Amazon guild by surprise, the Gwaridorn Elves gained the upper hand. Megildur could hear clashing metal and screams of battle as they ran for the coast. However, he needed to escape and discover how his mother knew of his demise, and how she convinced her kin to go to war against the Amazon guild.

CHAPTER 27: Voyage

They reached the coast and encountered several ships moored along the shore. They were magnificent vessels with massive sails and a hull large enough to carry several armies. Vanya guided them to the grandest of them all. The three boarded and they discovered Honoria's supposed friend, Scyleia was aboard.

Honoria screamed, reaching for Scyleia's throat. "Traitor!" Honoria almost managed to reach Scyleia before Vanya stopped her.

Vanya yelled out, "Restrain your anger! Scyleia is the reason we are here to help you!" She forced Honoria into one of the ship's seats, without the help of Megildur and Gaal. "My people notified me of your journey to the Amazon guild. Scyleia used the Bard network while we were sailing and we picked her up along the way. She told me how she was unable to help you on her own. Scyleia is trying to make amends for her actions, so please try not to judge her too harshly." Vanya motioned to a deckhand, who turned to the rest of the crew and began to set sail for the open sea.

Scyleia conceded, "Thank you Vanya, but Honoria has every right to be angry with me. I was too scared to take on the entire Amazon guild." She placed a hand on Vanya's shoulder.

Honoria lashed back at Scyleia, "That is the first statement out of your mouth we can agree on!" She stood from the seat and walked to the bow of the ship. Megildur was about to follow when Vanya stopped him.

"Let her go, she needs to come to grips with her friend's actions," Vanya commented. "Now tell me what you were doing in Amazon territory? That is no place for any man."

"We heard a rumor that Shadowbane was last in the Dwarf safehold on Stormvald," Megildur replied. "So when we arrived in Thieves' Den to find a Bard, we found Honoria. She helped us with a rather tense situation involving a Half Giant who wanted to turn Gaal into a rug." Gaal opened his eyes wide and nodded his head nervously. "She told us of a friend at Fort Irsadeng who would be able to give us passage across the sea to Stormvald."

Scyleia admitted, "Honoria was partly correct. I could have helped her, but the Amazon guild either kills, or makes slaves, of men. It is not something I believe in, but they took me in when I was near death from an attack on my village several years back. The Ranger's Brotherhood, from Wood's Hollow safehold, destroyed my home and I barely escaped. I crawled to the shore of a nearby stream and a few Amazon Scouts found me. They brought me back to health at their safehold and the Queen offered me a place in their guild. I felt, at the time, it was the best place for me."

"I understand your reasoning," Megildur replied. "However, Honoria feels betrayed and may be a harder soul to receive forgiveness from. Thank you for getting word of our predicament to the Bard's network. I am not sure we would have survived without your deeds." Scyleia gave a slight smile at Megildur and glanced to the bow of the ship to see if Honoria was still there. She wanted to explain to her friend but did not know if she had the courage.

"Where shall we make port, M'Lady?" One of the mariners asked Vanya.

"Set sail for Stormvald," Vanya commanded. "Be sure to land on the southwestern shore, otherwise the Dwarves will detect our presence." The sailor bowed to Vanya and departed to carry out her commands. She turned back to Megildur to see the surprised look on his face. "Your father is not the only one with royalty in his blood. My father is King of the Gwaridorn Elves, making me a Princess. We rule over the seas and do not bother ourselves with petty land disputes or trying to conquer the outlying villages, as the Dar Khelegur do."

"Well, I am glad you came ashore to rescue us," Gaal interjected. "Now if you will excuse me, M'Lady, I am going to see if I can forage for some food."

"Oh yes, speaking of that," Vanya replied, beckoning for one of her crew. "Follow this crewman, Gaal. He will take you to the supplies you will need. There is plenty of food to choose. It will be cold on Stormvald, so be sure to grab blankets and warmer clothing."

Gaal squealed, "Oh M'Lady, thank you for your generosity." He turned to follow the Gwaridorn crewmember.

"Thank you Mother, we needed more supplies," Megildur responded. "Gaal better not pack too much this time." The last part Megildur whispered to himself.

"I expected you would, since I was certain the Amazons kept your packs and gear," Vanya replied. "However, one of my men did find your armor that you possessed when you left Aelarnost. He found it when surveying the Amazon safehold. It's with your supplies already and you can collect some new weapons before you depart."

Megildur boasted, "Maethorion gave me that armor, originally forged for…"

"Oh, I know who they intended it for," Vanya interrupted. "The Elves forged the armor for Sillestor the traitor!" Just mentioning the name disgusted Vanya. "Just be certain that you do not follow down the same dark path, when you recover Shadowbane. Death and misery have followed that weapon for many people over the ages." Vanya now showed concern for her son on his journey. "I am sure if the Dwarves do not already have the sword, they know who does. Of course, they will not tell you. They despise all other races. They will enslave anyone they find within their safehold." That warning sank deep within Megildur's gut.

"I have no idea how we will get inside Korvambar," Megildur sighed.

"Well not to make matters worse for you, but you not only need to get inside the perimeter," Vanya added. "You'll need to infiltrate the depths of the Halls of Haganduur as well." Megildur was impressed with his Mother's knowledge.

Megildur gasped, "Oh no, I forgot about the armory within the Halls of Haganduur. I am not a burrowing rodent! Now I have no way inside. The only thing we can do now is have Gaal use his stealth abilities, but I dare not send him alone into the depths of the Dwarf safehold!" Megildur appeared distressed at the thought of sending his friend into danger. He did not want to have Honoria and himself wait outside when Gaal braved the tunnels under Korvambar.

"Relax my son, I have a solution for you," Vanya replied. She revealed a folded up cloth. "These are transparency cloaks, two of them. They will allow both Honoria and yourself to accompany Gaal on this section of the quest." Megildur's expression changed from dismay to delight at the sight of these gifts. Now he could fulfill the quest the All-Father laid out before him. "Now, I must warn you of the limitations of these cloaks. They only hide what they cover, so make sure you do not let go of them or you will be fully visible at the worst possible moment. In addition, they are not as powerful as the stealth ability a rogue uses, like Gaal."

Megildur exclaimed, "This is fantastic! Now all of us can infiltrate the tunnels under Korvambar and find Shadowbane." Megildur accepted the gifts.

"Now, tell me more about your journey since you left Aelarnost," Vanya inquired.

Megildur told his mother about his travels thus far and Scyleia took the opportunity to check on Honoria. Scyleia walked near the bow. She could see Honoria leaning over the ship, crying. Honoria heard someone approaching and wiped her tears away. The Bard noticed it was her treacherous friend and her sorrow turned to anger once again.

Honoria lashed out, "What do you want now? Did you come up here to drive the dagger deeper into my back?" Her Nephilim rage began to show as she confronted Scyleia.

Scyleia murmured, stepping backwards. "No, I just wanted to tell you I am sorry." She did not want to anger Honoria further. "I feel awful about what happened. I knew I could not free you and your friends on my own. That is why I left, to notify Megildur's people. I knew they would be able to help."

Honoria demanded, "Why did you not tell me that your new guild hated men so much? You made me not only look deceptive to my companions, but also like a fool!" Honoria's anger subsided now and humiliation set in.

Scyleia countered, "I did not see any reason to tell you since, well...you are female. They would have accepted you."

"Honoria, Gaal and I never felt that you deceived us," Megildur added, walking up from behind the Nephilim. "Remember, the Amazons captured you as well."

"I still do not feel I can fully forgive you, since you betrayed my trust," Honoria told Scyleia. "However, I thank you for your actions that led to our rescue. I just hope I can trust you again one day."

Scyleia vowed, "I will earn your trust again, I promise. Thank you Honoria."

Honoria chided, "So why are you here, Megildur? Didn't think we could reconcile without you?"

Megildur laughed, "I was actually afraid you might throw her overboard!" Honoria punched him on the arm for saying that. "You can't blame me for thinking that, I watched how you dispatched that Vampire at the campsite."

"You killed a Vampire?" Scyleia asked. "I thought it was Megildur who..."

Honoria grumbled, "Pay no attention to him!" She took Scyleia by the arm and guided her away from Megildur.

Megildur chuckled and turned to check on Gaal below deck. After looking around a bit, he managed to find the storage hold and Gaal. The Shade was feverish with excitement over all the weapons and supplies. Seeing his custom-made Elven armor blending in with the rest of the armory impressed Megildur. A sword along the far wall particularly interested the Aelfborn Lord. The blade was long and the workmanship was incredible. The blade shown so bright it could bring light into the darkest of places.

"That's a Jen'e'tai blade," Vanya commented, entering the room. "It's the preferred weapon for a Blade Master."

"What's a Blade Master?" Megildur asked.

"Dedicated swordsmen," Vanya described. "Jen'e'tai in ancient tongue means the Path of Truth. Blade Masters learn to strike with incredible speed. They're known as the whirlwinds of steel." Megildur stared at the blade in amazement while his mother told him of the Blade Masters. "But that's enough history for tonight, I am sure you have not slept for some time."

"What makes you say that?" Megildur asked. He noticed what direction his mother was glancing and he followed her eyes. There was Gaal, curled up on several sacks of food, asleep. "Alright, you may have a point. I will take him to an empty room and both of us shall sleep before we arrive in Stormvald."

"You will find some quarters down the hall," Vanya mentioned as Megildur dragged Gaal to a vacant space. "We should be along the shores of Stormvald by morning. Sleep well."

Megildur did find accommodations with two empty beds. Neither he nor Gaal had the energy to change, so both of them passed out atop the bedding. Before he closed his eyes, Megildur rubbed his chest and remembered the injury inflicted upon him before his rescue. It angered him that he did not get to kill the Amazon Queen himself, the one that scarred his chest. He cleaned the wound, but still the yearning for vengeance consumed the Aelfborn until his fatigue caught up with him.

Megildur was too exhausted to worry about what awaited them on the shores of Stormvald. He just fell fast asleep, for once.

CHAPTER 28: *Arrival on Stormvald*

Megildur woke to what he thought was the next morning, but it was well into the afternoon. He sat up in bed and stretched. Apparently, he undressed some time during the night, most likely out of habit. He looked to the other side of the room to find Gaal's lower half in bed and his upper half was hanging over the side. Megildur was unsure if last night he left the Shade that way or if Gaal thrashed about during the night. The Aelfborn Lord stepped down to the cold floor, put on his clothes, and nudged his friend to wake him. It was good fortune that Shades did not have hair or his would be a mess after the night he had. Gaal rolled over and fell out of bed, landing on the wood floor. He gazed up at Megildur, who was now laughing at him.

"Have we arrived yet?" The half-conscious Thief asked.

"Not sure, but you need to get up," Megildur replied. "Let's get topside and see where we are." Megildur finished with his boots, but Gaal had a long way to go.

The two went up to the deck to find Vanya, Scyleia, and Honoria all huddled under a large blanket laughing and conversing like old friends. This was a disturbing sight to Megildur, his mother laughing with his friends.

"What's going on here?" Megildur demanded, unsure if he wanted to know.

Vanya greeted, "Oh Megildur, Gaal, there you two are. I was just talking with these two about the old days and some of your current quest." Megildur wanted to scold his Mother for talking behind his back. "We have food for you both. Come, sit down." Gaal scurried over for the food and drink the women offered them. However, Megildur just stood there staring at them. His mother updated them on their voyage across the inlet. "Our ships are the fastest in Aerynth. We made the crossing to Stormvald in one night. We docked a short time ago but I figured you needed the sleep. It will most likely be your last warm rest. The girls came topside right before we landed and we have been talking ever since."

Honoria interjected, "Yes, since we were already awake most of the night talking we felt the ship slowing to dock. We needed to catch up. We haven't seen each other in months." Honoria wrapped her arm around Scyleia in a friendly manner.

"Whatever. Just hurry up and eat something," Megildur replied. He picked out the food he wanted. "I want to get to that Dwarf safehold fast and get this quest over with!"

Vanya and the girls looked at each other in shock. "He's under a lot of stress," his mother whispered to the others.

After they filled their bellies, Megildur, Gaal, and Honoria went down to the armory. They collected their packs and some warmer clothes. Stormvald was an icy continent with less than desirable summers, and even harsher winters. Moreover, this being winter it was definitely going to be harsh on their journey. Megildur also collected his armor but when he looked to the weapons, the Jen'e'tai sword was gone. Megildur grumbled under his breath and rolled his eyes. Vanya, along with two other crewmembers, walked into the room carrying items.

"I wanted each of you to take items that would help complete the rest of your quest," Vanya said.

"For Honoria, something every Bard needs." Vanya unveiled a small harp. It appeared crafted from gold and the strings shown as bright as moonlight, as did Honoria's face when she gazed upon it.

Honoria gasped, "Oh it's beautiful! Are you certain you want me to have this?"

"Of course I do," Vanya replied. "It was crafted by the Gwaridorn Elf Bards and I wanted you to wield it from this day forward. Its melody is like no other and you will find it has many capabilities." Honoria accepted the gift and held it tight. "Now, for our crafty friend, Gaal." He turned around but still managed to have food in his mouth. "These are serpentine daggers, they are very fast, and light, just as a Thief must be on his feet." Vanya smiled at the Shade while presenting the daggers to him.

Gaal muffled his gratitude, due to the mouthful of food. "Thank you, I will use them well." He managed to take the weapons from Vanya, after dropping some food.

"Now, Megildur, for you." Vanya turned around to take one last item from her Elven crewmember. "The Jen'e'tai sword of a Blade Master. I know it's not as prestigious as Shadowbane, but I am certain it will serve you well."

"I wondered who took it!" Megildur snatched the sword and realized by his mother's shocked expression that he was being a jerk. "Thanks. I will guard it closely."

"I have given you these items not so you will guard them, but that the weapons may guard you." Vanya smiled, gazing upon her son and his companions, dressed for battle. "Oh Honoria, you may want to grab another weapon of your choosing. A Bard can only defend with melody so much." She walked with her son to the deck to disembark from the ship. Once they reached the gangplank to leave the ship Megildur turned to his mother.

"I will be back from my quest soon, I hope," Megildur rumbled. "Thanks for all you have done for us." He reached out and quickly hugged his mother. Vanya squeezed him tight and Megildur winced.

"I know you are under tremendous pressure, but try to relax and not let the stress get to you," Vanya whispered, embracing her child. "You have a good group of friends. Be safe." She started to cry a bit and realized she cannot make him look too weak in front of his friends. She pulled back and restrained her emotions, "Besides, I owed you for saving your sister and me from Aelarnost. Take care of yourself and your companions."

"Of course I will, Mother," Megildur responded, rolling his eyes. He turned to see his traveling companions had already crossed the gangplank, plus one. "Scyleia, what are you doing ashore?"

Scyleia vowed, "I am going with you. The way I see it, I still owe you for what happened in Fort Irsadeng."

"You do not owe us for anything," Megildur countered. "I don't need another mouth to feed or another girl to protect!" Megildur noticed his response displeased Honoria, so he changed his answer. "Alright, you can come. But Honoria is responsible for you!"

Honoria blurted out, hugging her friend, "Yes, I will be responsible for her!" Gaal did not look too pleased, but that was his way.

Megildur picked up his gear, turned to wave one last time to his mother, and started walking north along the shoreline to Korvambar. They needed to walk a fine line between the shore and the mainland, since one side had hostile ships and the other contained hostile beasts. The terrain was frozen and dense with trees in some areas. Megildur moved inland slightly, but also made sure he could see the shoreline as well.

Megildur turned inland a bit to find some cover. The sun was high in the sky; from what they could see past the constant layer of clouds covering them. Honoria and Scyleia played around with the fact that they could see each other's breath. Gaal was thinking about making snowballs to throw at Honoria. Megildur kept to himself, perturbed with the group's optimism. The Aelfborn Lord decided to make camp after several attempts to keep the others on track.

Gaal blurted out, "Alright. I will grab some wood for a fire, but I doubt we will need much since this cold air is so refreshing." He sneered at Honoria who was shivering due to the frozen wasteland. Megildur and Scyleia did not look too comfortable. However, they appeared to be able to tolerate the cold compared to the Nephilim. "Is it too cold for you Honoria?" Gaal smirked. The Shade enjoyed teasing Honoria. That and food were his two favorite things during this quest. Honoria just glared at Gaal. The Shade was cold too, but he would not let the Nephilim know.

"That's enough!" Megildur commanded. "Gaal, go get the wood and make it a lot. Otherwise, I can let Honoria skin you alive for teasing her. The thought of skinning a Thief would please her. I am certain it would change her disposition from miserable to happy, for a few moments at least." Megildur turned his attention to Scyleia. "Help me prepare some food." Scyleia was eager to comply, since the activity would keep her warm.

Gaal returned with the wood and created a fire large enough for not only the food, but to warm everyone as well. They did not need to worry about the Dwarves spotting the fire. They were still far enough away from the safehold. Megildur and Scyleia made a stew, with various meats and vegetables they combined. Gaal took the food to Honoria as a peace offering.

"Here you go. This should help warm you." Honoria reluctantly accepted the food.

"Did you put enough poison in it to kill me fast, or am I to suffer awhile?" Honoria inquired, sniffing at her food like a wild animal. Scyleia glared at the Thief and imagined it could be true. After all, poison training is common among rogues.

"I would not poison your food!" Gaal countered. "I only meant to make amends for how I acted earlier!" Offended by the accusation Gaal spun around to walk away.

"Wait, I am sorry," Honoria apologized. She grabbed Gaal's wrist before he stormed off. "Thank you for the food. I did not mean to offend you. I know you were just poking fun at me." Honoria smiled at Gaal letting him know she was being sincere.

"True, I was just having some fun...at your expense," Gaal admitted. "Are we square now?" Gaal asked his Nephilim companion while extending a hand of friendship.

"Yes, I agree," Honoria replied when she shook his hand. "Now sit down with me and enjoy some of this food that Megildur and Scyleia made." Gaal agreed, received a bowl of the stew from Megildur, and sat down with Honoria and Scyleia. Megildur served himself a bowl and joined his friends for some laughter and tales of old. The Aelfborn Lord did not laugh often. Instead, he kept rubbing his chest and scowling. Gaal kept the fire going so that it would not get too cold for Honoria.

Once they had their fill of stew, the companions got back on their way. Megildur noticed a storm moving in and wanted to find shelter before their visibility of the terrain diminished. Unfortunately, they were unable to find any shelter while traveling northward before the snowstorm was upon them. Gaal spotted a cave off in the distance and since they did not have much of a choice, the group went inside. Megildur took the lead, drew his sword, and surveyed the cave for any unwanted creatures. It was hard to see but Megildur did catch the odor of raw flesh and blood. He did not find any beasts and hoped it was an abandoned shelter...for what type of creature he did not know.

"Well it's not much, but I fear if we go back outside we would not survive the storm," Megildur claimed. "It smells like death in here but I am certain death would find us if we braved the storm outside." The rest of the group agreed and they tried to make the best with what they had. They all huddled close to one another for heat, gathering any wood for a fire was not an option. They stayed close to the entrance since they were unable to see deep into the cave. Hopefully, nothing else was in there with them. Megildur drifted to sleep with the certainty they would survive the night in the shelter, so long as its previous inhabitants did not return.

CHAPTER 29: Icy Adversaries

Megildur whispered, "Gaal, wake up!" He nervously shook his friend and covered his mouth. Gaal's eyes popped open. "We are not alone in this cave. I need you to vanish from sight and see if you can distract the beast near the back of the cavern. I will get the others out."

Gaal muttered, "You want me to do what?"

Megildur hissed, "I didn't say I wanted you to battle the creature, just distract it! Now move so I can get Honoria and Scyleia out!"

Gaal grumbled, "Alright, I will go play with the vicious man-eating monster." He vanished from sight and reappeared minutes later at the back of the cave, just off to the side of a Shaarduk creature. The Thief made sure he was out of striking range but close enough to attract the beast's attention. He could see Megildur was ready, so he began flailing his arms to make the beast notice him and not his friends. The distraction began to work, because the Shaarduk creature charged toward Gaal. When the creature turned its back, Megildur woke Honoria and Scyleia.

Honoria mumbled, "What is wrong with you? I was…"

Megildur shushed, "Quiet! The inhabitant of this cave just woke up and we need to go, now! Gaal can only hold its attention for so long!"

Honoria realized he was serious, she turned to see Gaal vanishing and reappearing in different spots, like playing a game of cat and mouse with the enormous, and now angry, beast. Scyleia awakened at that time and noticed the other two looking at the rear of the cave. She turned to see Gaal waving his arms but she did not see the beast.

"Why is Gaal flapping about like a bird?" Scyleia asked. The beast then came into view and she could see why. "By the All-Father!"

"Unless you want to meet Him, move!" Megildur commanded and grabbed both Honoria and Scyleia by the arm. He whisked them out of the cave before the creature noticed.

He found cover for them by some nearby trees and returned to the cave entrance to see Gaal still annoying the Shaarduk. The Shade turned to see Megildur signaling that they were clear, just as the Shaarduk hurled a large rock at Gaal, knocking him to the ground. The beast raced to the fallen Thief, as a predator would. It grabbed Gaal's leg and opened its mouth. Blood from the beast sprayed all over Gaal. The creature's head rolled from his body. Gaal looked up to see Megildur standing over the decapitated Shaarduk, holding a bloodied sword. Megildur thrust the bloody weapon into the frozen cave floor and offered Gaal a hand to help him back to his feet.

Gaal exclaimed, "Thank you for finally helping! I thought it was going to disembowel me!" He accepted Megildur's assistance. "That thing looked infuriated while I was provoking it."

Megildur laughed at Gaal, "Well you can be very annoying. I can see why people keep trying to kill you. Remember the brute in Thieves' Den?" Gaal at first glared at Megildur's laughter but then realized he does have a tendency to upset those around him. However, he was content with this fact.

Gaal insisted, "Well, I distracted the beast for you, but I hurt my ankle. The least you can do is help me outside." Megildur threw Gaal's arm over his shoulder. Honoria and Scyleia were waiting. They both were in shock to see Gaal limping and covered in blood.

Honoria exclaimed, "What happened to you? You look like the beast thrashed you senseless."

Gaal jested, "Thanks, I would not want to look half dead and have nobody notice. At least the blood is not mine. Megildur slayed the beast just before it had me for a snack."

"Well it's good he did." Honoria beamed knowing Gaal was okay, or at least his mouth was. He was still able to make sarcastic responses. "I hear Shades taste horrible!" Gaal glared at Honoria. "Set him here on the rock and I will tend to his ankle." Honoria wrapped his ankle with some cloth, to help the injury heal. "Here, drink this bottle. It will help with the pain and allow the injured part of your leg to heal faster."

Gaal reluctantly accepted the liquid but decided to smell the potion before tasting it. He blurted out, "Oh, I am not drinking this vile swill!" His face scrunched up and the Shade looked like he was about to vomit. "It smells worse than that creature in the cave, I can only imagine how bad it tastes!" He pushed the drink back to Honoria, who by now did not look pleased.

Honoria rebuked, "It's either this or you will not be able to complete the quest!" She pushed the drink back to him. Gaal still did not want to try the potion.

Megildur interjected, "Either you drink this or I will leave you in the cave with that dead creature! I am sure his friends will be along soon to check on you!" The Aelfborn glared at Gaal.

Gaal looked terrified at the thought of going back in the cave, so he scowled at the potion, pinched his nose, and poured the liquid down his throat. "Yuk!" Gaal exclaimed. "That's ghastly!"

Honoria scolded Gaal, "Oh, give me that phial you baby!" Honoria took the empty phial from Gaal and put it back in her bag. "I expected a Shade to be tougher than that, I guess I expected too much!"

Gaal glared at Honoria and turned back to look at Megildur, who was busy rubbing his chest. Gaal wailed, "Did you hear her rude comment?"

"Well, you are acting like a baby!" Megildur bellowed, rubbing his chest. "Now on your feet! If you stay on that rock too long you are likely to freeze and never get a chance to regain your manhood!"

Gaal just scowled at Megildur, hoping he was joking but also curious why he was so angry. "It's lucky for you I am starting to like you, or I would have to regain my 'manhood' by gutting you!" Gaal jested, trying to appear harsher.

Megildur snapped, "Try it baldy!" Megildur reached for his sword but was unable to unsheathe it before Honoria jumped between them, restraining the Aelfborn's hand.

"At least my mother did not have to save me!" Gaal chided.

"She saved you as well, idiot!" Megildur countered.

"Stop it!" The Nephilim hollered, moving Megildur away from the others. She looked at him inquisitively, "What's the matter with you?"

"Nothing!" Megildur released his grip on the sword and began to walk past Honoria. She placed her hand on his chest to stop him. Megildur winced in pain, clutched his chest, and unintentionally exposed part of his wound from the encounter with the Amazons.

"What happened? I didn't hit you that hard." Honoria inquired.

Scyleia rushed to Megildur's side and pulled back his jacket. "Look at this injury." Both Scyleia and Honoria knew what this meant, looking at each other in horror.

"What, it makes him a creep?" Gaal interjected, now rubbing his ankle.

"No, the scar has disrupted the mystical tattoos. Aelfborn receive these markings upon birth," Honoria responded. "That explains his outbursts."

"So it does make him a creep!" Gaal asserted, wiping the creature's blood from his head and clothes.

"Gaal!" Honoria lashed back at the Thief. "If the markings are not intact, he will die of madness." She looked at Scyleia, "Do you know where we can find the herbs?"

"In this desolate frozen land it will be impossible to scavenge for any plants," Scyleia answered. "What are we going to do?"

"Stop panicking," Gaal interjected. "I know where you can find herbs, but I can't travel there like this and the old hag will not give you the herbs for free."

"Let me worry about that," Honoria replied. "Which direction and how far?"

Gaal pointed east. "It'll take several hours, but you should make it there and back before night. Do not mention my name. Last time I was there, we had a bit of a misunderstanding."

Honoria sneered at Gaal and told Scyleia, "Take care of Megildur and Gaal the best you can. I will get the herbs we need and be right back."

Scyleia agreed as Honoria began her trek eastward. She traveled for several hours without seeing any structures, nor beasts fortunately. Not many guilds settled on the tundra, except Dwarves and Barbarians. The Dwarf safehold was much further north, but Honoria still needed to stay alert for bandits and Thieves. She took her Nephilim form and flew until her stamina faded. Then she walked until her feet hurt. She found a stump on which to rub her feet. She looked up from her foot massage and noticed a smokestack rising in the distance. It was coming from a small hut surrounded by rocks. She put her boots back on and approached the front door. She was about to knock when a foul stench overwhelmed her senses. She restrained her desire to vomit. She knew Megildur's life depended on her success.

Honoria was about to knock on the door when a voice told her to enter. She pried the door open and saw what looked like an old woman standing over a boiling pot. The old woman had her back to the door and did not turn around. Honoria entered, "Excuse me, I am here..."

"I know why you are here, and what you want," the old woman interrupted. "Do you think you can fix that boy's mystical markings? It takes a skilled hand to perform the ritual."

Shocked by the woman's knowledge, Honoria responded, "Yes, I have seen it done before and even assisted once. I just need..."

"I know, I know. I am not a dolt!" The old woman cut in again. "Now, can you pay for the herbs it will require?"

"Of c-course," Honoria replied. "I have this necklace..." Before she could pull the chain over her head, the old woman made the necklace levitate from Honoria's neck to her decrepit hand, without even touching her.

"Yes, yes, this will do nicely." The old woman touted, with her back still facing Honoria. "Chaos jewelry is so enticing! Here's what you require."

The old woman made several circling motions with her index finger. This action pulled numerous herbs out of jars on a nearby shelf, once again, without the old woman even touching a single item. When complete, all of the required herbs danced through the air and piled into a leather pouch. Honoria grabbed the bag of herbs and shoved it into her knapsack. She turned to thank the old woman and found herself face to face with her. The old woman had no eyes, only stiches where lashes and lids used to be. Her complexion reminded Honoria of withered fruit left out in the hot sun, and it smelled the same. This caught Honoria off guard.

"Y-your eyes!" Honoria squealed out.

"Everyone has a price to pay," the old woman chuckled. "Now you tell that pasty Thief that the 'old hag' still expects him to pay for what he has taken from me. I will accept gold or personal belongings from him!" The old woman shrieked.

"I will relay the message," Honoria shouted, scurrying to the door. "Thank you!" She ran into the wilderness toward her friends.

"I got the ingredients!" Honoria shouted upon reaching the camp. "Here, can you mix them?" She handed the herbs to Scyleia, who agreed to mix the herbs. Honoria turned to Gaal next, "Nice woman you sent me to."

"You asked," Gaal retorted. "Did she mention me?" He seemed a bit worried.

"Yes, she expects payment for something you took," Honoria answered. "In one form or another."

Gaal shuttered at the response, "Sure, I'll get right on that."

Honoria did not have time to worry about Gaal. They needed to repair Megildur's tattoos before it was too late. The Nephilim picked up Megildur. His body drenched in sweat; he kept rambling nonsense. His insanity was growing worse. She placed him further away from the fire, on the ground, so he would not thrash around too close to the open flame. Scyleia approached with the herb mixture in a small bowl with a brush dipped inside. The mixture made a dark ink with a glimmering metallic substance flowing throughout. Honoria exposed his torso and wasted no time with repairing the mystical markings. She wielded the brush with precision and haste. Scyleia chanted in a language Gaal had never heard before. When Honoria finished the last stroke, Megildur let out a deep sigh and passed out.

"He will need to rest now," Honoria told the others. "He should fully heal by morning." Scyleia smiled at Honoria, but Gaal looked skeptical.

In the morning, Megildur awoke feeling better, as Honoria predicted. The Aelfborn stretched, rubbed his chest, and approached Honoria and Scyleia. "You repaired my tattoos. I was a bit out of sorts last night, but I remember you painting on my chest as Scyleia muttered something." He gave a slight smile to both of them. "I didn't know you possessed the skill of doing that. Thank you for saving me."

The four of them traveled at a slower pace for most of the morning because of Gaal's injury. Once they stopped to rest, Gaal had a bit more time to recover and the medicine seemed to be working. The pace was faster for the afternoon, now that Gaal did not need assistance to walk. The group traveled for as long as they could in the harsh frozen wasteland, trying to compensate for the time lost. Exhaustion overcame all of them and Megildur had to find shelter, hopefully an empty shelter this time. The best he could find was a large grouping of rocks that formed a circle. It blocked the wind while Megildur worked on getting the fire ready. Normally Gaal would have done this task, but Megildur felt guilty over the way he treated his friends during his bout of madness.

"There, that should keep us warm for the night," Megildur claimed after he started a roaring fire in the middle of the rock formation.

"Now that the emergency is over, I was meaning to ask. What was that thing that attacked Gaal in the cavern?" Scyleia inquired.

"Oh, you mean the Shaarduk creature." Megildur began. "They stand on two legs like a man, but resemble a bear, and they have the temperament to match. These fierce beasts are indigenous to this region. I had never seen one until now, but I have heard stories. Once the inhabitant of that cave awoke, we became unwelcomed guests."

Honoria added wood to the fire, intrigued by the tale. Megildur then changed the subject and became somber.

"In my madness, while I was experiencing physical and mental anguish, I had a nightmare." Megildur continued. "I was screaming at my Desert Flower, Zabrina. I am not even sure why, but it made me feel awful. I was dripping in sweat when I awoke. It was so real. Do you think she will forgive me?"

Scyleia countered, "There is nothing to forgive. Love is unconditional." Silence befell the group.

Honoria pulled out the small harp Vanya gave her. She began to tell the tale of Beregund Bladeseeker. His first quest to recover Shadowbane from the Dwarf stronghold occurred over a thousand years ago during the Age of Days. Beregund slayed Giants, crushed a deadly serpent, and decapitated an acrimonious drake in order to recover Shadowbane. The tale gave Megildur courage that he could succeed. He felt that if Beregund could accomplish such a task by himself, the Aelfborn could also succeed with the help of his newfound companions. Of course, Honoria left out the part where Ithriana betrayed Beregund by poisoning him. She felt Megildur did not need any discouragement.

"Thank you for that tale, Honoria," Megildur said after the Bard finished her story of Beregund. "We should try to get some sleep. We need to try to recover some of our lost time tomorrow, if our crippled Thief can endure." Gaal did not look pleased with Megildur's jab at the Shade's demise. "I will take first watch and I will wake Honoria after a few hours." Honoria agreed and the three of them rolled out their beds to prepare for sleep. Megildur began his patrol. He made a wide circle around the camp during his patrol so he could give his friends a chance to get some rest without disturbing them. He also let the campfire diminish to a low flame, so it would not attract any undesirables.

Megildur leaned against a rock, envisioning what his life would be like once this quest was over. He pictured Zabrina in a silk dress, sitting on the grass with him. Her golden hair was flowing in the breeze and he would rub his hands across her body.

Before he froze to the rock he leaned against, he noticed a light off in the distance. This snapped the Aelfborn out of his daydream. The glow was faint but looked like a campfire. The others had been asleep for several hours and it was almost time for him to trade guard duty with Honoria, so he decided to wake her.

Megildur whispered, placing his hand on Honoria's shoulder. "Honoria, it's your turn to keep watch on the camp."

Honoria grumbled, "What? Oh, okay, I am getting up." Once she was awake and ready for her shift as guard, she joined Megildur just outside the camp perimeter. He stared at the light in the distance. "What are you looking at?"

"I see light over there," Megildur replied. "I think it might be another camp, but the question is, are they friendly or hostile?" Honoria looked concerned over the thought of the inhabitants being hostile. "I am going to sneak up on the camp and see what they are doing. You stay and watch the others."

"Are you sure you do not want me to wake the others?" Honoria asked Megildur. "Gaal can sneak up on the camp using his invisibility."

"No, he needs his rest," Megildur retorted. "Besides, if I am to be High King one day I need to know what danger I am placing someone in when I give the command for them to do this very same act." He raised his eyebrows at Honoria. "I'll be right back."

They stood three times taller than the average man and their skin was pure white, like the snowy environment they lived in. Their hair and beards were a pale bluish-white color, giving them the appearance of frostbite. Many wielded gigantic clubs and hammers with their colossal muscles. Storm Giants! His father told him stories of these enormous inhabitants of Aerynth. He found a boulder to hide behind so he could maintain a safe distance and still observe the giants. Watching, he discovered there were several giants in the camp and they were cooking some beast, or at least that is what it looked like. They cooked an animal above the campfire, until the giants decided to devour it rare and still bloody. These colossal beings proceeded in tearing the limbs off their meal. They appeared to have veracious appetites, only exceeded by their immense strength. Megildur decided he had enough of both information, and disgust, from watching their eating habits. He crept back to his camp to find Honoria, nervously awaiting his return.

Honoria inquired, "What did you find? Were they hostile, like everything else in Aerynth?"

"I found a camp of Storm Giants," Megildur replied. "And I did not stay around long enough to ask them if their intentions were hostile or not." Honoria scowled at Megildur for his attempt at humor. "I believe we are safe, so long as they do not know we are here. Keep your eyes on the camp from here and be sure to patrol the perimeter occasionally. I am going to get some sleep, if I can." Megildur joined the others, huddled around the dwindling campfire, still fast asleep. He thought if they made good time tomorrow, they could reach Korvambar, the Dwarf safehold, by nightfall. With all the trouble they encountered so far on this journey, he wondered about finding Shadowbane inside the Halls of Haganduur. He heard tales of Thieves infiltrating the Halls of Haganduur but no tales of the Thieves making it back out alive. Maybe they would be the first, maybe?

CHAPTER 30: *Korvambar*

Gaal cheered, "Good morning, Lord Megildur!" The Shade was standing over him.

Megildur grumbled, "Good morning, Gaal." He was still trying to wake up. "Besides being one of those annoying morning people, how are you feeling and where's Honoria?"

Gaal boasted, "I feel strong enough to steal from all of Aerynth. Honoria is still patrolling the camp."

Megildur examined his surroundings; he was still worried what would happen if those Storm Giants discovered his companions. With everyone being this alive and energetic, the group just might be able to reach the Dwarf safehold by sunset. Of course, they could just be active to stay warm, but that was even more reason to accelerate to their destination.

Megildur rallied everyone to one location, he wanted to get going. "Now that our Thief friend is feeling better, we need to push forward and see if we can make it to Korvambar by sunset. It would be easier to sneak inside under the veil of darkness," Megildur commented. All were in agreement. "So let's grab our gear and head out." In moments, everyone packed and continued on to Korvambar.

Since Gaal's ankle had fully healed, the group made good time. They all decided to continue instead of stopping at midday. Fortunately, they did not encounter any more beasts or giants, at least not today. Before they knew it, they had traveled all day without stopping. Megildur noticed Gaal's stomach growling so loud, he worried it might attract unwanted attention.

The sun started to fall behind the snowy range. Even though darkness filled the valley, the travelers could see an aura emanating ahead of them, growing in intensity. The group was unsure what could produce that much light, except a safehold. They all decided to climb atop a small hill and crouch down to survey the light ahead.

Megildur reached the top of the hill and could see the safehold, he gasped, "Korvambar!" The brilliance and magnitude of the Dwarven safehold impressed the Aelfborn and his cohorts. The walls that secured the compound were stone but embellished with gold markings of the Dwarf guild. At the safehold's back was a dormant volcano. So the story goes, Thurin chose this spot for his stout offspring due to its heat source. Even though the volcano is dormant, an abundant source of lava still flows within. The Dwarves tap this rich heat source to keep their forges operational. Night and day, they work deep within the planet's crust. Megildur spotted an opening in the volcano. "That's the entrance into the Halls of Haganduur. We need to get through the compound in order to access the doors leading into the Halls of Haganduur."

Gaal exclaimed, "I never knew a race so small could produce such a majestic safehold!" He was busy ogling the Dwarves golden adornments.

"It may be majestic, but it's well fortified," Megildur replied. "We will remain here long enough to determine the best time to sneak inside their safehold. Honoria and I will use our invisibility cloaks and Gaal of course can sneak in using his own invisibility powers. We will be unable to see one another and will stop when no Dwarves are around. We must make sure we are all still within range of one another. Look for a stronghold deep inside, since

I doubt they would store Shadowbane in an unprotected armory." Megildur turned to Scyleia. "I will need you to watch our backs. Stay here and guard this spot. Also if they should capture us, you may have to save us again." He could see her disappointed expression about not accompanying them inside.

The gate into the compound was easy enough. Dwarves coming and going made it effortless for the trio. Inside the gate, they found a small stable to gather. The sound of the animals muffled their voices. The stable gave the perfect view to the massive doors leading inside the volcano. This was their target, now it was all a waiting game.

Gaal hissed, "Megildur, the doors to the Halls of Haganduur are opening! It looks like they are exchanging the guards. This is our chance to sneak inside."

"I agree," Megildur whispered. "Now, once we are past the doors we all need to stop when it's clear." Honoria and Gaal nodded and vanished from sight. Megildur pulled his invisibility cloak over his head.

All Scyleia could do now was watch and hope they made it inside before the giant doors closed. They remained open for a few minutes longer, until the exchange of guards finished. The massive doors collided shut with one another, causing a resounding bang.

Megildur did manage to make it inside before the doors slammed shut, but he was unsure of the others. He waited until the last of the Dwarves were out of sight before pulling his cloak down and revealing his location. "Honoria, Gaal, did you both make it inside?"

Gaal grumbled, popping out of his rogue stealth. "Yes I did. Now, can you move off my foot?"

Megildur chuckled, "Oh, sorry. I did not see you there. Where's Honoria?"

Honoria murmured, "I made it in, but Gaal pinned me against the wall!" She pulled down her cloak. "Get off me, you oaf!"

"Alright, we need to keep our heads here, or the Dwarves will take them!" Megildur interrupted before Gaal and Honoria had a chance to pursue their argument. "We also need more room to explore down here, if we are going to find where they are holding Shadowbane. Gaal, you follow that far wall and stop before going down any major halls. Honoria, take the wall we are next to. I will stay in the middle of this hall and watch for any Dwarves. If it is clear at the intersections, I will lift my cloak and make contact. If I do not, then assume someone is coming. Everyone ready?" Both Honoria and Gaal nodded and once again vanished from sight.

Megildur pulled his cloak over and proceeded down the middle of the hall. The dimly lit halls made it easier for the trio to sneak past the Dwarves undetected. When he came to the first intersection he looked both ways down the shorter halls and found no guards. Megildur pulled back his cloak revealing just his head and whispered. "I doubt they would leave it in an unprotected area so close to the entrance. We are looking for a heavily guarded room deeper inside these halls." He looked further down the main hall to spot another stopping point. "Let's meet along that railing ahead and get a better view of the area." Megildur heard both of his companions agree. The railing was a short distance down the main hall and appeared to lead into one massive room. The Aelfborn pulled his cloak back over his head and proceeded down the hall.

Once they reached the railing, Megildur discovered staircases to the left and right of their location, leading down to the floor below. When he looked past the railing, he could see a massive room. The chamber was so large he could fit his small village inside here, several times over in fact. In the center of the room was a stone statue of a bearded man in front of an anvil. The statue wielded a blacksmith's hammer in the right hand and the left hand was empty. However, the left hand was different from the right. The left hand was silver and metallic, which made it stand out from the stone.

Honoria whispered from under her cloak, bumping into Megildur, "Thurin! He is the God of Forge and Craft, the same one who crafted Shadowbane for the Elves in the Age of Twilight. He is the Father of the Dwarves, shaping the race in his image during Aerynth's creation."

Gaal chuckled, "He used a distorted image back then, cause he looks a lot taller than the Dwarves." He was still invisible, somewhere around Megildur.

Honoria lashed back at Gaal, "Hold your tongue, you blasphemous fool! That's all we need right now is for a God to spite us down at one of his own shrines."

"Both of you need to hold your tongues!" Megildur interjected. "This is a mission requiring stealth, not a religious debate! Now, we need to get to that large hallway behind the statue."

Gaal gasped, "You mean the one that has nearly a dozen Dwarf guards?"

"Where else do you think they would put something so valuable?" Megildur asked the terrified Shade. "Do you want to wait for us outside? Honoria and I will recover Shadowbane."

Gaal snapped, "Of course not!"

"Good, cause I need you to draw the guards away," Megildur replied.

Gaal panicked at Megildur's suggestion, "What? Are you insane? Dwarves may be short but they are strong! They would like nothing more than to rip apart a Thief found in their stronghold!"

Megildur responded, "I am sure that would please them. However, we need to get past those guards and into that hallway. I am certain their armory is there, since most of their people guard it. What else would they guard so dearly?" Megildur took a deep breath and decided to change tactics from pleading with Gaal to flattering his ego. "Besides, you're the one with stealth and sabotage skills."

Gaal boasted, "That much is true." A few moments of silence later, and a deep breath, the Shade spoke. "Alright, I will do it. Stay here and you will know when I have their attention."

Megildur whispered into the air, "Thank you my friend." He did not know if the Thief was still near him or if he had already departed. He watched the Dwarf guards for any sign of Gaal. Megildur noticed a pitcher float from its pedestal and follow a nearby guard patrolling the area. The container smashed into the guard's head and Gaal revealed himself to the other Dwarves.

"Could you point me to the nearest tavern, my short little friend?" Gaal taunted the guards.

"Stop the abomination!" One of the Dwarf guards roared, charging the Shade. Gaal took this as his cue to turn and run down a newly discovered hallway opposite of the one Megildur needed to get into.

"That's the opportunity we need," Megildur commented. "Let's move down the stairs on the right." The Aelfborn proceeded down the stairs hoping Honoria was still beside him. He cautiously reached the bottom of the winding staircase and examined the area for any Dwarf opposition. He crept forward toward the grand hallway and found Gaal had successfully cleared the section. Just before reaching the lone door in the hall, he ran into an unseen object. "Honoria, is that you?"

Honoria whispered, "Yes, I was waiting for you before peeking inside. Are you ready?"

"Ready as I will ever be," Megildur answered. "Let's get inside before more Dwarves arrive." He watched as Honoria forced open the door revealing an even darker room. He waited a moment, for Honoria to have enough time to make it through the doorway, and then he stepped inside and closed the door behind him. Megildur exclaimed, removing his invisibility cloak, "This is no armory!" For as far as he could see, this vast room contained barrels upon barrels. "It's a storage hold."

Honoria pulled back her cloak. She opened the spout on a nearby barrel, emptying the liquid into her hands, and tasting the contents. "Ale, these barrels must be full of Dwarven brewed ale!" There must have been over a hundred barrels in just the first row where they stood. Determining the height of the ceiling and depth of the walls, there were thousands of more barrels that filled the room.

"Well I heard the Dwarves enjoyed their ale," Megildur declared. "But I thought they would value their forges and armory higher than their drink!" Megildur leaned back against a barrel near him, amazed and shocked, trying to contemplate his next move.

"We do value our forges and armory more than the drink, which is why you will never see them, half-breed!" A shadowy figure bellowed from the now open doorway behind Honoria. The figure stepped forward along with other shadowy figures of the same height, one wielding a torch that revealed them all. The Dwarves had found them. "Does this abomination belong to you?" Another Dwarf dragged Gaal into the room by the back of his shirt, bruised and bloody. Megildur and Honoria went to Gaal's side. "We were about to slit his throat when I realized a Thief would not so blatantly reveal himself, unless he was just a distraction for other Thieves. Now, instead of killing all of you and allowing you to just return to your own safeholds, I will force all three of you to work for me, mining minerals deep inside the world." The Dwarf tilted his head back and began laughing at Megildur and his companions. This angered Megildur beyond control. He reached past one of the Dwarf guards and grabbed a loose board from a barrel.

"Noooo!" Megildur screamed out, swinging the board with all his might. He knocked the chuckling Dwarf to the ground. The Aelfborn used the board to knockdown another unsuspecting Dwarf, before two other guards retaliated by beating down Megildur with large wooden clubs. Honoria took her Nephilim form and knocked several Dwarves against the barrels before more of them tackled her and held her arms behind her back. She returned to her Human form, slightly battered. Even more Dwarf guards entered from the hallway and began dragging Megildur and his companions out of the storage area.

The lead Dwarf bellowed, "Wait! You can take the wench and the abomination to the mines. I will torture this half-breed with my own hands for his treachery!" The Dwarf securing Megildur dropped his semi-lifeless body to the stone floor, leaving the lead Dwarf to exact his revenge. Megildur, who now laid face down on the floor, was defenseless when the Dwarf stood over his back and unsheathed a golden dagger from his waist. The Dwarf grabbed Megildur by the back of his hair and dragged the blade down his back. "If you try that again half-breed, I will torture your friends, and make you watch!"

A voice thundered so loud it shook the stone structure, "Stop!" This sound startled the Dwarves, who dropped Megildur, Honoria, and Gaal. The Dwarves then backed themselves against the walls. They all looked around the massive room but were unable to determine where the command emanated from, until an enormous figure materialized before them.

All of the Dwarves gasped at once, bowing to the new figure in the room, "Father!"

Megildur lifted his head far enough off the floor to see who the Dwarves called Father. He was an enormous man who stood twice the height of Megildur. The man had a thick beard and wore a metallic glove on his left hand. He even overshadowed the statue next to him. The Aelfborn realized who this was...Thurin himself, Father to the Dwarf race.

Thurin commanded, "Rise Megildur, my children will harm you no longer. Your friends may rise as well." Thurin could see that Gaal and Megildur were slow to ascend due to their injuries. He turned to one of the Dwarves kneeling before him and commanded, "Bring forth a Priest to heal these travelers!" The Dwarf disappeared from the room to carry out Thurin's order. Soon after leaving, the Dwarf guard returned with another Dwarf who carried what appeared to be a medicinal bag, the travelers assumed this must be the Priest. He went to Megildur first.

Megildur grumbled, pushing the Priest toward Gaal, "See to my friend first." The Aelfborn rose to his feet and turned to Thurin. "Thank you for intervening. A life of mining deep inside Aerynth did not sound too appealing for my friends, nor did the thought of torture." Megildur nursed his injuries, glaring at the Dwarf who threatened him. "We meant neither disrespect nor hostility toward your children, we were..."

"You were looking for Shadowbane, to fulfill the quest the All-Father gave to you," Thurin interjected. "You will not find that which you seek here. You need to stop following rumors of where Shadowbane might be and start looking where it was last. For over a century now, the sword has remained embedded in the Stone Tree in the center of the old Kierhaven ruins. No one has removed it and no one shall, except for Cambruin's heir." Thurin smiled down upon Megildur.

Megildur replied with a perplexed tone, "But the last time anyone went looking for the ruins of Kierhaven, they found nothing. All that remained was a vast sea." He was even more confused.

Thurin chuckled, "Kierhaven is not gone, just lost. If someone seeks to travel to a lost realm in Aerynth, they can use the Lharast Portal."

"The Lharast Portal? I have heard tales of the full moon portal, but did not know it really existed," Honoria jumped into their conversation, followed by a glare from Megildur. "Sorry, I guess interposing is a fault in all Bards."

"Quite alright. The tales you heard were correct, my young Bard, the portal does exist," Thurin replied to Honoria's interruption with a smile. "However, this isn't an easy object to reach. It is on the isle of

Oblivion and guarded by the Lich Queen herself, Ithriana. What can you tell us of her, young Bard?"

"Ithriana was the daughter to Elf Lord Sillestor and she's the one who persuaded Beregund to recover Shadowbane from the Dwarves during the Age of Days," Honoria replied to a very impressed Thurin. "But I thought Caeric Blackhammer killed her during the Age of Kings when he recovered Shadowbane from her for the High King Cambruin?"

"Ithriana has risen from the dead before," Thurin cautioned. "Whether it's from the curse Beregund placed on Shadowbane or dark Elven magic from her kin, she's forever undead and impossible to kill." The God of Forge and Craft could see this news weighed heavily upon the already discouraged Aelfborn Lord. "Do not fret young Aelfborn Champion. Just because you cannot kill her, does not mean you cannot stop her, at least long enough to make it through the portal." Thurin looked toward one of the Dwarf guards. "Have the Forge Master fetch the Morloch's Betrayer of Fire and the Morloch's Betrayer of Truth!"

The Dwarf bowed to Thurin and walked past him to the back of Thurin's statue. Megildur watched the Dwarf wave his hand and say something in Dwarvish, "Knurlnien." Dwarf runes shown on the stone like fire and a door opened up for the guard.

"By the All-Father, no wonder no one has infiltrated the armory or forges inside the Halls of Haganduur!" Megildur proclaimed. "They are even deeper underground and protected by magical Dwarven doors!" Megildur whispered to Honoria, "Do you know what he said to open the door?" This even perplexed the Bard.

"Translated in your tongue it means Heart of Stone," Thurin responded. "And I would expect this knowledge to remain inside these halls!" Thurin scowled at the three companions who frantically shook their heads in agreement with the Father of the Dwarves.

The Dwarf who went below into the forges returned a few moments later carrying two daggers. One glowed red like the embers of a raging fire and the other glistened white like fresh snow after a storm. Thurin took both daggers from the Dwarf and dismissed him.

"These weapons will aid you in your battle with the Lich Queen," Thurin explained, handing one of the weapons to Megildur and the other to Gaal, who was now back up on his feet. "Though Ithriana has few weaknesses, you will find fire and holy attacks work best against her malevolent wrath. You will come across the Lich Queen inside her keep, deep inside the Plain of Ashes region on the isle of Oblivion. Once you leave this safehold, head south to the runegate and take the black portal. Good luck on your quest, Lord Megildur." Thurin turned to leave the travelers when Megildur made a request of him.

"Mighty Thurin, could I ask one more request of you?" Megildur beseeched the God of Forge and Craft. The powerful one turned around with a raised eyebrow to the Aelfborn. "Someone journeyed to Korvambar and his family never heard from him again. He is the father to a friend of mine, Marie. I was hoping you knew of his whereabouts."

"I know of whom you speak of," Thurin replied. "I have heard his daughter's cries. However, he violated my children's home and is being imprisoned for doing so."

Megildur conceded, "I understand Mighty Thurin, but his intentions were to recover Shadowbane and honor Cambruin...and the Gods.

Could you show mercy upon him and his family by allowing him to return home?"

"Knowing what strife lay ahead, you stop to plead for another man's life?" Thurin asked. "I can see why the All-Father chose you, Aelfborn. I will have him released at once to return home." The God turned to one of his children, who bowed to his father and left to carry out his wishes. Thurin gave the Aelfborn a slight smile and vanished from sight.

Gaal chuckled, "Well, I would take that as our sign to leave. I am ready, how about you...Lord Megildur?"

"Unappealing as the snowy weather is outside, it feels more inviting than this place right now," Megildur commented because of the glares they were receiving from many of the Dwarves. "How about you, Honoria, are you ready to travel?"

Honoria anxiously nodded her head, without saying a word. She was leery of a nearby Dwarf who was ogling her. She was unsure if this was a mischievous stare, or was he trying to flirt? Saying anything might provoke him and either way he intended the look, it revolted Honoria.

The three companions went straight for the exit. Anywhere in Aerynth right now felt more inviting than staying with these Dwarves. Several of them followed the travelers to the door, including Honoria's newfound friend. Once they made it past the doors leaving the Halls of Haganduur, the Dwarves slammed them shut. Two other guards escorted them outside the safehold walls and proceeded with slamming those gates as well.

"Charming little people, wouldn't you agree Honoria?" Gaal mocked. He noticed her flirting Dwarf inside the halls.

"Shut up, you whelp!" Honoria lashed back at the Shade. "Let's get Scyleia and our gear. I want to get as far away from this place as possible." The words barely escaped her mouth before Scyleia appeared, looking frantic.

"Are you alright?" Scyleia asked the group as they scrambled to gather their gear.

"Yes, but we need to make haste to the runegate south of here," Megildur replied. "We can explain along the way." They packed up their equipment and proceeded south, before the Dwarves got too restless.

CHAPTER 31: *Bound for Oblivion*

Megildur and his companions trekked south, straight down the middle of Stormvald this time. They attempted to avoid all signs of life and they told Scyleia of their encounter with Thurin and his Dwarf children.

"So Kierhaven's lost, not destroyed, according to Thurin?" Scyleia inquired. She was trying to analyze the information the God of Forge and Craft gave the others. "So since Thurin told you to look at Shadowbane's last known location that would take us to the Elven fortress Kierhaven atop Mount Telorinadreth." Scyleia looked deep in thought, as did the others, trying to process this recent knowledge. "Of course, in order to reach the lost fortress, we must travel to the Lich Queen's Keep and confront Ithriana for access to the Lharast Portal."

"I would say that sums it up," Megildur replied with a concerned look on his face. He understood that he must recover Shadowbane. However, in order to accomplish this, they must not only defeat Ithriana but also they must engage whatever awaits them in Kierhaven. Honoria could see the concerned look in Megildur's eyes.

"Do not fret about what we must accomplish," Honoria reassured the troubled Aelfborn. "The Gods would not have sent you on this quest if they did not have the confidence you would succeed."

"Besides, how can you fail with an epic Thief, a Vampire slaying Nephilim Bard and...what are you again?" Gaal commented, looking at Scyleia.

"I too am a Bard!" Scyleia countered Gaal's attempt at an insult.

Megildur bellowed, "Let's not start with the ribbing again! We will make camp over by those rocks and head out at first light. With any luck, we can make it to the runegate before the sun sets tomorrow."

The others could tell that Thurin's news disturbed the Aelfborn Lord. He did not fare too well against the last undead atrocity he encountered and the thought of engaging another did not comfort him.

Megildur felt they gained enough distance from the Dwarves to start a fire. Gaal collected firewood and started a blaze to offset the freezing wind and snow. After the campfire was going, Megildur looked around but was unable to find Honoria and Scyleia.

"Where are the others?" Megildur asked Gaal.

"Who knows, I saw them walking that way a short time ago," Gaal replied, pointing past the rock formation they used for shelter.

Megildur proceeded in the direction Gaal pointed. He rounded the rock formation and saw Honoria and Scyleia back to back chanting. They stopped and began walking back toward the camp as Megildur was in range of hearing what they were reciting.

"Oh Megildur, I did not know you were there," Honoria admitted. Scyleia also looked shocked to see him standing there watching them.

"We had not been in touch with the Bard network in some time," Honoria replied. "We just needed to update. Plus, we researched some new spells we can use against the Lich Queen."

Megildur grumbled, "Alright, well the fire is ready." He walked back to the camp and just stared into the fire. Honoria and Scyleia knew there was no comfort for him in any words they could offer, and Gaal was not the consoling type, so the evening passed in silence. Megildur stood to address his companions, "I will take the first watch. All of you should get some rest and we will leave at first light." He left to circle the encampment, checking for possible threats. He walked around the camp a few times and returned to the campfire to find the others had turned in for the night. He perched himself atop one of the closest rocks by the flames and contemplated how he would defeat the Lich Queen.

Megildur sat there thinking of his dilemma. A bright light shown in his eyes. The sun peeked up over the horizon. Without realizing it, he sat up all night worrying about the quest. He heard someone approaching from behind. He turned his head to see Scyleia was approaching.

"Did you stay awake all night? Why did you not wake one of us to take over?" Scyleia asked.

"I could not sleep, so I felt I might as well make myself useful," Megildur sighed, rubbing his worn eyes.

"I understand why you worry about your quest and I know you do not trust me after what happened in Fort Irsadeng," Scyleia remarked. "But you do not have to bear this burden alone. All you have to do is ask other guilds for help and I am sure you can rally more support."

"No others!" He retorted. "The All-Father gave me this responsibility and if I'm to be King one day, I need to be a man today." He stood up and seemed upset by Scyleia mentioning the thought of him needing assistance. It made him feel that she doubted his abilities. "Wake Gaal and Honoria, we need to proceed to the runegate."

"I apologize for my bitterness since leaving Korvambar," Megildur confessed. "Thurin's insight into locating Shadowbane, and our destination to reach it, distressed me. I had hoped we would find the sword in the Dwarf safehold and be returning to our homes by now." The Aelfborn turned to Scyleia, "I know those were words of comfort you gave me this morning, were not intended to cast doubt upon my abilities, but this is something I must do on my own." He turned to face all of his companions, "I will understand if you want to use the runegate to travel home now, I can continue on to the Lich Queen's Keep alone."

Gaal, Honoria, and Scyleia looked at one another, pondering the Aelfborn Lord's words. Honoria stepped up to Megildur and placed a hand on Megildur's shoulder, "I think I speak for all of us, we are with you until the end."

"Just try to make sure it's the end of the quest, not us!" The Shade Thief added.

Megildur boasted, "Well it looks like I have my army. Through the runegate, for tonight we camp in Oblivion!" The companions turned and followed their leader, and future High King, to the runegate. The four of them stood in the center of the platform and examined each of the three gates. One was a multicolored mist, one was a bright white cloud, and the last one was a thick black smoke.

"So where do these portals go?" Scyleia asked. "I've never traveled through one."

"I traveled through the runegate in Sea Dog's Rest through a custom portal opened by Zeristan in the center," Megildur replied. "Thurin told us to take the black portal to reach Oblivion, but does anyone know where the others lead?"

"I remember reading an ancient tale about the runegates during their formation, after the Turning," Honoria interjected. "It talked about the multicolored portal leading to Maelstrom and the white portal leading to Sea Dog's Rest."

"Well since our destination is on Oblivion, we go through the black smoke," Megildur commented. He approached the portal and placed a hand near the outer edge of the smoke, he could feel the energy hum within. The smoke would bend and sway to the movements of his hand. The Aelfborn gave one last look to his companions, took one large step and vanished into the smoke. Megildur once again saw the glowing circles, the same as when Zeristan transported him to his home. The symbols faded and Megildur was standing on the runegate in what he assumed was Oblivion now.

Oblivion lived up to its name, it was bleak and depressing. The ground was barren, the sky was ominous, and the stench of death was in the air. It did not feel as if any life ever existed on this forsaken land. Megildur stepped off the runegate and examined the area around him for any trouble, but for once, it appeared safe. He turned to watch each of his friends materialize on the runegate, until all four were there.

"Well, looks like we are on Oblivion as Thurin directed." Megildur remarked. "But does anyone know the way to the Lich Queen's Keep from here?"

Megildur glanced around at his companions but both Honoria and Scyleia had the same blank expression as the Aelfborn Lord.

"We go west," Gaal declared, starting to walk in that direction. Megildur looked puzzled by the Thief's statement. Gaal stopped and faced Megildur so he could speak soft enough for only the Aelfborn to hear.

"I used to scour this island looking for unsuspecting travelers to steal from."

Megildur whispered back to Gaal, "Glad you are on our side." He pulled back to address everyone. "We go west."

The four of them grabbed their gear and started walking west. It was not long until they reached a river. Megildur did not like having to cross another river but this one appeared still and dead, much like the land around him.

"If we tried to go around, it would extend our journey by several days," Gaal commented. "It's an inlet from the northern sea. It flows down to a lake just south of here."

"No," Megildur replied. "We will cross here."

The friends looked at one another, knowing they had little choice. None of them wanted to stay on this island longer than necessary, so crossing the river here was the best choice. Honoria could have taken her Nephilim form and flown over the water, but she did not want to make her friends suffer alone. They slipped into the water, one at a time, and crossed by swimming as fast as each of them could. The water reeked of dead sea organisms, which matched the floating remains all around them. They arrived on the other side with all four of them looking like beached sea life. The air lacked enough heat to dry their clothes, but the air was just muggy enough to make them miserable.

They continued west for some time before reaching any signs of life, if you could call it that. Megildur saw a creature walking on two legs but hunched over. Its skin was dark, with no fur. It was hard to see from a distance, but it appeared to have hooves instead of feet.

"What's that beast?" Megildur asked. "Some sort of demon?"

"That's a ghoul," Gaal replied. "You will find this island is swarming with those, along with skeletons, vampires, and worse."

"Well since he's moving north, we will travel southwest and see about making camp," Megildur commanded. He turned to Gaal, "Can you scout ahead and see if there are any sections free of demons, vampires and other undesirables?"

Gaal chuckled, "I will see what's available." He vanished from sight to survey the area ahead, without anyone spotting him. He was gone for about thirty minutes before he reappeared. "I found a spot near a tree up ahead, it looks clear and I can't spot any 'undesirables' either visibly or on track." Scouts, Rangers, Huntresses, and some others, like Thieves, have the ability to track enemies in wide open areas, though it does not detect animals. A handy feature to possess for just such an occasion.

"Ok, we will make camp there for the night," Megildur decided. "I will need you to check our track often in this forsaken land." Gaal agreed and guided the others to the area he found.

On Oblivion, the sun never showed itself, just bleak and gloomy skies. By the time they made it to the campsite, the sky had changed from dismal to a darker shade of dismal. Megildur started a fire close to a tree, concealing the light from the flame in one direction. He worried about uninvited guests seeing their campfire and dropping in.

"Stand close to the fire and dry your clothes," Megildur said. "I do not want to keep the fire this large for too long. We should reach the Lich Queen's Keep tomorrow. Once we get past Ithriana, one way or another, we will use the Lharast Portal to reach

Kierhaven...wherever that may be." The travelers did not look comforted by the thought of having to face Ithriana.

Gaal joked, "I guess 'one way or another' our journey will soon be at an end."

This made the others laugh. That was another one of Gaal's talents, using humor to diffuse a tense situation. This helped Megildur loosen up a little, since the burden of having to save the world was a bit overwhelming at times. They sat around the fire in silence, contemplating Megildur's words. They let the fire dwindle once their clothes were dry. Each of them rested as Gaal took first watch. They envisioned their pending encounter with Ithriana, but none thought of what peril awaited them if they do make it through the portal.

CHAPTER 32: *Undead Disturbance*

Gaal woke Megildur sometime during the night. Something was definitely wrong, Megildur could tell by the look of dread on his face.

"What's wrong?" Megildur asked the Shade.

"I tracked a Vampire Thief coming in from the east," Gaal replied. "He'll be here any minute." Honoria and Scyleia awoke from the commotion.

"We have a Vampire Thief approaching," Megildur announced.

"Honoria and I can reveal the Thief once they are close enough," Scyleia admitted. "If you two can attack the Vampire once they are visible?"

"Are you certain about this, both of you as bait?" Megildur inquired.

Scyleia looked over to Honoria. "Yes, now put on your cloak and wait for our signal," Scyleia insisted.

Gaal vanished from sight and Megildur put on his invisibility cloak. Scyleia and Honoria laid down around the campfire. They knew this would give the Thief the best opportunity to steal from them. A few moments passed, Scyleia felt a slight tug at her waist and knew the Thief was making his move. She rolled on her back and cast a spell into the air that not only revealed the Vampire, but also slowed the Thief's movements. Honoria also rolled over and cast a spell that would cause some damage to the would-be Thief. Once they exposed the Vampire, Megildur and Gaal revealed themselves and began their assault. Fortunately, Thurin gave Megildur and Gaal the perfect weapons for this type of encounter. Gaal first snuck around behind the Vampire and plunged his dagger into the back of a fellow Thief. This caused an effect of releasing a fire power against the Vampire. The blood-sucking Thief turned to face Gaal, raised his dagger, but was unable to complete his blow thanks to Megildur. The Aelfborn plunged his dagger into the side of the Vampire. It released an intense light, which due to their unholy nature caused severe damage to it. Another power Vampires are vulnerable to. The Thief slumped downward. Megildur moved around to face his enemy.

The Vampire Thief hissed at Megildur, "I will not forget this, whelp!" Megildur held his sword to the Vampire's throat.

Megildur bellowed, "Good, then let me see if I can leave you with a lasting impression, bloodsucker!" He pulled his sword back, gaining enough strength to strike the Vampire, and decapitated him. The Thief's lifeless body toppled to the ground and his head rolled several feet away. Megildur turned to Gaal and asked, "How does your track look now?"

"Let me check," the Shade replied, gazing off in the distance to check for enemies on his track. "I see another Vampire. A Scout this time, no wait, the Scout is gone. It must have been traveling with this Thief and evacuated, sensing his friend die." Gaal turned to walk back to his friends, "Track is all clear now."

"Well, I will be unable to sleep after that fight," Megildur admitted after removing his dagger from the Vampire and wiping it off on its corpse. "Put some more wood on the fire so we can warm up a bit, before we continue on to the Lich Queen's Keep. I think the sky has lightened up, a little."

The Aelfborn was correct, dawn was a few hours away, but nobody could tell in Oblivion. The sky was always cloudy and bleak. The four of them warmed themselves by the campfire for a short time before

Megildur suggested they depart for the Keep. They traveled for some time in silence until Megildur spoke up.

"That was an impressive ambush back at the camp, Scyleia," the Aelfborn Lord commented. "I doubt we could have revealed him, let alone defeated the Thief, if you had not cast that spell against him."

Scyleia beamed, "Thank you, M'Lord." She gave a slight smile and continued walking.

"Yes, that was a good plan," Honoria added, bumping playfully into Scyleia.

The group continued walking for several more hours before seeing any activity, living or undead. Off in the distance they noticed a grouping of trees. They were not in their path, which was fortuitous for the explorers. The trees appeared dead and decaying. Below what branches remained, skeletal forms were visible. They moved in a circular motion around the trees, almost as if they were guarding...nothing. This caused Megildur to shiver a bit and then hasten his comrades on their way. Gaal would periodically stop to check track but he discovered the track was clear each time, until now.

Gaal exclaimed, "I got three Vampires on track!" This caused the rest of the group to halt.

Megildur fretted, "What direction are they coming from?" He dropped his gear and clutched his dagger, the Morloch's Betrayer of Fire. He also kept his Jen'e'tai sword at the ready.

"Checking now," Gaal replied. "West, they are west of here."

Megildur bellowed, "West? You dolt! Of course there are Vampires in that direction, what do you think Ithriana is?"

"Oh, good point," Gaal confessed, picking his gear back up and standing sheepishly next to his friends.

"Sorry, I thought our Vampire friends were back from earlier."

"Well I guess this is a good time for everyone to get their gear and weapons ready," Megildur said, pulling out his armor and invisibility cloak. This encounter with the Lich Queen would be the first real test of this armor Maethorion gave Megildur. He felt this was fitting, since they forged the armor for Sillestor and now Megildur wore it for battling the Elf Lord's daughter. "Are we ready?" Gaal, Honoria, and Scyleia followed the Aelfborn Lord toward the Keep.

As the Keep came into view, Megildur spouted off, "Gaal will use his Thief stealth, and Scyleia will wait here, just out of sight from the undead at the Keep. I wish we could take you with us, but without any stealth you will be an easy target."

Scyleia acknowledged, "I understand, good luck."

"You both wait for me just outside the door to Ithriana," Megildur commanded Honoria and Gaal. "I want us to enter at the same time, to increase our chance of success." The Aelfborn put his cloak on. "Let's go!"

None of them could now see where the other two stood. Someone bumped into Megildur; this was expected with all of them being undetectable. Megildur was glad his friends could not see the apprehension on his face. The sheer size of this malevolent place increased the dread in the Aelfborn's heart. Skulls and enormous bones used as large braces comprised the outer walls. Past the walls was an open courtyard with a massive building within the center. The outside guards paced back and forth, making navigation through them difficult without hitting anyone, or anything. Megildur stopped to look at the main archway and noticed a massive skull just above it, too large to come from a

Half-Giant. He assumed it was from a full sized Giant. Megildur looked back down from the archway just as a Vampire Scout materialized blocking the opening. The Vampire sneered directly at Megildur, as if the bloodsucker could see the Aelfborn Lord. It then waved its hand into the air to cast some sort of spell. There was a spark of light in the air and Megildur could then see Gaal in front of him and Honoria to the right.

"Oh no, I can see both of you!" Megildur announced.

"Our cover is blown!" Gaal retorted.

The travelers realized the guards detected them. All five of the guards drew their weapons. Megildur, Gaal, and Honoria also drew their weapons and prepared for battle. They thought the situation could not get worse, but it did.

Gaal shouted as he deflected an attack from a guard, "Uh, Megildur! We have more on track now!"

Megildur demanded, also trying to deflect numerous attacks, "How many?"

"It looks like...oh no," Gaal gasped. "Dozens of Elves!"

Megildur suspected the Elves could be from Aelarnost, in retaliation for them taking Caunion. He knew the three of them could not handle the five guards and numerous vengeful Elves.

"Pull back to Scyleia!" Megildur commanded. "Honoria, see if you can slow these guards a bit!"

The Bard waved her hands and cast a spell, slowing the guards. The guard's swings were half their original speed. The three of them turned and ran back to where they left Scyleia. Megildur approached Scyleia and could see her standing out in the open with a frantic look on her face. Her arms were down at her side. Something was wrong but the

Aelfborn did not know what. Honoria also noticed as the three of them approached her friend.

Honoria inquired, "Scyleia, are you alright?"

Scyleia screamed out, threw her hands around to her back, and fell. Megildur could see what was affecting Scyleia. A shape materialized over her motionless body, the Vampire Thief they encountered earlier. He was holding a blood-covered dagger in his left hand. He stabbed Scyleia in the back to avenge his death at the hands of Megildur.

The Vampire hissed, "I told you I would not forget, whelp!" The Thief vanished, leaving their friend bleeding on the ground.

Honoria screamed, "Scyleia!" She rushed to her friend's side and held her tight, "Stay with me!"

Scyleia muttered, "I am sorry, I did not see the Vampire Thief coming. I do not want to return to Fort Irsadeng. They will...torture me for...helping you escape. Don't let them..." The Bard beseeched her companions not to leave her in the Amazon safehold with her last breath, leaving Honoria crying over her friend's body.

Gaal gasped, "Megildur! Look, back at the Keep!"

Megildur turned to see the worst scenario he could imagine unfolding. Not only had the guards broke the slowing spell, but they also had reinforcements. Another two dozen guards joined the original guards and all were advancing on Megildur, Gaal, and Honoria. With a legion of undead progressing from the Keep and a large group of vengeful Elves coming from the other direction, it could get no worse.

CHAPTER 33: *Ithriana*

"Honoria, we have to move now!" Megildur begged his friend to leave Scyleia's body. "I promise if we make it out of this mess we will save her from the Amazon guild, but we have to get out of here now!"

Megildur reached down to help Honoria up from the ground. A flaming arrow soared past Megildur, a bit too close for comfort. The Aelfborn heard an agonizing shrill, from the one receiving the arrow he assumed. Fearing for his friend Gaal, he spun around to see the Vampire Scout standing next to him with a flaming arrow protruding from his chest. Two more flaming arrows and even a blast of fire followed the first arrow. The blast of fire propelled the Scout to the terrain, his lifeless body landed next to Gaal.

"Look to the east!" Gaal exclaimed, pointing in that direction.

Megildur turned to see a massive group of Elven Scouts, Rangers, and even Channelers proceeding to their location. He stood up and unsheathed his sword, but he wondered which direction to defend first. West of them was the undead guards and advancing from the east, an Elven army. Megildur began to move against the Elven army as another arrow flew well above him and struck one of the undead guards. This puzzled him since twice now an Elf did not assault Gaal, Honoria, or him.

Honoria blurted out, "Megildur, look over there!" She put her hand on his shoulder to stop his attack.

"Mother!" Megildur gasped, looking in the direction Honoria was pointing. He now realized the Elves charging were from the Gwaridorn tribe, the same as his mother, and not from the Dar Khelegur. Megildur was unable to determine which Elven race advanced upon them at first because of the dismal surroundings. The two Elven races were close in appearance. Only slight skin variations distinguished the two. The Gwaridorn's skin has a greenish hue while the Dar Khelegur's skin is alabaster in color. Nevertheless, Megildur was ecstatic they were on his side. Vanya spotted the three companions and rushed to them.

Discovering no harm befell her son, Vanya sighed. "Megildur, it's good to see you're alright."

Megildur cried out, "Gaal, Honoria, and I are alright, but a Vampire Thief killed Scyleia. We vanquished it earlier today and the bloodsucker returned with the Scout your group just defeated." He pointed to the Vampire Scout's body.

"I will send two Scouts to deal with the Vampire Thief!" Vanya commanded, motioning for two from her group to find the remaining Vampire. "Let us handle the undead around the Keep. You three should sneak inside using your stealth. You still have the cloaks, right?" Megildur told her they did, looking down at Scyleia. "I know you are worried about your friend, but you cannot save her if you do not complete this quest. Now go!"

Megildur knew his mother was right and this would be the best time to sneak inside the Keep. He put on his cloak and disappeared from sight, followed by Honoria and Gaal. The Aelfborn turned and continued on to the Keep's entrance. Since his mother's tribe was fighting with the undead of the Keep, Megildur crept past the archway without any resistance. Once inside the courtyard he found the vast edifice and the doors leading to Ithriana. No undead remained inside the courtyard with the Elven army at their backs. He removed his cloak so his friends could see him. Gaal appeared out of stealth just before reaching Megildur but Honoria was not there yet.

"What happened to Honoria?" Megildur asked Gaal.

"I am already here." She replied, removing her cloak. "I did not want to be first one to remove my cloak." She was still visibly distressed over the loss of her friend.

"Don't worry about Scyleia, we will save her," Megildur reassured Honoria. "But I need your help now. If we do not function as a team against Ithriana, we will never make it through the portal. So, are you with us?" Honoria took a deep breath and agreed. "Good, now I want to try to sneak past her if possible. Gaal, follow along the walls to the left side of the Keep. Honoria, take the right side. I will do my best to find the portal and not run into Ithriana. Confronting someone of her malevolence would be our last option."

Gaal and Honoria agreed that encountering Ithriana would not be wise. So all three of them went invisible once more and Megildur opened the door. The trio navigated a maze of hallways that turned left and right, but never gave a choice of altering routes. It was as if they were being guided to a single point inside the building. They finally reached what Megildur assumed was their destination. There sat a throne on the opposite end of the room. Behind that was an archway containing a green glowing aura. Megildur assumed that was the Lharast Portal. He took a few steps toward the portal, something unexpected happened, laughter.

"Did you feeble mortals think you would evade my detection?" A voice echoed from the dark. "I changed the halls within my Keep to guide you straight to me. Between the abomination, the chaos demon, and the half-breed, I am not sure which one smells the worst! You did not provide me with a very good selection. Could you not have brought along an Elf or at least a Minotaur thrall? They are so much fun to snuggle up to after I've drained their blood, but you will have to do." There was a long silence, none of the companions wanted to give up their location. "What, no banter from the inferior beings? Alright, let's finish this!"

An intense light radiated from the center of the room, followed by a blast of energy. The three travelers, along with Ithriana, were now visible in the room. Most were near the center, including the Lich Queen, who hovered above the floor. This was the same as the first Vampire Megildur encountered.

Ithriana teased, "That's better, now we can play!" Like a predator with its prey, she decided to romp with Megildur, Gaal, and Honoria, now that she exposed them.

Honoria jested, "So you want to use magic? I can play that game too!" The Nephilim transformed into her chaos demon form and ascended into the air.

With one wave of Ithriana's hand she forced Honoria down and with a wave of her other hand she blocked all three of them from using any powers. With incredible speed, the Lich Queen struck each of the companions with her bare fists, driving each of them to adjacent walls. Their flaccid bodies toppled to the flooring. Megildur and Gaal were motionless from the intense blows, so the undead Queen focused her attention on Honoria. The Bard was already weak, bleeding, and slumped over, which pleased the Vampire.

Ithriana taunted Honoria, "I expected more from you, being a chaos demon!" She picked the Nephilim up off the floor by her neck. "Pathetic!"

Megildur, seeing his friend in trouble, unsheathed his sword and charged Ithriana. Without looking in the Aelfborn's direction, she swung Honoria around using her as a club and pelted Megildur with her body. This bludgeoned Megildur but also rendered the Bard unconscious. Gaal saw his opportunity to attack. Ithriana turned her back. Being the Thief that he was, backstabbing was a common assault. He drew his serpentine daggers and crept up behind the Lich Queen, she held Honoria in her clutches. Before he could get within striking distance, Ithriana vanished from sight, dropping the Nephilim to the surface. Gaal spun around in a circle but did not see his opponent. An icy cold hand reached past his neck, followed by the rest of the freezing cold arm. The Lich Queen had materialized behind the Shade, squeezing the life out of him with her arm completely around his neck.

Ithriana bellowed, "You are all worthless and frail!" She continued to squeeze the life from Gaal. "I would be doing the world a favor by keeping you here to torture for an eternity!"

"So you can only attack us using cheap tricks and deceit?" Megildur scoffed, pulling himself up from the floor. The Aelfborn Lord knew this would be his lone opportunity to distract Ithriana. He hoped she would loosen her grip and allow Gaal to live.

"What's this?" Ithriana chided as she released Gaal. "Do you dare challenge me, boy? I have crushed hundreds of men who tested my powers!" By this time, the Lich Queen had made it across the room and now had Megildur by the throat, lifting him from the ground. She used her other hand to impale Megildur through his chest. Her nails shattered against Megildur's armor. If not for this elite armor, Ithriana would have pierced the Aelfborn's heart and prematurely terminated his life...and quest. "Ah, what is this? You have the audacity to don my father's armor in my presence? That will not save you!" The wicked Queen once again cackled at her prey. "What made you think you could come here and defeat me?"

Megildur chortled as the Vampire squeezed his throat, "Because I know your weakness!"

Ithriana boasted, "I have no weaknesses, feeble mortal! What are you babbling about?"

Megildur gathered his last bit of strength and spat, "Your arrogance!"

Ithriana wasted time crowing about herself and Gaal regained his energy. He picked up his weapons, one of them being the dagger Thurin gave him, and crept up behind the Lich Queen. The Shade plunged the dagger into her back. The weapon unleashed its fire damage upon Ithriana with a bright fiery light emanating from the wound. She let out an agonizing shrill, so high pitched that both Megildur and Gaal covered their ears. Once the Vampire released her grip on Megildur, he pulled out his dagger that Thurin gifted to him and plunged it into her chest. This dagger released its holy power with a light even brighter than the last one, but caused the same result in Ithriana, agonizing pain. She spun around, smiting both Megildur and Gaal in opposite directions. This action also forced the daggers from her body. The still screaming Lich Queen then faded away in a cloud of thick black smoke.

Megildur sat up from the floor and muttered, "Gaal, are you alright?"

"I feel like that Half Giant in Thieves' Den sat on me, but I will be alright," he replied. "Where's Honoria?"

Gaal and Megildur rushed to Honoria, as fast as they could in their current condition. Megildur elevated her up slightly to try to revive the Nephilim. She was still in her chaos demon form. They would have to assess her injuries at a later time. She started to awaken after a few moments.

Megildur pleaded, "Honoria, wake up!" He shook her. "We have to move, now."

The Bard opened her eyes and sat up further. "Where is she? Did you vanquish her?"

"I do not know about vanquishing her but she has retreated, for now," Megildur replied. "Can you stand? We should vacate this place."

"I think I can move," she winced, trying to stand. "But I feel like a worg's chew toy."

Megildur and Gaal helped Honoria stand and continue on to the portal. The companions picked up their belongings along the way, since they figured they would need all their resources for the next part of the quest. The three stood before the Lharast Portal. Nobody knew what awaited them on the other side. However, anything at this moment was an improvement over Ithriana.

Gaal, of course, broke the silence first. "Well, we didn't just come this far to just stand here waiting for the Lich Queen to return." He released Honoria's arm, now that she was able to stand on her own. The Shade looked at both of his friends and stepped into the green glowing portal.

Megildur and Honoria looked at each other. "Ready?" She asked.

"No, but do you want to wait and see if Ithriana returns?" Megildur smiled at Honoria and both of them stepped into the portal.

CHAPTER 34: The Terror of Terrors

Megildur again saw the glowing circles, similar to the ones from the runegate. Once the symbols faded, he found himself, and Honoria, somewhere else entirely. The air was dank and a dense mist enveloped the surround landscape. They could not see far into the distance, just a few yards or so ahead of where they walked. The Aelfborn also found it hard to breathe due to the thin air. It felt like they were at a high altitude, which would explain the cloud-like atmosphere. Honoria was regaining her strength and able to walk unassisted now.

"Where's Gaal?" Megildur asked. They had not seen him since arriving. Honoria looked just as lost as Megildur. "Better find him before we encounter anyone else." They walked a few feet. The Shade Thief materialized in front of them, and with a shocked look on his face.

Megildur scolded, "Gaal, you must stop doing that!" Both the Aelfborn Lord and Honoria had to catch their breath after Gaal startled them.

"You two are going to want to see this," Gaal proclaimed. He turned and guided the others past a few dead looking trees, through some green foliage, and stopped next to a ledge. "Don't get too close, but look down."

The three of them stood next to one another and looked over the edge. All they could see were clouds and nothingness. Shocked, and a bit terrified, the companions took a few steps back.

Honoria stammered with a puzzled look on her face, looking at her surroundings, "W-where are we?"

"It's supposed to be the ruins of Kierhaven, but I do not know where in Aerynth Kierhaven was supposed to be," Megildur replied. "We could be at the top of a mountain peak or perhaps we are in the clouds above Aerynth."

"Well, that would explain the atmosphere around us," Gaal remarked, also looking at the surroundings. "Are you really thinking what I think you're implying? Is that we are standing on solid ground floating in the clouds. Kierhaven is a hovering island!"

"Let's survey the area, but stay close," Megildur commanded. "And for All-Father's sake, DO NOT fall off the edge!"

The three friends split up and went in different directions. Dead trees and harsh shrubbery covered the area, so they found it impossible to move silently with the constant snapping of twigs. Every bush snagging them like they had claws of their own. It was difficult to move about and eerie to think that each tug could be something other than just dead foliage. Each of them had to proceed with caution...wherever they were.

Gaal shouted, "Hey, the ground is..."

The Shade's silence concerned Megildur. The ground trembled and the air was fouler. Megildur changed his direction toward Gaal, fearing the worst had happened to him. Before long, he saw much of the mist up ahead circling in a vortex funnel motion. Trying to investigate his friend's location, and the mysterious behavior of the mist, he observed Gaal running in his direction.

"Get down!" Gaal shouted, diving for the Aelfborn Lord. He tackled him and covered his own head.

Unsure of why his friend just attacked him, Megildur looked back in the direction Gaal ran from. He noticed a giant stream of fire projected in the air above them. He too covered his head but could feel the intense heat from the flames on his back. A few moments of blistering heat, Megildur looked back to see the source of the fire...a dragon.

Megildur yelled, "Move Gaal!"

Gaal scrambled to his feet, followed by Megildur. Both scurried away from their behemoth aggressor. Honoria heard the yelling and sprinted toward them, but Megildur grabbed her by the arm and forced her to join them in evading the predator. Gaal found a spot behind some jagged rocks to hide and guided the others to him.

Megildur peered around his refuge to examine the monster. Crimson scales swathed the monstrosity from head to tail. The crevices between its scales glowed like molten lava, which matched the intense heat the dragon emitted. When it opened its mouth all that Megildur could see were rows of jagged teeth encompassing the inferno within the dragon. Two long spikey horns adorned the top of its skull, running toward the monster's spinal plates. It stood several stories high with an even longer wingspan. Razor-like claws resided on each appendage except for the tail, but that appeared deadly due to its magnitude alone. The Aelfborn stared into the bright yellow fiery eyes of the beast and dread filled his heart. Megildur withdrew back to the safety of his friends.

"What are we running from?" Honoria demanded to know.

"A massive dragon!" Gaal exclaimed. "I explored the area and stumbled across him. He was just as pleased to see me as I was to see him!"

"That was not just any dragon," Megildur added. "Did you see his eyes? One of them appeared wounded with what looked like a shaft of a spear embedded within."

"Oh, by the All-Father!" Honoria gasped. "You mean it was..."

"Yes," Megildur interrupted. "That dragon is the Terror of Terrors. The one the Irekei call Kryquo'khalin. The same dragon that awoke from deep within Aerynth centuries ago and almost destroyed the Elven race. It's the reason Thurin crafted Shadowbane, so they could use the weapon to defeat him if he ever returned."

"I heard the one weapon to wound the dragon was the Spear of Kolaur. Kolaur was a Dark Chaos Lord," Honoria commented. "Kenaryn took the weapon as his prize for helping the All-Father and the other Gods defeat the hordes of chaos before Aerynth's creation. Kenaryn renamed the spear Callanthyr. After he broke off the tip of the spear in the dragon's eye, Thurin took the remaining piece of the spear to forge Shadowbane. Thurin used the metals from the chaos weapon and mixed them with minerals from deep within the world to..."

Megildur hissed at Honoria, "We do not need a history lesson right now! We need a plan to recover Shadowbane, not a lesson in Metallurgy!" The Aelfborn could see his words wounded his friend. "I'm sorry. I shouldn't have let the burning blood of my kin govern my anger."

"Thank you," Honoria responded. "As for a strategy, I can recall many tactics from epic battles but none of them involved a dragon. Most people avoid the drakes residing in the northlands, for obvious reasons." She had a look of frustration on her face, "Even if we did have a plan, we have not found Shadowbane."

"I spotted a stone tree, as the dragon discovered me," Gaal added. "It's in that direction." The Shade pointed, remaining behind the rock formation for safety.

The ground stopped trembling for a moment, which made the travelers even more nervous. They heard a deep and sinister laugh that chilled them to the bone. This caused their bodies to quiver. Then the unexpected happened, the ancient drake spoke. "So you come before me seeking glory and riches, then hide like cowards?"

Megildur did his best to contain his fear. "Gaal, you vanish using your stealth and climb into that tree." The Aelfborn pointed toward a distant tree. "Honoria, try to lure the dragon to you but do not get too close. The dragon will walk below Gaal and he will jump onto the dragon's head and distract it by attempting to wound its other eye."

Gaal's eyes widened, a look of terror now filled his coal black eyes. With a terrified voice he spoke, "You want me to do what?"

"Unless anyone has a better plan, this is the best I can devise," Megildur replied. "I'm the only one that can pull Shadowbane from the stone tree and I can't do that if that dragon has roasted me alive!"

"We're not certain anyone can pull that sword from the tree!" Honoria remarked.

"True," Megildur sighed. "If retrieving Shadowbane is impossible, do you think the All-Father would have given this task to me? Or that Thurin would have returned to Aerynth, after being gone for hundreds of years, if they did not know I could?" His friends conceded. "I know you're terrified just thinking about what we must do, but it's that fear that lets us know we are still alive. Aerynth has been in complete anarchy since the Traitor used Shadowbane for that one treacherous act. This is our moment to restore that balance that the world needs so desperately. With this one act we can right the wrongs, open the gates to Heaven and Hell, and finally have a place we can call home." The Aelfborn Lord placed a hand on each of his friend's shoulders. "We must have faith that the All-Father knows best. I cannot do this alone. So are you with me?"

Honoria and Gaal looked at each other and the Shade replied, "It's an insane plan. None of us will make it, but if we die here today, at least we can return again if we fail!" He smirked at Megildur, who shook his head in disbelief.

"We are with you," Honoria replied. "Let me apply a spell to increase our resistance to fire. I will need to keep recasting it, but at least it will help against that dragon."

"Thank you both," Megildur sighed. "I will rush for the Stone Tree once you have the dragon's attention. Good luck!"

Megildur watched Gaal vanish and Honoria move into a better position to see the dragon. The Nephilim waited for a few minutes and then she began making noise and waving, in order for the dragon to notice her. It did not take long until a fireball raced past the Bard. It would have struck her, if she had not jumped to avoid it. She led the dragon down a path, away from Megildur's objective, and toward Gaal. The Thief dropped from the tree, once the beast was below him. He pulled out his dagger but found it challenging to attempt an attack, he hung on to save his life during this wild ride.

Megildur could see the back of the dragon. He scrambled to his feet and sprinted in the direction Gaal pointed out. He encountered dense mist on this side of the ruins, likely because no dragon existed here to burn off the haze. He stumbled around like a drunken blind beggar looking for his next mug of ale, but eventually found the tree. The colossal Stone Tree looked like other Trees of Life, except for its composition, solid rock. Embedded into its trunk he found a sword with a black blade and gold wire spun around the hilt. Megildur snuck toward the tree and could see this was truly Shadowbane. The guard of the sword had the mark of the same beast his friends now battled. The closer the Aelfborn Lord got to the sword, the brighter the rune markings shown on the blade. He gripped the hilt of the sword tight, closed his eyes, and pulled with all his might. The blade moved, but only budged an inch before something hit Megildur from behind. The force knocked him against the stone tree and then to the ground. He looked up to see the attacker had dark red skin and looked half-crazed, an Irekei.

The Irekei shouted, "I won't allow you to harm Kryquo'khalin!" He grabbed Shadowbane and yanked with all his strength, but the sword would not dislodge for the desert dweller.

Megildur knew his companions could not contain the dragon and he needed to act fast to help them. He scurried to his feet, unsheathed his Jen'e'tai blade, and commanded the Irekei "Move away from that tree, I must vanquish the beast to save Aerynth!"

This displeased the Irekei, who responded by stepping back, drawing his sword, and striking at Megildur. The Aelfborn was able to block the attack and counter with his own. The agile Irekei dodged the assault. This exchange of swordplay went on for several minutes until the Irekei disarmed Megildur. The Irekei held his sword to Megildur's neck and backed him into the hilt of Shadowbane. It shocked the Aelfborn that he came this far and faced so many adversities, only to fail at the end of his quest.

"On your knees, half-breed!" The Irekei commanded.

Megildur was out of options for the moment, so once again an adversary forced him to drop to his knees. The red-skinned man raised his sword above his head to strike him down. Megildur knew it was now or never. The Aelfborn Lord raised his hands, grabbed the hilt of Shadowbane once more, and heaved with all of his remaining strength. Finally, the mighty sword escaped from its imprisonment in the old Stone Tree. However, the blade found a new space to occupy, the Irekei's skull. The assailant dropped his weapon and collapsed, being the first one struck down by Shadowbane in over a hundred years. Megildur rose, planted one foot on the Irekei's flaccid chest, and pulled Shadowbane from his head. He wiped off the blade on his rival's apparel and for a brief moment held the sword up to admire its craftsmanship. That moment came to an abrupt stop. Megildur heard an ear-piercing scream from Honoria. The Aelfborn sprinted in his friend's direction.

Megildur could hear the dragon speaking. "Now, my dilemma is whether to eat the pasty one first, or the spicy demon. Oh, what a difficult decision I have to make."

The ancient beast let out another sinister laugh. He had Honoria pinned to the ground under his front left claw and Gaal gripped tightly in midair within his right. The dragon opened his gigantic jaw and pulled Gaal into range of its horrible breath. This was apparent by the nauseous look on the Shade's face.

Just before the beast could devour his pale friend, Megildur flew through the air from a nearby tree branch and landed inside the beast's jaws. He grabbed onto one of the dragon's massive teeth with his left hand and held onto Shadowbane with the other hand.

Megildur bellowed, "Try chewing on a half-breed!" He plunged the gleaming ebony blade deep into the roof of the beast's mouth and into its skull. The dragon's jagged fang pressed firmly against Megildur's forearm but his armor proved its worth by averting the piercing of his limb. The monster began to thrash from side to side, which threw Megildur and Gaal away from the beast. This action also freed Honoria from the scaly claws of the dragon. The beast struggled in agony trying to dispel the sword and still manage to kill his prey. Alas, the dragon, unable to escape from the blade, reared up and collapsed. The ground trembled and shook as the giant dragon fell. The sky thundered, as if trying to announce the terror's dreadful end.

CHAPTER 35: Separate Ways

The Nephilim crept up to the carcass of the dragon. She peered at Megildur and Gaal, "Is it dead?" She took her finger and poked the enormous drake's tail, holding her breath that it did not respond. She slowly backed away just in case resurrection was one of its abilities. "You know, just to be certain."

Megildur laughed, "Well I am not checking for a heartbeat. Let's just collect what we came for and get back through the portal."

"So, we completed our quest?" Gaal asked. "We're finished?"

"Well we retrieved Shadowbane as the All-Father commanded," Megildur replied, walking over to the dragon and yanking the mighty sword from its corpse. "But I'm certain we're not done. Let's get back and see how the Gwaridorn Elves faired against the undead army, they may require our assistance."

Before reaching the mystical entry, Megildur turned back to see the dragon's carcass had vanished. This not only puzzled him, but distressed him as well. Did the dragon regain consciousness and slither away? Maybe he just respawned? He did not want to tell the others. He was trying to hurry his friends along without alarming anyone to the dragon's disappearance.

Megildur guided his friends through first. When he went through his companions were waiting inside Ithriana's Keep. To their surprise, the main room where they engaged the Lich Queen was still empty. Weapons at the ready, they remained alert for any unexpected confrontation.

"Let's get outside," Megildur insisted. He did not want to have another encounter with the undead queen. Honoria and Gaal made it through the doorway before the door slammed shut behind them, trapping Megildur inside. The temperature of the air plummeted and the Aelfborn could see his breath. Creaking emanated from every corner of the room, as if the building was breathing.

A sinister voice crawled down Megildur's spine, "Did you really think this was over, boy?" He heard Ithriana's voice, but she lacked physical form. "I have died many times before, but I am still here. Death does not want me, only misery."

Megildur's voice crackled, "I defeated you once, I can do it again. And this time I possess Shadowbane, the weapon that vanquished the Terror of Terrors!"

With an ominous laugh she bellowed, "You fool! Do you believe that you destroyed Kryquo'khalin? He's older than I am and survived attacks from more worthy opponents than you!"

"I am not afraid of you!" Megildur replied. He was trying to control his emotions. By this time, he wielded Shadowbane and was ready for anything, he hoped.

Ithriana chuckled, "You reek of fear boy! Do not be afraid, I need my beauty sleep before I disembowel you and hang your entrails on my wall. You may leave, for now."

Megildur leaving her in a weakened state from their first brawl, reached for the door exiting her Keep. Megildur's friends barged in, weapons drawn.

"Megildur, are you alright?" Honoria asked. "What happened with the door closing?"

Megildur snarled, "Just a goodbye wish from Ithriana. We should get far away from her Keep, before she regains her full strength." The Aelfborn was trying to remain calm, but that encounter chilled him to the bone, literally.

The three travelers made their way outside and into an ongoing battle between the Gwaridorn Elves, his mother's tribe, and the undead army. It did not appear that the Elves were doing well, so Megildur decided to end this. With Shadowbane still in hand, he walked to the edge of the skirmish and thrust the ancient sword into the sky. The clouds parted, allowing the sunlight to burst down upon him, and reflected on the dark blade. Instead of absorbing the light, as you would expect anything black to do, it caused the blade to emit shadows in every direction. However, instead of evil lurking and thriving in these shadows the undead army met fear and dread. These soulless creatures did not rejoice in Shadowbane's reflections but instead absconded for the safety of the Keep. This was the first time in over a hundred years anyone in Aerynth had seen the last sword forged by Thurin. Silence fell upon the remaining Elven armies, but one word emanated from everyone's lips…"Shadowbane!"

Vanya sighed, approaching her son, "You retrieved Shadowbane?" She embraced her son, after he lowered the weapon. "Thank you for saving us from those creatures. I am not sure how much longer we would have lasted. Are you injured?" The Elven Princess motioned for her healers to attend to Gaal and Honoria, who both looked a bit ragged.

"I am fine," Megildur replied. He pulled his mother aside and whispered, "Thanks to you and your army. That was just the distraction I needed."

Vanya proudly responded, "Son, you are the heir to Cambruin and rightful successor to his throne in Mellissar. You have rule over the Kingdoms of Men and allegiances from many races in Aerynth."

"Mellissar?" Megildur inquired. "You mean New Mellissar, right?"

"No, I am referring to the High Kingdom Cambruin formed. Mellissar became the capital, reuniting the Kingdoms of Men," Vanya educated her son. This was all new to him since Vanya and Aedan kept the truth of their noble heritage from Megildur and Aranel. "I think a familiar tutor might be able to explain this better than I can. He did live during the time of Cambruin, after all." Vanya looked past Megildur to another person approaching behind her son.

"Zeristan!" Megildur remarked. He met the old Wizard and embraced him. This lasted a moment until he realized his mother's entire army was staring at the new High King. "Uh, I am glad to see you." The Aelfborn regained his composure and gave Zeristan a slight grin. "So what kept you from assisting us this entire time? We could have used the most powerful Wizard in all of Aerynth."

"I suspect the All-Father would not have approved my helping with the quest He set you out upon," Zeristan replied. "And besides, I had to prepare for your arrival once you retrieved Shadowbane."

"How did you know I would succeed?" Megildur asked the wise mage.

"I never doubted your chance for success," he grinned at the Aelfborn champion. "Now, let's get you back to Mellissar for your coronation."

Honoria pleaded, "Megildur, wait! What are we going to do about Scyleia? We cannot leave her in that awful place after all she has done for us."

"She is right," Vanya interjected. "We would not have known you needed help on Oblivion, if not for

Honoria and Scyleia. They sent the request for assistance along the Bard's network."

Megildur looked puzzled, "Request for assistance?" He turned to Honoria and stared.

"It was actually Scyleia's idea," Honoria commented. "Remember on Stormvald when we chanted with the Bard's network? It was then out in the tundra that we asked for help. If she did not think of asking, we would not have made it past the undead army."

"Honoria is correct," Megildur replied. "So here's what we will do. Mother, take Honoria and your army to Fort Irsadeng to rescue Scyleia."

"It would honor us," Vanya replied. She smiled at Honoria, who was happy to hear this.

Megildur continued. "Meanwhile, Zeristan, Gaal, and I need to gather a few friends and head to the desert. I also have someone I wish to save." He grinned at Zeristan. The Wizard knew exactly whom the Aelfborn referred to, Zabrina. Gaal, on the other hand, looked disgusted with the idea of traveling to the desert, but he did promise to repay Megildur in exchange for saving his life. Megildur turned to address all who were present. "We will meet in Mellissar, after saving a few friends, and rejoice in the new age of peace!" He thrusted Shadowbane into the air and the crowd cheered. The cheering died down. He turned to Honoria and placed a dagger in her hands. "You might need this." The Bard looked down to see she had just received the Morloch's Betrayer of Truth Thurin had given Megildur in Korvambar.

"Thank you, M'Lord," Honoria responded. "We will meet you in Mellissar once we rescue Scyleia." She looked concerned for the Aelfborn Lord. "You are going to the desert to save Zabrina?" Megildur nodded. "Be careful, the Temple of the Cleansing

Flame is powerful. I doubt they will release her willingly."

Megildur chuckled, "Oh I know they will not, that's why I am picking up some help along the way." Megildur laid a comforting hand on Honoria's shoulder. "You save Scyleia and we will meet in Mellissar. Good luck." Honoria worried about where Megildur was going, but knew he could handle himself by now.

Vanya had her Wizards started recalling the Elven army back to the Oblivion runegate, Honoria followed. They would have to travel through a few runegates to reach one on the mainland and then open a portal closer to the Amazon safehold. Megildur, Zeristan, and Gaal followed the Elven army to the runegate on the mainland, but Zeristan opened a separate runegate portal once Honoria, Vanya, and her army had made it through to their destination. The wise Wizard did not want to confuse anyone on which portal to use.

"Where are we going?" Gaal asked. "I thought we were going to the desert?"

"We are, but first we need to gather some old friends along the way," Megildur replied. "The Temple of the Cleansing Flame is not going to just hand over Zabrina without a fight."

Gaal gasped, "Those religious nuts? Oh man, I should have gone with Honoria!"

"Do not worry, pale one," Zeristan replied, stepping off the last runegate and applying the spell for fast travel on all of their boots. "Megildur has a plan."

The Shade rolled his eyes but continued with Megildur and Zeristan. He hoped this plan did not involve him dying since he still had no desirable home to return to. With that thought, Gaal remained steadfast in continuing his allegiance to the new High King.

CHAPTER 36: *Saving Scyleia*

Off the runegate, Honoria, Vanya, and her army turned toward Fort Irsadeng. They made good time since they did not travel with siege weapons or servants. All who traveled with Honoria and Vanya were fighters, rogues, mages, and healers. They did not plan to overthrow the Amazon safehold; they just wanted to secure a friend's safety.

Their hastened pace made for a quicker return to the Amazon safehold. Allowing them to return within a day and arrive under the cover of darkness. Vanya divided her army into five factions, one for each corner of the safehold and her group. Several Scouts, Assassins, and one Bard, Honoria, comprised Vanya's unit. Once the four support groups were in place around the outer perimeter, Vanya moved her group forward.

She advanced on the weakest point where she thought there would be fewer Warriors on guard. The Elven Princess spied a guard along the wall that detected her presence, so she seized her bow and released a single arrow. The guard dropped before alerting the rest of the safehold. However, Vanya knew it would not be long before the guard respawned, alerting the others. She pushed her way through a small opening in the perimeter fence and the rest of her group followed. Honoria guided them the rest of the way toward the holding cells where Scyleia would be. They reached the outer wall of the prisoner barracks. Honoria could hear voices inside. She stopped the group and listened for her friend. From the voices she heard, it sounded like the brute who bullied Honoria and her friends last time was now torturing Scyleia.

The brute bellowed, "You little wench, did you think I was finished with you? The beating I gave you earlier will not compare to what I will do to you tonight. Before you are about to die, I will bring in a Priestess and have her heal you again."

Scyleia murmured with what breath she had left, "Have you not tired of beating me yet?"

The Half Giant laughed, "I can do this all night!" Honoria could hear the brute smack Scyleia and her friend wince from the pain.

Honoria heard enough. She transformed into her Nephilim form for additional strength, threw on her invisibility cloak, and crept past the first door into the building. She could see where they held Scyleia. The Amazons shackled her friend to the wall, and it looked like she had been there for some time. Honoria moved into position behind the brute and unsheathed the Morloch's Betrayer of Truth that Megildur had given her.

The brute taunted Scyleia, clenching her massive fists, "Are you ready for more?"

Honoria bellowed, "Yes, I am!" She plunged the dagger into the back of the Half Giant with all her might.

A bright light, from the weapon's power, filled the room. Blood flowed out of the gapping gash along with a horrific howl from the Half Giant. The brute turned around with what life force she could gather and reached for the Nephilim. Grabbing her by the horns atop of her head, she forced the Nephilim's head back, attempting to bash her brains into the wall.

Vanya stepped inside the doorway with her bow aimed at the brute.

"No!" Honoria screamed out. "This bitch is mine!"

The Nephilim reached around to pull the dagger from the back of the Half Giant and plunged it into the brute's chest, ensuring her death. The Morloch's Betrayer of Truth held true to its reputation in vanquishing evil. Honoria tasted vengeance.

Vanya bellowed, "Grab your friend and let's get out of here! That brute will alert the others upon return!"

Honoria reclaimed her dagger and proceeded to free Scyleia from her shackles. Scyleia gasped, "You, you came for me?" She was half-alive and severely beaten. Honoria felt it would have been more humane if the Half Giant had killed her and ended her suffering.

"I told you I would," Honoria replied with a smile. She used a set of keys she found on the waist of the lifeless brute to unlock the shackles. Scyleia fell into her arms, unable to stand on her own. Honoria moved out of the building, assisting Scyleia, although they did not make it far before turmoil erupted.

A shout pierced the night air, "Intruders!" The alert came from the guard Vanya eliminated earlier.

They all knew this was no longer a mission of stealth but one of survival. Arrows and spells began flying from each of the four corners of the safehold. It was the Elven army trying to cover Vanya and her group. Fleeing was the only option since they knew they could not stay and fight. If, and when, an Elf kills an Amazon, the Amazon member respawns at this safehold. The Elven army was not so fortunate. They would respawn a half a world away. The Elves would all perish if this battle continued.

One of Vanya's Scouts ran ahead to secure the opening they came through earlier, but was unsuccessful. Some commotion radiated from that general direction. The Scout flew out from the darkness and landed on the ground. They could then see who the instigator of the scuffle was, the Half Giant. The same brute they vanquished in the prison cell earlier.

The brute laughed, "Did you fools think you could just walk in undetected and then leave without a fight?"

"No, but there are always other ways out," Vanya replied, motioning to one of her mages on a nearby corner of the safehold.

A circular beam of light surrounded the Half Giant and she could no longer advance upon Vanya and her group. The mage had surrounded the brute with a root spell. This stopped all movement in any direction. Then one by one, Vanya and her group vanished from the brute's sight, followed by the Elven army withdrawing from the safehold walls.

The Half Giant thundered, "They recalled, search the perimeter for them!"

The Elven healers had indeed summoned Vanya, Honoria, Scyleia, and the rest of her group out. The Amazon Scouts surveyed the surrounding area, but by the time they rallied their forces, the Elven army was gone. Vanya and her kin absconded back to the shore and departed on their ships. Scyleia was starting to show some signs of life, after a healer assisted her recovery.

Scyleia murmured to Vanya and Honoria, "Thank you so much for coming back for me. They began torturing me right after I returned to their Tree of Life." She started showing her weakness by drifting in and out of consciousness.

Honoria whispered, "Get some rest, my friend. We will talk after you get some sleep." She waited for a minute until Scyleia closed her eyes and she turned to leave the room with Vanya. "I owe you for saving Scyleia."

"It was the least I could do for the people who helped my son," Vanya replied with a smile. The smile faded as she spoke next of Megildur, "I do hope he's careful in the desert. Those Cleansing Flame cultists can be dangerous." Honoria stopped walking and looked at Vanya with empathic eyes. She had the same worried thoughts too.

CHAPTER 37: The Desert Flower

Megildur, Zeristan, and Gaal stepped off the desert runegate into blistering heat and dry sand. Instantaneously their spit dried up, their tongues swelled, and they felt grit in their teeth, among other places. All three travelers found the temperature and terrain undesirable. They preferred the lush forest regions of Aerynth.

Gaal grumbled, "Why are we down here again? This place is worse than Oblivion!"

"You think this is bad, try walking through this desert for days with no water and no clue where you are going," Megildur replied. "Oh yeah, watch out for Manticores. They will sneak right up on you!"

Zeristan grinned at the Aelfborn's comments. He reapplied the spell on all their boots to decrease their traveling time in this wretched place. "It's this way," Zeristan pointed to the west and the three of them departed.

For hours, they traveled until they reached their destination. There, spread out amongst the sand dunes, was the Temple of the Cleansing Flame safehold, "Gray Sands" in the distant horizon. Megildur hardly recognized the compound. The first time he arrived upon the back of a Half Giant and departed under the cover of darkness.

"Alright, here's what I need from you two," Megildur laid out his plan for Zeristan and Gaal. "I am going to need both of you invisible. Gaal, I want you to infiltrate the safehold and once I call for you, take their leader prisoner. Zeristan, I need you to help fight off any attackers outside the safehold. Also, I will need a lightshow in the sky from you. Sound good?" The two agreed and vanished from sight.

Megildur waited several minutes and then began walking toward the front gates. Once he was within shouting range of the safehold, he stopped. Archers lined the walls near the main gate and a voice from atop of the wall bellowed, "Stop there, heretic! What brings you before the Temple of the Cleansing Flame?"

Megildur roared, "That's a matter I wish to discuss with your leader."

The voice shouted back, "He does not concern himself with blasphemous peasants, now depart before I have you slain where you stand!"

Megildur grew tired of this debate and decided to escalate it by commanding, "You bring him before me, or I will devastate this safehold and leave no one standing!"

They must not have taken kindly to this threat. The archers released several arrows at the Aelfborn. Before they could reach their intended target, Zeristan appeared in midair and disintegrated the arrows, leaving dust particles to fall from the sky. The Wizard then released several energy bolts at the archers along the wall, knocking each of them off the structure and onto the ground. Once again, the Wizard vanished from sight. Several moments of silence went by before someone appeared at the nearby corner wall to address Megildur.

With an arrogant tone the voice demanded, "Why do you bother me, you irreverent whelp?"

Megildur returned the arrogant question with one of his own, "Are you the leader of the Temple of the Cleansing Flame?"

The voice retorted, "Yes, I am their ruler! Now what do you want before I release my army to decimate you and that annoying Wizard?"

Megildur commanded, "I am Lord Megildur, future High King over the Kingdoms of Men, and I demand the release of Zabrina and her mother!"

"You want who released?" The ruler inquired, sounding thoroughly confused. "And who did you say you are?" One of the guards stepped up to his master and whispered something in his ear. "What, you risked your life coming before me for a slave? What will you offer for the slave's release?"

Megildur bellowed, "I will allow your insolent head to remain where it is and I will let your buildings stand!"

The ruler laughed, "One boy and a single Wizard against the strength of my army?"

The Aelfborn Lord snickered, "Who said I only brought one other person with me?" He looked into the air in the Wizard's direction, "Now Zeristan!"

The Wizard materialized and released a lightshow high into the sky above his head. This puzzled the ruler of the Gray Sands safehold, who just stared at Megildur in disbelief. Within moments of the lightshow, the ground began to rumble, growing in intensity. One of the guards near the ruler shouted and pointed to the horizon. Countless numbers were now within visual range, coming over the sand dunes. The line of soldiers kept going on and on. The safehold was besieged. Megildur's "friends", the Centaur Cohort and the Church of the All-Father, comprised the encompassing army.

The overwhelmed leader threatened, "I could just order her removal from our Tree of Life and have her executed! She would respawn to an unknown location somewhere in Aerynth and you will never find her!"

"If so, your fate will be hers!" Megildur countered. "Gaal, now!"

Upon hearing his friend's command, the Thief materialized behind the Gray Sand's ruler with a dagger to his throat. The ruler's eyes widened at both the thought of the pain from the blade and the sight of the surrounding armies closing in. Even though he would just return inside his own safehold, he knew the Thief would keep playing this game of cat and mouse. Also, he detested the thought of his guild losing to a half-breed.

The leader commanded, "Release the wench and the old hag!"

Moments later, the gates opened. Zabrina stood behind them with her mother and both appeared tattered and bruised. She dashed from the safehold, which did not surprise anyone considering her mistreated condition. Megildur ran to her and the two shared a deep embrace in the middle of the blistering desert.

Zabrina murmured, "M-megildur, I prayed I would see you again one day!" She pulled back from the Aelfborn and looked down at the ground, feeling embarrassed by her outward appearance. She attempted to hide her bruises with her frayed clothing.

Megildur whispered, "You look as beautiful as the first time I saw you, my Desert Flower." He lifted her chin and kissed her weathered lips. They found comfort in each other's arms. He stroked her hair and motioned for a healer to attend to Zabrina's mother. Concerned for their condition, Megildur asked. "Now, what happened to you after I left? Why are you bruised and beaten?"

"They blamed me for your escape," Zabrina replied. "They tortured us to ensure my obedience."

Megildur's blood began to boil at the thought of the woman he loved tortured because of his escape. "Who hurt you?" Zabrina pointed at a guard just inside the gates. Megildur signaled for Bowen to come forward. The Centaur Master Archer approached the Aelfborn Lord. Megildur pointed and Bowen released a single arrow with such power that it threw Zabrina's tormentor several yards back.

The Temple of the Cleansing Flame ruler looked down at his fallen soldier and glared at Megildur, "You will pay for that!"

"Not today," Megildur replied. "Gaal, let's go!" The Shade waved his hands and disappeared. Megildur turned to ask Zeristan a question, who was nearby at the time. "Can you provide some assistance as our forces withdraw? I prefer to avoid a fight."

"A wise decision, Lord Megildur," Zeristan smirked. He rose into the air and released a stun effect into the safehold, rendering the inhabitants unconscious.

Maethorion and Atreus motioned for their armies to pullback. They began recalling all back to their safeholds. The armies disappeared as quickly as they had arrived. The sand dunes looked desolate now that the armies had dissipated. Only Megildur, Zeristan, Gaal, and Zabrina remained.

Megildur tended to Zabrina. The young desert flower had a concerned look on her face. "What's wrong?" Megildur asked.

Zabrina murmured, "I did not expect you to order that man's death."

"Do not worry. He will respawn soon," Megildur replied, placing his arm around Zabrina and walking away from the safehold. "But maybe this time he will be a bit more respectful to beautiful damsels." Zabrina smiled at Megildur.

Before Megildur and his close friends were out of sight, the safehold citizens started to wake. The ruler looked out from the walls of his city and spotted Megildur off in the distance. Seeing no army to protect Megildur, the Temple of the Cleansing Flame ruler sought revenge.

The ruler bellowed, "Templars and Confessors destroy the heretics!"

Megildur heard a shout in the distance and turned back toward Gray Sands. He saw several Half Giant Templars and Human Confessors charge out of the gates of the safehold, bearing in their direction. Knowing his remaining armies already withdrew; Megildur unsheathed Shadowbane and looked at his few remaining friends, "Looks like they still have some fight left in them." He turned to Zabrina, "Run ahead and stay with the others so we can engage in battle with this group."

"I want to stay with you," Zabrina replied.

Megildur pleaded, "But if you die, you will return back inside Gray Sands. I could not stand the thought of them hurting you anymore."

The two lovers debated as the Templars and Confessors continued their charge. Without warning, the sky grew dark and the clouds gathered. A terrible rolling thunder resounded, followed by ominous lightning bolts striking the advancing Templars and Confessors. A chain lightning followed their trail back to Gray Sands and devastated the safehold. When the sand and dust settled, Megildur and his group could see the Temple of the Cleansing Flame army, along with the rest of Gray Sands, lying motionless.

Megildur exclaimed, "By the All-Father!"

"Nobody but Him would have that much power, or wrath," Zeristan replied. "I think that's our cue to depart."

Megildur and the others agreed and departed, before He unleashed more of His wrath.

CHAPTER 38: *Royal Preparations*

Zeristan stepped onto the platform and waved his hands. The portal for the closest runegate to Mellissar opened. Megildur and his confidants arrived at the runegate. Zeristan announced, "Lord Megildur, your portal awaits." He was bowing in the Aelfborn's direction.

Megildur turned to Zabrina and motioned for her to move onto the platform first. She stepped into the portal and vanished within. The flashing colors and moving patterns frightened her. She felt defenseless in an unfamiliar environment. Her first instinct was to scream out, but she found her voice without volume. Megildur followed right behind her and found Zabrina stumbling on the next platform. He rushed to her side.

"Are you alright?" Megildur asked with concern.

"I have never done that before," Zabrina replied. "What was that image of flashing lights I saw?"

"That happens whenever you teleport somewhere," Megildur responded, helping her off the platform, to avoid any collisions with others coming through. "Just be happy you did not end up in the mist with everyone talking all at once." Zabrina looked at him with a puzzled expression. "It's a long story, one that I look forward to telling you later." For the time being, that answer appeased Zabrina's curiosity.

Zeristan delegated the task of keeping the portal open in the desert to another mage from Greensward Parish, so that he could guide Megildur and Zabrina to Mellissar. Once he stepped off the platform, the

Wizard approached both of them. Zeristan resounded, "M'Lord, M'Lady; this way to Mellissar." He motioned with his hand and began walking beside the couple. "I also need to prepare both of you before we arrive in the capital."

Megildur inquired, "Prepare for what exactly?"

"Well, the Kingdoms of Men have not had a High King for over a hundred years," Zeristan educated the new royalty in the ways of Aerynth, walking toward Mellissar. "Most of the fragmented world is now lawless, as both of you have witnessed firsthand. Many will want to keep it that way. Now do not be too concerned, we have one less major obstacle. Due to some 'divine intervention', many in the capital support your claim for the High Throne." Zeristan was recalling the shocking scene whereas lightning struck down Queen Bronwyn on the steps of Mellissar Castle.

Megildur asked, "Divine intervention? You mean like what happened back in the desert?"

Zeristan chuckled, "Yes." He walked in between the two and put an arm around each of them. "Now, the High Steward requires a week or so to notify everyone and set the date for the coronation. You can take that time to get a little more, acquainted." Both Megildur and Zabrina blushed at the old Wizard's remark but then Megildur thought of something.

Megildur requested, "Zabrina, can you walk with Gaal for a moment? I need to speak with Zeristan on an urgent matter." Zabrina agreed and turned to face the Shade Thief.

Gaal jested, "Come to hang out with a real hero?" Zabrina chuckled at his comment and walked alongside the pale one.

Megildur pulled Zeristan aside to talk, "I have an imperative request of you." The Aelfborn took the old man away from the others but Zabrina could see him making gestures with his hands. At first, the flustered look on Megildur's face worried her, but Zeristan's confident reaction reassured her. Next, the Aelfborn called Maethorion over to make a request of the Elven guild leader. The Elf agreed and departed to complete Megildur's request.

Zeristan and Megildur rejoined Zabrina and the Wizard finished explaining all the work done to the capital for Lord Megildur's arrival. This was the first time that Megildur, Zabrina, or Gaal had ever seen the capital for the Kingdoms of Men. The work done to the capital was evident, now that they rebuilt the walls and freed the structures of undergrowth. The castle towered over the fortifications and shone brighter than ever. Megildur and Zabrina were the first to pass through the gates. The High Steward, Sir Adelard, greeted them.

Sir Adelard bowed and announced, "Lord Megildur, welcome to Mellissar. I am your High Steward, Sir Adelard. I served the last High King and I offer my services once more, if you so desire."

"Thank you, Sir Adelard," Megildur replied. "I look forward to your assistance during this process." Megildur looked past the High Steward and noticed his father and sister approaching from the castle entrance.

Aranel screamed, running to her brother, "Megildur, your back!" She jumped into his arms and hugged Megildur. She hopped down and looked at her brother's sheath. "Shadowbane! Can I see it?"

Megildur unsheathed the weapon and placed it into her hands. "Careful." He looked up at his father, who grabbed his son and hugged him before the Aelfborn could say anything.

Aedan rejoiced, "I am glad to see you safe and alive." He pulled back and wiped his eyes before the tears flowed, "I am proud of you." Realizing they were not alone, he looked past Megildur and saw someone new. "Who is this radiant beauty?"

Megildur responded, "Father, I would like you to meet Zabrina. I met her in the desert, after they captured me. She and her mother helped me escape." He looked at Zabrina, "This is my father, Aedan."

"Pleased to meet you, Zabrina," Aedan said, greeting the Human female. He turned to Megildur. "Your mother is not back yet, but I received word that they are well and sailing back as we speak. Let's get you settled inside."

"Rest and enjoy your newfound excitations," Zeristan added. "I have another task I must attend to. Please excuse me." He winked at Megildur and waved his hands, teleporting to the nearest runegate.

Sir Adelard showed both Megildur and Zabrina to their rooms, but not before showing off the castle. The rooms were enormous and lavishly decorated. The grand hall alone could fit all the residents from Megildur's home village. Being a gentleman, the aging knight showed Zabrina her room first, Megildur stood in the hallway. Before they left her to explore her own room, Megildur took her by the arm and kissed her hand, promising to return tomorrow morning. This would give her enough time to acclimate to her new surroundings. As for Megildur, he went to his room and collapsed on the bed without even undressing first. He had not slept in an actual bed in a long time, succumbing to sleep was not an issue.

Sometime after falling asleep, someone knocked on the door. The sluggish Aelfborn pulled himself out of the soft cozy bed to see who disturbed his slumber. Maethorion stood before him.

Maethorion proclaimed, "Lord Megildur, I have the person you requested in the grand hall. I apologize for the delay."

Megildur mumbled, "Delay? How could you have accomplished this so fast?"

The Aelfborn Lord's reaction confused Maethorion, "Fast? You asked this of me two days ago."

Megildur's eyes widened once he came to the realization that he slept for two days straight. "I will be out in a moment. Thank you for this favor."

Maethorion bowed and left the doorway, so Megildur could change out of his tattered clothing. It shocked him that he slept so deep. He also left Zabrina for so long, which distressed the Aelfborn to realize this. He found some water to clean himself with and dressed in some clothes that he found next to his bed. He proceeded down to the grand hall to welcome the person he asked Maethorion for, Marie. The handmaiden was so excited to see him she ran up and hugged him. Acknowledging that this was not a proper way to greet a Lord, she stepped back and curtsied.

Marie cheered, "Thank you so much for saving my father. He did not know why the Dwarves released him, but I knew it had to be at your request."

"You are welcome," Megildur replied. "I'm just thankful Thurin intervened or I may have joined your father in the mines, or worse." The Aelfborn shuttered at the thought. "Now, I have asked Maethorion for your freedom and he has granted my request." Marie's eyes glistened at the thought of being free. "With your newfound freedom I would like to offer you a position in the High King's court as assistant to someone very special."

Marie beamed, "You found her? The girl you always thought of during your journey to Aelarnost?"

"Yes," Megildur blushed. "Her name is Zabrina and she is even more beautiful than I remember." Megildur realized he was daydreaming and snapped out it, Marie wiped the grin off her face.

She answered, "I accept. It would be an honor, your Majesty."

Megildur chuckled, "I am not King yet. I still have one more challenge and then I must confront most of Aerynth at the coronation." He cringed at the thought of facing so many people but knew it was unavoidable.

"So, are you ready to meet her?" Marie nodded in agreement and Megildur led her to Zabrina's room. On the way, Zeristan met them in the hallway. "Please wait here for me, Marie." Megildur walked off to the other side of the hall to confer with Zeristan. Marie could see the Wizard hand him an intricate wooden box. Megildur opened the box. A glimmer of light shone from within. It was almost as bright as the shine in Megildur's eyes at the sight of the contents inside the box. He closed the container and thanked Zeristan for the item. Megildur proceeded with Marie to Zabrina's room. He knocked on the door and a moment later Zabrina answered.

Zabrina bubbled, "Oh Megildur, I'm glad to see you. Please come in."

"I have someone else to see you also," Megildur replied. "Zabrina, this is Marie. She will assist you while you are here." He gestured for Marie to come inside the room.

Marie entered the room and curtsied to Zabrina, "I am pleased to assist you."

This offer shocked Zabrina a bit, but she greeted Marie, "Thank you. I'm pleased to meet you as well, but I'm not certain I need anyone." She turned to Megildur, "Do I need someone?"

"You will, especially after the coronation," Megildur replied.

This surprised Zabrina. Servitude was all she ever knew, not having people waiting on her. Zabrina was just ecstatic to be in such a majestic place that she did not even question why. "I only hoped you, Lord Megildur, might offer me a station working close to you. I am certain anything you have to offer will be more than I ever dreamed possible."

"I already have something in mind for you," Megildur replied.

Marie quickly dismissed herself and departed the room, leaving the two alone. Marie waited outside in the corridor just in case they summoned her. She had a wonderful feeling that something miraculous was about to occur, but she kept it to herself.

Megildur took Zabrina by the hand and guided her to the balcony outside her room. Megildur's voice trembled, overlooking the valley below, "The All-Father himself laid my destiny before me to reclaim Shadowbane and to lead Aerynth out of darkness, as the High King. However, I do not wish to take this path alone." He turned to face Zabrina and knelt down on one knee. Megildur opened the intricate wooden box he carried and revealed a shimmering ring. The gem was a square cut diamond, but the glowing effect was from an image below the diamond. Three interlocking circles formed the image with an almost magical aurora to them, the symbol of the All-Father. The same image Megildur had on his shoulder.

Zabrina gasped, "Oh that's beautiful. I have never seen anything like this. Are you asking...?"

"Zabrina," Megildur took a deep gulp. "Will you marry me and be the Queen Aerynth deserves? You saved me once in the desert. My life was in danger. Save me once more by accepting this ring."

Zabrina was finally able to catch her breath. She looked deep into Megildur's eyes and wept, "I accept, but it's you who have saved me." She wrapped her arms around Megildur and kissed him. She was so excited she almost knocked Megildur over. She then knelt down beside him. He removed the ring from the box and slipped it onto her finger. Zabrina felt a surge of energy run up her hand and deep within her soul, causing a warming sensation that traversed her body.

Megildur fretted, "Are you alright? What happened?"

Zabrina reassured, "I am alright, I think. I guess this was more excitement than I am used to." She was a bit dizzy but regained her composure.

There was a knock at the door but before Megildur could stand to reach it, the door opened a bit. "My Lord, may we approach?" Sir Adelard requested before entering the room. He knew he might have interrupted something, but he felt this was important.

"Yes," Megildur replied. Zeristan, Sir Adelard, and Marie proceeded inside the room.

Sir Adelard proclaimed, "The invitations have went out, the coronation will commence in one week from today."

Megildur boasted, "Perfect! That will allow enough time to prepare for our wedding!" With a smile beaming from ear to ear, he wrapped an arm around Zabrina and pulled her closer. Marie squealed and ran to Zabrina's side to see the ring.

"This will make me your Lady-In-Waiting," Marie told Zabrina.

"Congratulations to both of you," Sir Adelard commented. "This will not allow enough time to invite guests for the wedding."

"We will have the wedding just after the coronation," Megildur proclaimed. "All of Aerynth should witness this event."

Sir Adelard looked concerned. A wedding would require much more planning and he was uncertain about how the inhabitants would perceive a new Queen as well. The new High King being an Aelfborn already agitated most. He knew he could not sway Megildur from this decision. "Very well My Lord, I will make the necessary arrangements." The High Steward left the room, followed by Zeristan and Marie, leaving Megildur and Zabrina alone, again.

Zabrina stepped out onto the balcony to admire the ring against the light of the setting sun. Megildur enjoyed just gazing at her beauty with the backing of the sunset, until Zabrina looked up to see his admiration of her. She walked back inside to Megildur, who was now blushing. She proceeded in caressing his face with her soft gentle hands, working her way down to his chest. Unbuttoning his shirt, she exposed his chest and began kissing his skin. Wanting to help her in any way possible, Megildur removed his own shirt and then started helping Zabrina off with her clothing. With the fire of their passions elevating, she guided him to the bed and left nothing of their newfound love unexplored. They spent the rest of the night enjoying each other's company and forgetting the world around them. Neither of them knew true love before this moment but they found it tonight, in the arms of each other.

CHAPTER 39: The Ceremonies

The week progressed quicker than either of the two new lovers preferred. They enjoyed using this time to become acquainted with each other. Preparations for the wedding took much of their time. Clothing, flowers, and food were just a few of the items needing their approval. In between, they were able to find brief moments to be together.

Vanya, Honoria, and Scyleia arrived in Mellissar the day after Megildur proposed to Zabrina. The engagement surprised his mother, but even more surprising was how soon the wedding was to commence. On the other hand, the engagement did not surprise Honoria. She knew Zabrina was all Megildur could think of during his quest for Shadowbane.

The eve before the ceremonies was upon them. One ceremony to crown Lord Megildur the new High King. The other, to bind the love between Megildur and Zabrina, then she can take her rightful place as the High Queen of Aerynth. This shall be a celebration that Aerynth will never forget.

Honoria and Gaal met the two young lovers entering into the castle, after a late afternoon walk in the nearby forest. The plan was simple, the Bard and the Thief would separate the lovers and give them one last night to celebrate before they locked themselves in matrimony.

Honoria greeted the royalty, "M'Lady, you need to come with me. M'Lord, you can go with the rest of the livestock." She brushed him aside, taking Zabrina's arm and guiding her deeper into the castle.

Megildur grumbled, "Livestock? What did she mean by that?" He turned to Gaal.

Gaal chuckled, "Come with me, Lord Monogamy. We must celebrate before they shackle you to just one woman. Follow me." The Shade guided Megildur through a dark corridor and down some stairs. He opened an iron cell door and Sir Adelard, Sir Mardiock, Atreus, Bowen, Thaddaios, Maethorion, Turwaithion, and Zeristan greeted them.

Megildur exclaimed, "What's this? Why have we gathered in the dungeons?"

Zeristan uttered, "Reelaxmeeboy. Thiis ceelibration iss fer u." Megildur could tell the elderly Wizard began drinking without him.

Gaal announced, "Yes, the old drunk is correct. We are here to enjoy one last night of festivities before Megildur plummets into a life of servitude. And let me guess, my new profession for the new High King shall be the Court Jester!"

Zeristan blurted out, "Iweel driiink too thaaat!"

Bowen handed a mug of ale to Megildur. Gaal forced the Aelfborn into a chair in the corner. A creaking sound emanated through the room and the others separated so Megildur could see the iron door that just opened. A red skimpily dressed Irekei woman slinked out of the open cell door and toward Megildur. She began dancing close to Megildur, rubbing up against him. She exposed more of her crimson flesh.

"You should enjoy this!" Gaal proclaimed. "Every man knows Irekei women excel in dexterity and aggressiveness in the bedroom!"

Megildur exclaimed, "Let's have the host of this party enjoy some of what he arranged!" He stood from the chair and forced Gaal to sit in his place. The Shade was shocked at first, but the Irekei woman started rubbing against him and he lost all thought of Megildur's needs. The Aelfborn snuck to the side of his friends and then around behind them. Due to the ale, or dancing, nobody noticed Megildur sneak out an exit near the back of the dungeon.

Meanwhile, Honoria took Zabrina to a secluded room in the castle where she greeted Marie and a mass of other women she did not know.

Honoria declared to the room, "Ladies, we are here tonight to celebrate Zabrina's last night of freedom." She took a glass of wine for herself and handed another to Zabrina. "Long life to our future High Queen!" All of the women toasted Zabrina, she sipped from her goblet of wine. "Now bring in the entertainment!" Honoria bellowed.

A Human male walked into the room and began dancing around the crowd of women. He wore tight leather clothing and they all seemed to enjoy him thrust himself against the excited females in the room. Zabrina withdrew to the back of the crowd with sheer panic in her eyes, which Marie observed.

Marie admitted, "You know M'Lady, there's another door behind us which leads out into the hallway."

Zabrina smiled, "Thank you Marie. If anyone notices, just tell them…" She was unsure what excuse she should use.

"I will advise them you were not feeling well from all the excitement and needed to retire for the evening," Marie added.

Zabrina smiled once more and slipped out. She entered into a hallway and found her way to the main hall, where she met her future husband walking up the stairwell.

Zabrina burst out, "Megildur, thank the All-Father it's you! Those women were getting crazy!

They were bringing in some guy to dance for all of us."

Megildur admitted, "That's nothing. They escorted me down to the dungeons and had an Irekei woman trying to seduce me!" Zabrina glared at Megildur. "Don't worry. Before she made any progress, I pushed Gaal in front of me so he could enjoy her company." Megildur pulled Zabrina close and kissed her, "You are the only exotic woman for me." He looked around the hall for a place to hide away with his soon-to-be-bride before the big day. "Now, where can we go?"

"If you are through with the dungeons, there's a nice view of the moon from the cathedral steeple," Sir Adelard advised, appearing from a side doorway. He then vanished from sight.

At first, the elderly knight's sudden appearance startled the two lovers, but afterwards they rushed off to the steeple to be alone. After some romantic, and passionate, embraces they both leaned back into each other's arms and enjoyed the full moon. They were sure that their friends were having a good time in their absence.

Megildur did not understand why the others, such as Gaal, thought of marriage as a life of servitude. All he could think of was spending his life with Zabrina. His one regret was that he could not provide his mate with offspring. Unfortunately, he was sterile due to the curse transferred upon his race by the Elven Queen Silesteree Allvolanar. The Aelfborn High King would just enjoy his time with his newfound love and try to accomplish what the All-Father expected of him in one lifetime.

The moon soon disappeared behind the surrounding hills and the sun rose up behind the slumbering couple, who were still in the cathedral tower. Inside the castle, many others were searching for the bride and groom. They needed to prepare them for the ceremonies. Marie found Sir Adelard.

Marie pleaded, "Sir Adelard, have you seen Lord Megildur and Lady Zabrina?"

Sir Adelard grinned and walked on, "I have not, but if I wanted to get away from people I might visit the cathedral steeple."

Marie understood the High Steward's not so subtle hint and ran for the cathedral. She opened the small door to the tower and found both of them still asleep. She was glad they found happiness together, but she needed to hurry. "M'Lady, we must get you dressed." Megildur and Zabrina both awoke at the same time. "You must dress as well, Sir."

The three of them hurried back to the castle and found everyone running around. Aedan and Vanya were guiding the guests to appropriate seating in front of the castle steps, Aranel accepted the wedding gifts. One of the items she received was a glowing box that sloshed from side to side as the young Aelfborn walked. Aranel set down the container and began to open it, Zeristan placed his hand on top of the box.

Zeristan warned, "I would advise against opening that box, little one."

"Why?" The curious Aelfborn asked. "What's inside?"

"It's a sea creature from your mother's tribe, the Gwaridorn Elves," Zeristan educated Aranel. "They filled the box with a suspension fluid, so that once someone pours the creature from the box into water, it will grow...fast." Aranel's eyes grew big. The old Wizard laughed at her expression and noticed more guests had arrived. "I think you have more gifts to receive." He patted her on the head and went off to find Megildur. The Wizard tracked him down inside his room, still getting dressed in his royal attire.

Megildur scoffed, "This outfit is dreadful. Sir Adelard insisted I must wear this! I would prefer to wear the armor that Maethorion gave me."

"You're receiving the High King's crown and getting married, not sieging a fortress," Zeristan replied. "You represent all of Aerynth as the High King, not a mere knight, no offense Sir Adelard." The aging knight glared at the Wizard. "Now, are you ready to stand on the steps of the castle and address your guests?"

Megildur gasped, "Address the people? Stand on the steps of the castle?" He took a deep gulp. "I thought we were having the ceremonies inside the cathedral? And why should I address the guests?"

Zeristan asserted, "The cathedral cannot hold over a thousand guests and you must address them since you are assuming the role as High King over all of Aerynth."

Megildur exclaimed, "A thousand people?" Zeristan put his arm around Megildur and walked with him. They proceeded down to the grand hall, leading to the outside steps of the castle. He gave him a reassuring look and a hand upon his shoulder, just before the doors opened.

Lord Megildur walked out of the castle and the crowd cheered. He took his position at the top of the stairs. He gave a timid wave, since this was his first time before so many people. Megildur turned back to look at the front of the castle and could see Maethorion standing there in full ceremonial robes.

Megildur leaned over to Zeristan and whispered, "Why is Maethorion in those robes?"

Zeristan whispered back, "Well, you need a Priest to marry you. Who better than the High Priest of the Church of the All-Father?" The Wizard smirked at Megildur and returned to standing upright next to the groom.

Maethorion bellowed out over the cheering, "I now have the honor of crowning our new High King of Aerynth, Lord Megildur." The cheering from the crowd diminished and the guests returned to their seats. Megildur turned to face Maethorion, the High Priest continued. "Please kneel and commit to the oath." He pulled out a book that had the mark of the All-Father. "Will you solemnly swear to govern the people of Aerynth, and the realms within, according to the statutes set forth by the All-Father, and establish new laws and customs of the same?"

Megildur replied, "I solemnly swear."

Maethorion continued, "Will you, to the best of your power, cause Law and Justice, in Mercy, to execute in all your judgments?"

Again, Megildur replied, "I will."

Maethorion took the crown Sir Malorn had recovered from Cambruin's remains and placed it on Megildur's head. Maethorion bellowed, "Rise and face your people as High King Megildur!" He rose and turned to an energetic crowd praising his name. All except a limited few who will bide their time and detest the new Hierarchy. Letting the applause continue for a few moments, Megildur raised his hand to silence the crowd.

The murmurs from the crowd diminished when the music began to play. Megildur looked out from the steps to see a pure white horse approaching with a vision of beauty riding atop of a stallion. It was Zabrina and she wore a golden gown that shimmered almost as bright as her blonde hair. Her veil consisted of some type of lace that looked like golden snowflakes. She arrived at the opposite end of the crowd and met Sir Adelard. The High Steward placed a stool beside the horse, to provide the bride with an easier dismount from the stallion. She took the left arm of the High Steward and proceeded down the aisle. All of the guests gazed at the exquisite bride. Megildur advanced down the stairs to meet her. Sir Adelard presented her hand, which the Aelfborn Lord gladly accepted. He walked Zabrina up the stairs to face Maethorion. However, before the High Priest could begin, Megildur turned to face Zabrina and reached for her veil.

With a hastened whisper Maethorion advised, "High King Megildur, we do not unveil the bride at this time."

Megildur proclaimed, "I do not wish to shield my loves eyes from this event, nor do I wish to hide her beauty from the world." Since nobody wished to defy the High King, he continued with lifting her veil. Now that he could see her face, Megildur turned to face Maethorion, "You may proceed."

The High Priest grinned and began with the ceremony, "People of Aerynth, we gather here today before the All-Father to join these two. Commanded by the All-Father to complete a perilous task, Zabrina saved Megildur during his hour of need. Now, they have found love in each other and wish to nurture that love by binding their souls in holy matrimony. If any person finds grounds to object to this union, speak now or forever remain silent."

No one dared challenge the All-Father's chosen champion. The crowd remained silent. Maethorion continued with the ceremony by having the couple exchange rings and vows.

Zabrina looked into Megildur's eyes and recited her vows first. "Megildur, from the moment I met you I knew you were a true man. I have found love and security in your arms. You have given me more today than I ever dreamed possible. I will always love you." She received Megildur's ring from its bearer, Aranel, and placed it upon his finger.

Megildur did his best to restrain his nausea, because it was his turn now. "Zabrina, the first time I smelled your sweet scent I knew I could not exist on this world without you. You are my heart, my soul, and my love. I will never let harm befall you again. I will always love you." He too obtained the remaining ring from Aranel, gave her a slight smile, and placed it upon Zabrina's finger. By this time, Zabrina was crying, along with all the women present. Gaal, being the emotionless Shade he was, just looked toward the tables full of food and drink.

Maethorion bound their hands together with a leather strap and said, "With the binding of their hands, we have bound their souls together for as long as they both shall live." He then took the crown recovered, and cleaned, from the ashes of the late Queen Bronwyn and placed it on Zabrina's head. "I now present Megildur and Zabrina as husband and wife, your High King and High Queen of Aerynth. You may now kiss your bride."

Megildur took that opportunity to grab his new bride and give her a long and intense kiss. Even the cheering crowd did not deter him from his objective. He stepped back, turned himself and Zabrina to the crowd, and raised their hands, still bound by the leather strap.

Megildur announced, "My people, I promise the following." He took a deep breath and gathered his strength, "From the rubble, we will rebuild! Out of the chaos, we will bring order! We will restore Aerynth to its former glory!"

He unsheathed Shadowbane from his waist and thrust the sword into the air. An intensified light shown from the sky onto the sword and the blade seemed to absorb the power from the sun. The pommel, guard, and the exposed hilt, reflected the bright light. The black blade emitted a dark glow. From the sky, a powerful roar of thunder emanated and an object descended from the Heavens. When the object reached the ground, everyone saw, it was the All-Father. Everyone, including the new High King and High Queen, knelt before Him.

"Rise, my children," the All-Father commanded. He turned to face Megildur. "You have done well, High King Megildur. I knew you would prevail in the quest for Shadowbane." He reached down and motioned for Megildur to hand him the mighty weapon, which the Aelfborn was more than willing to accommodate this request. The All-Father looked over the sword, "Thurin is such a brilliant craftsman. He always put a bit of himself in his work, such as the magnificent ring you wear, High Queen Zabrina." She looked down at her ring and then to Megildur. Both were surprised by the fact that Thurin crafted the wedding ring. The High King looked back at Zeristan, who was grinning by this point.

The All-Father handed Shadowbane back to Megildur and continued by addressing everyone within Mellissar. "Megildur has restored my faith in all of Aerynth, which I must admit had faltered after I witnessed such betrayal against your previous High King. From this day forward, the gates to Heaven and Hell are open once more. Every mortal shall have only one life to live on Aerynth, so live it well. Of course, with restoring mortality, I would imagine conflict on Aerynth to take on a new meaning.

Megildur, Zabrina, and their heirs will establish law and order to this once forsaken world."

Megildur interjected, "Mighty All-Father, being Aelfborn I will be unable to sire offspring." He glanced over to his bride who was saddened by this fact.

The All-Father reassured, "Do not worry my children. Immortality on Aerynth is not the only curse I lifted." The God then placed a hand on Zabrina's stomach, "She already carries your heir."

Zabrina's sorrowful expression changed to amazement with this news. She would now be able to have children with her new husband. She reached up and hugged the All-Father, "Thank you Almighty One!" The All-Father returned her embrace and turned to face the rest of the crowd, Megildur and Zabrina rejoiced at this information.

The All-Father proclaimed, "The Age of Strife has come to an end. All should rejoice as Aerynth now enters the Age of Aelfborn!" The God over Aerynth raised his arms and an intense glow radiated from his body. The people of Mellissar shielded their eyes. After a few moments, the blinding light was gone and so was the All-Father.

Over the next few weeks, Megildur secluded himself and Zabrina from the woes of Aerynth, to gain more bearing within their own lives. They both needed to contemplate everything that had occurred. In one day, Megildur became a King, a husband, and a Father...and his greatest challenge was yet to come.

ABOUT THE AUTHOR

By day, Paul Francois is a mild mannered IT professional. He has been in the technology field for over 20 years. One day, in 2011, he started pondering story ideas until they leapt out of his brain and onto paper... onto the computer to be precise.

Join him as he discovers which genre suits his writing style best. Fantasy, Sci Fi, Thriller, or perhaps...all of the afore mentioned genres. The road is dreary and his journey long, sit back and enjoy a tale as we travel it together.

###

Thank you for reading my book. If you enjoyed it, please take a moment to leave a review at your favorite retailer.

--Paul Francois

Connect with me:
Follow me on Twitter:
http://twitter.com/Authorfrancois
Like me on Facebook:
http://facebook.com/AuthorPaulFrancois
Subscribe to my website:
http://crusaderscrypt.com
Goodreads:
http://goodreads.com/author/show/8364313

48328623R00192

Made in the USA
San Bernardino, CA
23 April 2017